# WOLF

*An Allison Parker Mystery*

*Adair Sanders*

Copyright © 2018 Adair Sanders
All rights reserved

ISBN: 9781724017406

# TO MY READERS

I always think I am finished with this series each time the Muse walks away from the particular story I am writing. Truly, I had zero intentions of writing a 5th book in the Allison Parker mystery series, but I haven't been able to get Wolf Johannsen out of my mind. How weird is that, since he is a creation of my imagination? Clearly, Wolf wants me to tell his story, just as Allison wanted me to tell hers when she appeared to me during a writing class at the John C. Campbell Folk School in 2013.

So, this book, although a part of the Allison Parker Mystery series, will have a bit of a different perspective. How different? I have no idea, but I know Wolf will have his hand in the telling of the tale.

Enjoy.

*Adair Sanders*

# ROME

Five years was long enough to be dead. For the first year of the five, the man had often wished that he had not survived. The damage done to his body, both by the assassin and the drugs that had caused his heart to mimic death, had taken a very long and painful time to heal. Only his desire for revenge had kept him alive during the days and nights when he felt that his entire body was on fire.

A part of him knew it was dangerous to emerge into society, but he didn't care. The money that he had hidden before his death had supported him in hiding, and there was plenty left. He could live out his remaining years undetected, safely hidden on the remote island that had been purchased by a loyal soldier so many years earlier. The man did have a small regret at having to kill the one who had stood by him during his darkest hours, but the plan that the man intended to pursue could have no loose ends. Not until it no longer mattered.

He had debated a new identity, transforming plastic surgery, an unassailable back story. Wisdom and self-preservation dictated such measures if he wished to survive. Survival only mattered until the target was extinguished, until the sweet taste of revenge filled his senses, until he punished the one who had made him suffer. After that, survival was only lagniappe.

# CHAPTER ONE

Wolf Johannsen brushed silky-fine particles of sawdust from his hands and stepped back to observe his creation. Not bad he thought, as he circled the wooden sculpture. The raven wasn't perfect, but personally, Wolf thought the imperfections in the carving gave the bird character. Plus, it had been over a decade since Wolf had picked up the carving tools his grandfather had given him so many years before. The bird he had created was a far cry from the miraculous figures of animal, fish or fowl that his grandfather's skilled hands had cajoled from misshapen wood, but for someone with rusty skills, and not much skill at that, Wolf was pleased with the small raven.

Carefully, Wolf gathered the tools he had used over the past several days – the chisel with its flat edge, the gouge with a razor-sharp cutting edge, the short bent whose small, spoon-like dip had helped Wolf make quick, deep cuts as he brought the raven to life. The wood shavings and other detritus which covered the carving tools caused the voice of Wolf's grandfather to echo in the Swede's head. "Always clean and sharpen your tools when you finish, boy. You take care of those tools, and you'll be able to give them to your own grandson one day."

Wolf hummed softly as he cleaned each instrument with an oiled rag, then using a separate clean and soft cloth, wiped away the excess wetness. Satisfied that all of his carving tools were now pristine, Wolf pulled out the whetstone that had once belonged to his grandfather and began honing the steel edges of the wooden handled set. Finally, satisfied with his work, Wolf wrapped the instruments in a cloth tool bag and placed the rolled container in the utility cabinet behind his work bench.

His own grandson. The shadow of a sad smile creased Wolf's handsome face. Wolf's life had not left room for a wife and children. His grandfather would not have understood Wolf's decision to place work over having a family, but then Wolf's grandfather would never have chosen the shadow career that had prevented his grandson from revealing enough of himself to find a mate.

Sometimes Wolf wondered what had happened to the eager young man who had started Johannsen Consulting almost twenty years ago. Fresh out of Oxford with an advanced degree in astrophysics, Wolf had used a generous inheritance to capitalize his new company. First, an office in Stockholm, then two years later, one in London, and five years after Johannsen Consulting took its first client, an office in Atlanta, Georgia.

Johannsen Consulting had developed a confidential and classified list of customers. Wolf's expertise in theoretical physics, the result of a degree from Lund University in Stockholm, coupled with his work in astrophysics, had landed the entrepreneur with multiple lucrative military contracts. When the United States became the biggest consumer of Wolf's products, the Atlanta office seemed the next logical step. Wolf's company had found its niche and was rapidly making Wolf a very wealthy man. He had a core group of talented people working for him who also had small ownership interests in the consulting firm. The team that helped run Johannsen Consulting worked hard for several reasons, not the least of which was because they had a real stake in the success of the company.

Satisfied with his day's work, Wolf flipped off the overhead lights in the small out-building that he had reconfigured as a woodworking shop, stepped outside and pulled the door closed. "Satan's helvete lit," Wolf cursed in his native tongue, struggling with the recalcitrant door. The door and jam were badly warped. After forcing the lock into place, Wolf added another item to his mental to-do list.

Gravel crunched underneath Wolf's boot-clad feet as he walked the short distance from the woodworking shed to the back porch of the Old Fort Inn. Thinking about his grandfather had triggered another memory - the day Wolf had been approached by the C.I.A. It had started with a call from Ned Bakke, an affable civilian detailed to run oversight on several of the military contracts that Johannsen Consulting had entered into with the U.S. government.

"Wolf, how are you?" Ned had inquired. "I'm in town for a few days and wondered if we could grab dinner tonight? I've got something I want to run by you."

Assuming the meal was business related, Wolf suggested a quiet restaurant in the Buckhead area of Atlanta. "Do I need to bring any files with me?" he had asked.

"No, no," Ned had replied. "This isn't consulting business. I'll see you tonight and give you the details."

The pitch Ned had given Wolf that night had intrigued the Swede. The promise of American citizenship was alluring, especially since citizenship would be helpful to his consulting business if he expanded its scope in the United States. All the C.I.A. wanted Wolf to do was gather information. "You travel in Europe frequently. You're fluent in several languages. Your consulting business provides opportunity for access to government facilities. We think you'd be a remarkable asset for the Agency."

The porch door screeched as Wolf pulled it open. Lowering himself into a nearby rocker, Wolf frowned as memories of the true nature of his work for the C.I.A.

filled his mind. The first couple of assignments had gone off fairly smoothly. The information Wolf provided Ned Bakke after each European trip appeared inconsequential to the Swede, but his handler – for that is the role Ned Bakke had assumed – seemed pleased by the intel that Wolf was providing.

However, all that changed on the Rome assignment.

Neither Wolf nor the C.I.A.'s internal investigators were able to determine what went wrong, why Wolf's cover was blown, and who was responsible. But when the unknown man burst into Wolf's room in the small hotel near the Coliseum and pulled out a knife, the Swede had acted on an instinct he didn't know he had. Wolf killed his attacker, quickly formulated a plan to dispose of the body, and moved to another hotel on the other side of town. The next day he coolly completed his assignment, leaving town without further incident. No connection was ever made to the CEO of Johannsen Consulting. That fact and Wolf's handling of the attack had convinced Ned Bakke that Wolf Johannsen just might be more of an asset than the C.I.A. had anticipated.

Wet work. That is what Wolf's actions for self-preservation the April night in Rome had led to. There hadn't been many, but there had been more than a few. Assassinations, really, all in the interest of protecting freedom. At least, that is what Wolf had told himself for the ten years that he acted as a hired gun for the Agency's covert network. It wasn't so much the killing that bothered Wolf. The men he had assassinated were criminals at best, evil at worst. The world was well shed of them. No, what had begun to bother Wolf more and more over the years was the startling recognition that, not only was he naturally skilled at doing this sort of work, being the purveyor of Death just didn't bother him.

When the niggle at the back of Wolf's brain which asked if he was losing his soul became a full blown scream, Wolf knew it was time to make a change. So, after a decade of leading a double life, Wolf had negotiated the end of his relationship with the C.I.A. his exit timing had been perfect. Younger men and women, eager to have a role in the war against ISIS and other terror groups and with as much or more "talent" than Wolf had, were being recruited by the Agency. Fortunately, Johannsen Consulting had continued to prosper, even with Wolf's periodic absences. Returning full-time to the company he had founded had been easier than Wolf expected. In short order, it was as if he had never left.

And then F.B.I. agent Jake Cleveland called. Jake and Wolf had become acquainted during a mission involving both the C.I.A. and the F.B.I. Jake knew Wolf had retired, but he thought his friend might be willing to assist on a home-grown terrorism case that had the potential to cause hundreds of American deaths if the bad guys weren't identified and stopped. All Wolf had to do, Jake told his friend, was purchase a place in Ft. Charles, Alabama that the F.B.I. could use during an undercover operation one county over.

"You're sitting on plenty of cash, old man," Jake had laughed. "Find a place in Ft. Charles, pretend it's a second home, or a remote office, or whatever. We need a presence close to Auburn. Ft. Charles is the perfect location, but the town's too damn small for us to get in unnoticed, and besides, there're too many people in that town who already know me. I need a reason to be seen in Ft. Charles, and having my old friend living there will give me an excuse that no one will question. After this is over, you can sell whatever you've bought and go back home."

Wolf had reluctantly agreed to check out the town and give Jake what help he could. Wolf owed Jake, and he knew Jake's request was the agent's way of calling in the debt. So, Wolf had purchased an empty B&B, the Old Fort Inn, on whose expansive, screened back porch he now sat reminiscing. Wolf's role in the undercover operation War Eagle had both energized the Swede and reminded him of why he had quit working for the C.I.A. The terrorists had been stopped, but not without the loss of innocent American lives.

To Wolf's surprise, by the time Operation War Eagle had concluded, the gracious two-story antebellum Old Fort Inn had captured Wolf's heart. Modern technology made it possible for him to run Johannsen Consulting remotely most of the time. The grounds of the Inn were beautiful, and the rural setting and slow pace of Ft. Charles reminded him, for some reason, of his years growing up in Sweden.

Of course, if Wolf were perfectly honest with himself, he would have to admit that there was another reason he had decided to make Ft. Charles his home. During Operation War Eagle, Fate had unexpectedly brought a remarkable woman into his life. Allison. Allison Parker. Thinking about the petite blond dynamo made Wolf smile and a lower part of his anatomy respond accordingly. Intriguing, head-strong, iron-willed, smart and beautiful – Allison Parker was the unexpected possibility that had walked into his life six months earlier.

Wolf was taking the new relationship slowly. Allison was a widow, and Wolf knew he was the first man she had taken an interest in since her husband's death. "Damn it was hard," Wolf thought, then laughed at the irony of his use of words. He was hard just thinking about the woman, and he was frustrated because he knew better than to rush the physical part of whatever he and Allison were heading into, even though his body and his emotions urged otherwise.

Springing from the rocker, Wolf headed inside to shower and change. He and Allison were attending a party at Frank Martin's offices that evening. Heading up the stairs to his second floor suite, Wolf hummed a new tune. Ft. Charles really had become his home. He was looking forward to an enjoyable evening with new friends and an exceptional woman.

# CHAPTER TWO

Hosting cocktail parties was not Frank Martin's idea of fun. Not only was he having to wear a friggin' jacket, this afternoon Marty had suggested he might consider adding a nice tie to what she called his "ensemble."

"Frank, you're the host," Marty Hampton had explained for the third time. "And besides, you look so handsome when you get dressed up."

Frank was exasperated. How in the world had he let himself be talked into hosting a cocktail party at the offices of Martin Investigations? Shaking his head, Frank retrieved a plaid tie from the back of his closet. When was the last time he had even worn a tie? The Judge's funeral? Probably. And before that? Frank had no idea. Coats and ties just weren't a normal part of his wardrobe.

"Blast it to hell!" Frank groused at the mirror as he pulled the loop of the constricting instrument-of-torture tightly around his neck. "I look like a stuffed turkey." Frank figured he might be able to keep the noose on for a couple of hours without dying, but if the guests hadn't left by 9:00, he was getting comfortable, regardless of what Marty thought.

The fifteen-minute drive from Frank's house to his office gave the ornery P.I. a chance to calm down a bit and to acknowledge that he knew quite well the reason he had agreed to host a cocktail party at his place of work. After years of declared bachelorhood, Frank had become interested in a member of the opposite sex.

Frank had met Marty Hampton when he accompanied Charlotte Parker-Kaufman and her classmates to an outing at the Montgomery Zoo as a favor to Charlotte's mother, Allison Parker. Maybe he had mellowed after passing fifty, but whatever the reason, Marty Hampton had caught Frank's attention and kept it. The pair had been seeing each other now for almost five months. When Marty had suggested Martin Investigations as the locale for the elementary school's fundraiser, Frank had found it hard to say no.

"I think your office would be the perfect site for the kick-off of the spring fundraising campaign. You and Ms. Parker are heroes of a sort after the events of last October, and having the two of you as co-hosts would draw a good crowd." When Allison agreed to help with the event, Frank knew further objection would be futile.

The building housing Martin Investigations and the law offices of Parker & Jackson occupied a good half block of downtown Ft. Charles real estate. A small parking lot for clients of both businesses already held several vehicles. Frank recognized Marty's Camry and his secretary's Kia Soul, but the identity of the owners of the remainder was unknown to the reluctant host.

The digital clock on the dash of Frank's Ford F-150 glowed 6:45 as he pulled into the nearest parking spot and shut off the behemoth's engine. "Crap," Frank muttered as he heaved his body from the truck's interior. "Late already." Marty had asked him to be there by 6:30. Chagrined, Frank hoped the rest of the evening would be better than the start. On the other hand, he thought as he hurried towards the front door of Martin Investigations, maybe all the prep work would be done and he could just grab a brew.

"Frank, I was getting worried about you!" Marty Hampton called out, beckoning him to join her by the bar that had been set up on the far wall of the firm's large reception area. "How do you think everything looks?" she asked when Frank reached her side.

"Where did all this stuff come from?" Frank asked, taking in the comfortable-looking furniture scattered around the room. The reception area of Martin Investigations had been completely transformed. "What happened to all my furniture?"

"It's in temporary quarters next door. Dawn likes to bring in her own staging for events she caters in business locations," Marty explained, referring to Dawn Deakins, a local party planner. "You remember Dawn. She handled your cousin Sean's wedding reception at Allison's last September."

"Yeh, I guess," Frank fudged. "Where's Allison? I didn't see her car in the lot."

"She got delayed. Something about a sick rabbit. Wolf called and said they'd be here as soon as they could," Marty explained. "I could barely hear Wolf over the crying in the background. I think it was Mack. Poor baby." Giving Frank a quick peck on the cheek, Marty discreetly reminded Frank of his role at the evening's event. "People want to hear about some of the cases you and Ms. Parker have been involved in. That's part of the reason they are here tonight. Regale them with some stories and then ask them to donate to the fundraiser."

Steeling himself to the task, Frank grabbed a beer and made his way towards a small group gathered nearby. Soft music coming from the string quartet that Dawn Deakins had hired provided just the right overlay to the rise and fall of animated conversations as the large room began to fill with attendees.

Just as Frank reached the group a familiar voice caught his attention. "Hey, Frank. This is great. I had no idea you could put on such a class act."

"And I had no idea you were a comedian." Frank raised his beer in a mock salute to the county's head law enforcement officer.

Sheriff Toby Trowbridge grinned, "Frank, you are the easiest target in the world. Quit being so damn sensitive."

Frank frowned at his longtime friend. "You know I hate this kinda' stuff. Makes me itchy. Marty told me I have to actually talk to these people." The P.I. downed the last drop of beer, tossed the empty bottle in the round, black disposal container parked at the end of the bar, and motioned the bartender for another. "What time is it now?"

"7:15. The party's just getting started. You've got at least two more hours of pressing the flesh before you can escape." Toby struggled to maintain a serious expression.

"Oh, sweet Jesus and Mother Mary," Frank moaned, pulling at the tie that was beginning to constrict blood flow to his head. "I don't care what Marty says." Frank flung the discarded tie behind a nearby chair. "If I'm going to be tortured, I'm at least going to be comfortable."

"Don't forget your jacket!" Toby called to Frank's back as his friend headed towards the entrance to take up his assigned duty as greeter-in-chief. Knowing Frank, Toby figured the navy blazer would meet the same fate as Frank's plaid tie. The only question was how soon.

# CHAPTER THREE

"I'm so hot I'm sweating!" Allison lifted her long blond hair off her neck, twisted it into a soft chignon and secured it to her head with a large hair clip she retrieved from her purse. The crisis involving her son's pet rabbit had put the Parker-Kaufman home in disarray just as Wolf had pulled up to the stone and wood cottage. Fortunately, Peter Rabbit had been discovered hiding under the back porch steps and returned to his large enclosed pen before any real injury had occurred to Mack's favorite pet. "Maybe I should have changed into something a bit cooler before we left," Allison frowned, fanning herself with a discarded envelope from the floor of Wolf's Mercedes. "My clothes feel damp."

"By the time we get to town, you'll be fine." Taking his right hand from the steering wheel, Wolf wrapped his long fingers around Allison's small hand. "And you look damn sexy with your hair up like that." Wolf grinned admiring his companion.

"At least one person will think so." With her free hand Allison turned the passenger side air vent towards her face, increased the fan speed and turned the temperature setting as low as it would go. The cold air felt wonderful. Allison hoped it would also cool the heat from the blush that was quickly spreading over her neck and face. There was no denying she was attracted to Wolf Johannsen.

"I've got to go to London next week," Wolf's non-sequitur interrupted Allison's thoughts.

"Is it something with your London office?" Allison had hired Frank Martin to do a thorough background check on Wolf Johannsen the previous year when Wolf had retained Allison's firm to close the purchase of the Old Fort Inn. Under normal circumstances, she would never have even considered such an invasion of privacy with a client, but Allison's instincts had told her Wolf Johannsen was more than he appeared to be. Frank's report had given Allison plenty of information about Johannsen Consulting and its office locations, all of which Wolf had subsequently shared himself, but nothing about the man's secret life. That information had come later. Now, as far as Allison knew, Wolf's shadow career was in the past. A trip to London was either for pleasure or something to do with Wolf's consulting business.

Wolf considered his next words carefully. "Yes, partially business. I need to meet with a new client who has come through the London office. It's better to be there in person for the first meeting rather than skyping." Nervously, and uncharacteristically, Wolf cleared his throat. "Uh, I was thinking I might make a pleasure trip out of it, as well."

Unsure of why Wolf was telling her all of this, Allison's Southern upbringing offered up the standard reply, "That sounds nice." Biting her tongue to ensure she didn't ask the wrong question, Allison waited.

"Well, um, I was wondering if you would like to go with me?"

"To London?" Silently Allison reprimanded herself. Of course he wants you to go to London. Stop acting like a moron.

"You'd have your own accommodations," Wolf quickly replied, "but yes, I thought it might be a chance for you to get away for a week, or two, and a chance for me to show you a little bit of what I do for a living. What do you think?"

The sight of a long line of cars parked along Main Street offered Allison an excuse to postpone an immediate reply. "I need some time to think about this, Wolf. And from the number of cars parked up and down the street, I'd say we need to join the party. Can I give you my answer later?"

"Of course." Wolf maneuvered the coupe into a vacant space along the street and cut the engine. "I need to be in London Thursday morning. Let me know by Monday, and I'll have plenty of time to make arrangements."

A few minutes later, the sound of clinking glasses, animated conversations and music greeted the pair as they opened the door to Martin Investigations.

"It's about time!" Frank boomed. "You're supposed to be hosting this nightmare with me."

Stepping on tip-toe, Allison gave her favorite curmudgeon a peck on a slightly whiskered cheek. "Frank, are you growing a beard?"

"Think'in about it" the P.I. retorted. "You got something against beards?"

"No, but Marty might," Allison laughed. Kidding her friend she added, "I think you'll look great– just like Blackbeard."

Leaving Frank to ruminate on whether or not he wanted to look like a pirate, Allison and Wolf moved separately into the crowded room, greeting friends, introducing themselves to those they didn't know, and otherwise becoming a part of the evening's festivities.

Sarah Jackson, the wife of Allison's law partner David, waved from a corner. Making her way to the other side of the reception area Allison hugged the woman who had become one of her closest friends in Ft. Charles. "Sarah, I'm so glad to see you." Pulling her friend towards a nearby hallway, Allison leaned close to Sarah, "I need your opinion on something."

Curious, Sarah allowed herself to be practically dragged to Frank's private office. Closing the door, Allison blurted, "Wolf asked me to go to London with him!"

"What? Really? When?" Sarah's questions fired rapidly. "You're going aren't you?"

"I don't know what to do," Allison moaned. "I really like him, and he said I'd have my own accommodations."

"So what's the problem?" Sarah waited for an answer.

"I'm scared. No, I'm terrified." Allison paced back and forth. "I had partners before Jim, but I haven't been with another man since Jim and I married, and certainly not since he died."

Sarah suppressed a smile. This was no joking matter to her friend. That much was evident. "Are you afraid you've forgotten how to have sex?"

"No. Yes – hell, I don't know!" Allison exclaimed. "All I know is that I really like Wolf, and I don't want to do anything to mess this up. If I say no, I don't want to go to London, will he think I don't like him? What if I go and he wants to have sex and I freak out? Or I'm really bad at it?" Allison grabbed Sarah's hands and pleaded, "Help me!"

Sarah Jackson smiled at her friend. This was not the first time the two women had talked about Allison's life since Wolf Johannsen had entered the picture. "Do you want to go on this trip with him?"

Allison nodded, "Yes, I do."

"Then that's your answer," Sarah replied. "Don't worry about what may or may not happen. Just listen to your heart and everything will be fine."

# CHAPTER FOUR

A frown creased deep furrows across Ned Bakke's forehead. The information that had been delivered to him this morning via secured email transmission was more than troubling. The source of the information was a trusted agent, but even so, Ned found what he had read hard to believe. And, if who the agent had seen was accurate, the potential ramifications were beyond what the seasoned C.I.A. man wanted to contemplate.

Punching in a quick succession of numbers on his desk phone, Bakke listened for the electronic sounds that assured he had accessed a secure line.

"Have you seen the report?" Even on a secure line, Bakke was hesitant to use the name of the deep-cover agent who had authored the worrisome report.

"I have. How confident are you of the information?"

"Confident enough to be calling you. She's one of the best deep-cover agents we have in the field. If she says she saw Vargha, I believe her." Bakke paused. "Vargha was Wolf Johannsen's last assignment. The kill was confirmed. Our contact viewed Vargha's body in the morgue."

"Obviously not," a terse reply interrupted Bakke.

"Either the man Johannsen killed was a body-double for Vargha, or we've got an imposter now." Bakke pointed out the only two options that explained what his agent had reported. "I'm less worried about whether this is the real Vargha or an impersonator. Frankly, the bigger question for me is why. Why is someone claiming to be Gyuri Vargha emerging now, five years after he was supposedly killed?"

"Can your agent get close to Vargha?"

"She says yes. It will be dangerous," Bakke replied, "but she knows the risks."

"Have you contacted Johannsen?"

"Wolf's been out of the Agency for over five years. Even if Vargha is alive, I don't think there's any exposure for Wolf."

"If someone had tried to kill me, revenge would be my first item of business."

"Wolf was always careful," Bakke countered. "In the ten years he worked for me he never had his cover blown. Whoever this guy is, Vargha or a lookalike, the odds that he knows Wolf's true identity are pretty low."

"Low but not zero," the voice at the other end of the

secured line reminded Bakke. "Reach out to Johannsen. Tell Wolf we're still confirming the guy's identity, but he needs to watch his back, particularly if he goes across the pond."

The call concluded, Ned Bakke leaned back in his chair and stared at the ceiling tiles in his drab government office. Ned was a company man. He'd risen high in the C.I.A. by following orders, not disobeying them. Ignoring the directive his boss had just delivered was crazy, wasn't it? And for what purpose? Every operative who worked for the agency knew that they never really left that life behind them, even when they retired or quit. Wolf would be no different. Johannsen would hear Ned out, weigh the likelihood of Vargha's existence and protect himself accordingly. Or not. All Ned had to do was make the call.

Later, Ned would rationalize his failure to call Wolf Johannsen by telling the investigatory panel that his orders hadn't designated a time-frame for notifying the ex-operative. It was more than reasonable, based on the information he had at the time, to decide to wait until the undercover agent had a chance to provide more information about the identity of the man who was supposed to be dead. How was Ned to know that withholding that information would have the result it did?

# CHAPTER FIVE

The weekend had passed without further discussion between Wolf and Allison about the London trip. One of the qualities that Allison liked about the Swede was his patience, at least where Allison was concerned. Although they had spent the better part of Saturday together taking Charlotte and Mack to the Montgomery Zoo, Wolf didn't raise the question of the London trip. The deep kiss that she and Wolf had shared when he left Allison's house after seeing Allison and her children safely inside had asked its own question. One that Allison was struggling to answer this Sunday afternoon.

Allison wasn't kidding herself. She and Wolf might have separate sleeping accommodations on the trip, but Allison was pretty certain that would not prevent their relationship from taking a very serious next step.

Wolf was forty-four and Allison would be forty on her next birthday. The idea of a sexual relationship with Wolf wasn't a moral dilemma for Allison. Not at her age or where she was in life. But Allison was concerned about the effect a more serious relationship might have on her children. Mack and Charlotte had come a long way emotionally since the loss of their father, and both children liked Wolf Johannsen, but would they accept him as a part of their family?

"Wait a minute, girlie," Allison cautioned herself. "The man hasn't asked you to marry him. You're way ahead of yourself."

But that was it, wasn't it? The core of Allison's dilemma. Taking the step to physical intimacy was, for Allison, much more than responding to her body's demands. If Allison slept with Wolf Johannsen, it would be because she was serious about him, not only as a companion for herself, but as a step-father for her children. Accepting Wolf's offer of the London trip was certain to bring that question front and center, maybe not immediately, but certainly eventually.

Sarah Jackson had encouraged Allison to go. "It's just a trip, Allison. It will be fun. And besides, you said y'all would have separate rooms. Nothing has to happen that you don't want."

Further internal debate was quashed by the sound of running feet rapidly approaching the den where Allison had cosseted herself. Launching herself onto the sofa with her mother, Charlotte asked, "Can you take me over to the riding club? Jerry promised to work with me this afternoon. You know I've got a competition coming up next month."

Overlook Riding Club and its owners, Marion Hutcheson and Jerry Kennedy, had played a large role in Charlotte's grieving process. Charlotte had spent hours at the riding club working with her Appaloosa, Diamond Girl. The time had been well spent – Charlotte healed, as much as any child heals from the loss of a parent, and she and Diamond Girl became real contenders on the horse show circuit.

"That sounds good." Allison smiled at the daughter who was rapidly approaching her teen years. "Give Jerry a call and find out what time works for her."

"I already called her," Charlotte admitted. "She said to come on now."

Allison shook her head in exasperation. "Okay," she acquiesced. "See if Mack wants to ride over with us, and I'll grab my purse and keys."

Halfway down the hallway to her brother's room, Charlotte stopped and called to Allison, "Hey, Mom. Why don't you call Mr. Johannsen and see if he wants to meet us there? I want him to see Diamond Girl running through her paces."

"What about Mr. Johannsen?" Mack emerged from his bedroom. "If he's going to be at the riding club I want to go."

Allison listened as her children happily bantered over which of them was going to get Wolf's attention at the riding club. Yes, maybe living in the moment and letting nature take its course was the right thing to do. Picking up the phone, Allison punched in the numbers for Wolf's cell.

"Yah?" Wolf's melodious voice ticked Allison's ear.

"Wolf, it's me, Allison."

"Yes, I know. Caller ID and all that" Wolf laughed. "What's up?"

Allison decided to lead with her children's invitation. "I'm taking the children out to Overlook Riding Club. Charlotte wants you to join us and watch her put Diamond Girl through her paces. Of course, unless you've got other plans."

"No, no. I'm just doing some chores around the Inn" Wolf replied. "Tell Charlotte I accept her invitation. What time should I be there?"

Allison glanced at her watch. "It's 1:30 now and it'll take me about 20 minutes to get there. Say, 2:00?"

"I'll be there," Wolf agreed. "Anything else?"

Taking a deep breath, Allison took the emotional next step that had occupied both her waking and sleeping hours for the past several days. "I'd like to go to London with you."

# CHAPTER SIX

By 11:00 Monday morning, Allison had handled three client conference calls, made final revisions to a set of Interrogatories she intended to serve on the plaintiff's counsel in the case she was handling for the local hospital, and executed the finalized settlement agreement she had negotiated on behalf of Nina Toldano on her wrongful-termination claim. Earlier that morning, during the partners' regular Monday briefing, Allison had made certain David Jackson could handle the only court appearance she had on her schedule for the time she would be gone on the trip with Wolf.

Satisfied that everything she could anticipate had been handled or would be taken care of in her absence, Allison reached for her phone to call Frank Martin. A new matter had come across her desk at the end of the previous week. Allison wanted to enlist Frank's help on the case before she left town.

Gambling was still illegal in many states, including Alabama, much to the chagrin of businessmen who saw gambling as a great way to make and hide money. Some states, like Mississippi, had solved the problem by enacting legislation that allowed gambling, so long as the casinos where the gambling took place were located on navigable waterways, such as the Mississippi River or the Gulf of Mexico. In those states, huge casinos sat on even larger floating barges, tethered to the shoreline by a permanent walkway. In 2017, Mississippi had more than twenty operating casinos generating millions of dollars for the state coffers.

The money generated by well-run casinos attracted the attention of many Native Americans. Because of tribal sovereignty, the right of Native American tribes to govern themselves within the geographic confines of the United States, Native American tribes were free to build and operate casinos on land owned by the tribe. Thus, not only did many tribes build and operate casinos on reservation property, they were free to build and operate casinos off the reservation proper, so long as the real estate upon which the casino sat was owned by the Native American tribe.

A few years back, Allison and Frank had met the granddaughter of the Chief of the Choctaw Tribe in Mississippi. Sharon Green, a Lauderdale, Mississippi, sheriff's deputy with a white-sounding name was pure

Choctaw. The Mississippi Choctaw tribe had become financially well-off after building two spectacular casinos on the reservation outside Philadelphia, Mississippi. Allison's chance involvement with Sharon Green during the Boudreaux matter had resulted in the new case that had landed on her desk less than a week earlier.

Mona Phillips worked at one of the casinos owned by the Creek Indian Nation in Alabama. Recently, Ms. Phillips had filed a charge of sexual harassment and constructive discharge against the Blue Wind Casino, alleging that her shift manager, an African American man, had touched her inappropriately, had used sexually charged language in speaking to her, and had made her working environment intolerable. A recommendation from the Choctaw Chief to his counterpart in the Creek Nation had resulted in Allison's hiring as defense counsel for the Blue Wind Casino.

"Hey Sheila," Allison responded to Sheila McMurray's cheery, "Martin Investigations." "Is Frank around?"

"Yes, Ms. Parker, he sure is. Hold on a minute while I transfer your call to him."

Allison had barely had time to take a quick sip of coffee before Frank's booming voice came on the line. "If you're calling to get on me about not making my appointment with Dr. Lopez, you can get in line," the P.I. huffed. "Marty beat you to it, and I've already rescheduled it for next week."

A wide grin covered Allison's face, but she forced a measured reply, "No, Frank, I wasn't calling about that, but now that you've raised the subject…."

"Oh, no you don't," Frank interrupted. "That topic is closed for conversation. If you've got somethin' else to talk about, fine. Otherwise, you can tell Marty I've made the appointment."

A laugh burst from Allison's lips. "Frank, I haven't talked to Marty since the party. I'm calling you on business. Business I want to hire you for."

"Harummph," Frank mumbled. "Business? What sort of business?"

Quickly, Allison gave Frank a concise run-down on the Blue Wind case and Ms. Phillips' claims. "I want you to do a little snooping for me. On the clock, of course. See what you can find out about our plaintiff from some of the people at the casino. I think they'll come closer to talking to you rather than the attorney who is handling the case for their employer. I want the truth, not what an employee may think the casino wants him or her to say."

"You want me to go in as a P.I. or just someone who's heard some gossip?"

"I'll leave that up to you, Frank. You'll know better once you're there."

"How soon do you need my report?" Frank scanned his calendar. "I've got some time over the next few days, but after that I've committed to another client for a week or more out of state."

Allison considered Frank's question. She couldn't do much while she was in London, but she'd want to get started on the case as soon as she got back. "Next week would be great. If I could have your report by the 10th that would be perfect."

"Consider it done," Frank replied, "and thanks for the hire. It will be good working with you on a normal case."

The call concluded, Allison typed a short memorandum for Frank, re-iterating Mona Phillips' claims and giving the P.I. all of the information the lawyer had been furnished by Blue Wind Casinos. Adding a number for Mike Oxendine, her contact at the Casino, and a copy of all the paperwork she had received from her client, Allison slipped the document into a slim manila envelope and rang her secretary on the interoffice line.

"Donna, I've got some information for Frank on the Blue Wind case. Please see that it's delivered to him first thing tomorrow. I'm heading out and I'll leave it on my desk."

# CHAPTER SEVEN

Frank studied the memo that Donna Pevey had brought over earlier that morning. In addition to the memo, Allison had included copies of other documents. Mona Phillips' personnel file was fairly sparse - just her employment application, tax withholding information, and a copy of the document she had signed acknowledging receipt of Blue Wind's employee handbook. There were two interview statements– the one given by Phillips herself and the one taken from Benji Smith, the man Phillips had accused of inappropriate behavior. The only other documents in the envelope were copies of the charge of discrimination that Phillips had filed with the Equal Employment Opportunity Commission, known in shorthand as the EEOC, and the three pages dealing with sexual harassment from the Blue Wind Casino's employee handbook. Either Blue Wind's human resources manager had not interviewed any of Phillips' co-workers, or he hadn't bothered to put a written summary of other interviews in the casino's investigative file. "Sloppy" Frank thought.

Opening a new browser on his computer, Frank typed in "Native American Creek Nation." The P.I. wanted to educate himself about Allison's newest client before he headed to the casino. Frank knew the Blue Wind was owned by the Creek Indians, but other than that, the P.I. knew little to nothing about the tribe itself.

According to Wikipedia, the Creek Indians, along with the Cherokee, Chickasaw, Choctaw and Seminole tribes, had been given the moniker "the five civilized tribes" in the 1800's by white settlers after the tribes accepted Christianity and European ways. " Figures," Frank thought. History was replete with white Europeans forcing their own beliefs on the people whose lands they invaded.

Frank was familiar with the story of the Trail of Tears, the removal of most of the Cherokee Indians from the Carolinas and Tennessee at the end of the 1800's. What Frank hadn't known, and what he was reading now, was that most of the Creek Indians had been relocated during that time as well. Reflecting on the Creek's and Cherokee's wholesale conversion to Christianity, Frank murmured "Didn't make any difference, though, did it?" After the expulsion, an eastern tribe of the Creek remained in Alabama, just as an eastern band of the

Cherokee remained in North Carolina, but the larger Creek Nation, known now as the Muskogee, had their headquarters in Oklahoma. The eastern tribe of the Creek, while affiliated with the larger community in Oklahoma, maintained its own government. It was that particular tribe which had become Allison's client.

Scanning the various sections in the Wikipedia entry, Frank was surprised to learn that the Creek were a matriarchal society. Children belonged to the same clan as their mother, not their father. Frank smiled as he considered that historical tidbit - maybe the Creeks were the original women's liberation movement. Because so many people were closely related within the tribe at large, marriage outside one's clan – be it Wind, Bird, Alligator or Bear – was required. Frank wondered if the Blue Wind Casino was owned by member of the Wind Clan of the Creek Nation. The name would certainly suggest that to be the case.

When Frank had first reviewed the Mona Phillips file, he had assumed that the alleged harasser, Benji Smith, would not be a member of the Creek tribe because he was African-American. Once again Frank was reminded that assumptions could often be wrong. The Creeks, along with some of the other "civilized tribes," had allowed freed African slaves to live among them. One of Smith's ancestors had obviously married into the tribe, giving his descendants membership in the Creek Nation.

Mona Phillips was not Native American. Her personnel file was bare bones, revealing only that she had passed the pre-employment drug test, that she resided on a rural route near the casino, and that she claimed no dependents for tax withholding. Frank would have a lot of digging to do on Mona Phillips.

Opening another browser, Frank typed in "Blue Wind Casino" and was quickly directed to the casino's web home page. The Blue Wind was a fairly large enterprise – hotel, full casino, two restaurants, three bars, a par 3 golf course and a large outdoor pool complex. Clicking on the link for "make a reservation," Frank reserved a room for the next two nights. Playing the role of a gambler might be the best way to start his on-site investigation. Money loosened mouths. If that didn't work, Frank could always reveal his P.I. status. Staying on the casino grounds for a couple of days and nights would allow Frank to observe Benji Smith, as well as talk to other employees who would have worked the same shift as Mona Phillips. According to Allison's memo, Phillips was on a medical leave now for the alleged emotional distress that she had suffered at the hands of her supervisor. Frank looked forward to talking to Mona's co-workers now that Phillips was no longer showing up for work.

# CHAPTER EIGHT

Rebecca Molinere cast a critical eye at the large canvases her assistants had placed at varying heights on the white walls in the main room of the small art gallery she owned on the Via de Monserrato.

"That one is too high," Rebecca pointed at the largest painting. "It's the focal point of the exhibit. Bring it down three centimeters."

Rebecca waited until the two men had repositioned the large painting, then began a slow walk around the room, examining the positioning of each of the remaining canvases. The slight nod of her head as she passed each masterpiece assured the assistants that their boss was satisfied with the exhibit. Soon they would be dismissed and able to take in a quick caffe before finishing up the work day.

Rebecca Molinere loved her job. Art and those who created it had been a passion for as long as she could remember. An undergraduate degree in Art History at Yale followed by an MFA at Tor Vergata University in Rome, Italy had paved the way for Rebecca's foray into ownership of the small gallery. Of course the fact that she was trilingual and had family money as well as connections in the business and art world hadn't hurt either.

Renee Depeche, an acclaimed French watercolorist, had been Rebecca's first introduction to the world of art. Some of Rebecca's earliest and fondest memories were of sitting in her maternal grandfather's art studio in Paris watching her Grand-Pere create beauty from the mass of colorful paints scattered around the studio. Thanks to her grandfather, Rebecca had met almost all of the famous painters of her grandfather's generation, as well as many of the up-and-coming artists in the next. By the time Rebecca opened Il Piccolo Paridiso, the gallery owner was on a first-name basis with most of the painters, agents and critics that mattered in the international world of art.

A soft vibration and muted buzz caught Rebecca's attention. Retrieving her cell from the back pocket of jeans that emphasized the woman's slim hips, Rebecca noted the caller's identity.

"Bastien, I expected your call several days ago. The show opens tonight."

"Ma Cherie, it's taken some time to get your

information to the right people and to receive instructions back," Bastien Dubois's heavily accented English flowed over the long distance line. "Only a few people at the very top knew about Vargha."

"I wouldn't have recognized him, except for Charlene just happening to be at the gallery last month when he, whoever he really is, walked in." Rebecca paused to recall the memory. "When Charlene introduced me, I knew the name sounded familiar. It wasn't until late that evening that I made the connection."

"Tell me again how your friend knew Vargha?" Bastien didn't believe in coincidences. Vargha's appearance at an art gallery owned by a C.I.A. deep-cover agent had raised all sorts of red flags in the Agency.

"Charlene has been a fixture in Rome society for the past thirty years. My grandfather Depeche introduced me to her before he passed away. Charlene told me she knew Vargha through mutual friends, but hadn't seen or heard from or about him in over five years. She seemed genuinely surprised to see him in the gallery." Rebecca knew why Bastien had wanted this information – Rebecca had the same questions and concerns as her handler. In her line of work, one could never be too careful. "What do you want me to do tonight if he comes to the opening?"

"Langley wants you to get close to him. How you do that is up to you. They need confirmation of his identity. Langley had reliable intel that Vargha was eliminated by one of its agents. If this guy really is Gyuri Vargha…

well, I don't have to tell you what that means."

Rebecca did know what that meant. If the man who had walked into her gallery was indeed Gyuri Vargha, then one of Langley's agents involved in the Vargha operation had lied. And that meant they had a traitor.

"I can't just ask the guy if he's the real Gyuri Vargha," Rebecca stated the obvious. "Do we know if he has any identifying marks, any particular background detail they may help me?"

"Vargha has a dragon tattoo on the inside of his upper right thigh. The dead guy that was ID'ed in the morgue had the same tattoo. That's why Langley thought they had a legit kill."

"Anyone can get a dragon tattoo," Rebecca interrupted. "I'm going to need something else."

"Langley's working on it. In the meantime, your instructions are to move on the target, find out everything you can about him, get him to trust you," Bastien relayed the orders from C.I.A. headquarters. "This guy is important."

"Important how?" Rebecca inquired.

"That's above my pay grade, and yours," Bastien replied. "What do you want me to tell Langley?"

"That I'll do my job," Rebecca's retort came quickly. "I've got to go. Guests will be here in about an hour and I need to look my best, especially if I'm going to use my feminine charms to seduce Mr. Vargha."

# CHAPTER NINE

Allison cast a critical eye over the slacks, shirts, skirts, dresses and jeans that covered the cream duvet. Thrown helter-skelter as Allison had pulled the clothes from her closet and tossed them on the king size bed, the assortment of casual, business and formal attire would need three suitcases to contain them all. And she hadn't even pulled out matching shoes, purses and jewelry yet.

"I don't know what to take," Allison complained to the small Schnauzer that watched her from one of the overstuffed chairs in the bedroom's adjacent sitting room. "Baxter, you pick" Allison commanded the small canine that had joined the family a few months earlier. Hearing his name, the four-legged love-bucket cocked his head and gave his mistress a questioning look.

Allison really didn't know what to pack for the

whirlwind ten-day trip to London, Paris and Rome that Wolf had enticed her to take with him. They would be staying at The Savoy in London, at the George Cinq in Paris and the St. Regis in Rome, all five-star hotels. Allison liked a comfortable accommodation, but her regular hotel of choice was more along the lines of a Hampton Inn. Would she have to be properly dressed to stay in those places?

Allison wasn't much of a world traveler. She made the chaperoned European tour the summer after she graduated high school, at the insistence of her father, Matthew Parker. For her honeymoon, Allison and Jim had spent a week in the Caribbean, and then a few years later, a short vacation at an adults-only resort on the Pacific coast of Mexico. Other than those two trips, travel for Allison had been for business or family vacations. Truth be told, Allison's favorite vacation was simply staying at home, working in the yard, and enjoying time with her family.

Wolf hadn't been very helpful, either. In response to Allison's questions about what she should pack, all the Swede would say is "something for a couple of nice dinners out and comfortable shoes for walking." "Men," Allison thought as she began to organize the mound of clothing into "take," "don't take" and "maybe" piles for further consideration. An hour later, after re-arranging her selections multiple times, Allison examined the end result with approval. Two cocktail outfits, a wrap-style dress that could be casual or dressy depending on accessories, three pairs of slacks, several shirts, two sweaters, and two pairs of nice jeans. Four pairs of shoes would have to do, as would only one cocktail purse. The oversize shoulder bag that normally doubled as an extra briefcase for the lawyer would do double-duty as Allison's everyday bag and airplane carry-on. The evening wrap that would work with both cocktail outfits would fit nicely into the bottom of the shoulder bag. No need for the largish wrap to take up precious suitcase room.

"You take good care of Charlotte and Mack while I'm gone," Allison instructed the little Schnauzer giving him a scratch between the ears. Saying goodbye to her children when she dropped them off at school earlier that morning had been harder than Allison had anticipated. Given the children's responses, Allison was pretty sure she would miss her children more than the other way around. Her children were growing up. One day soon they would prefer their friends over spending time with their mother. "Oh well," Allison thought. "That's the way it's supposed to be."

The chimes of the ancient grandfather clock that stood in the cottage's large foyer rang twice, reminding Allison that Wolf would be picking her up in less than forty-five minutes. Their Delta flight from Atlanta to London was scheduled to depart at 7:00 p.m. The four-hour window Wolf planned for the drive from Ft. Charles to the Atlanta airport should give the couple ample time to park in the long-term lot and make it through security before the flight boarded.

Every item on the handwritten list in Allison's hand had a line drawn through it, evidence that all necessary items were packed and accounted for in either the large black suitcase or the brown leather carryall. Gathering a light jacket from her wardrobe, Allison wheeled the suitcase to the front door of the cottage, placed the carryall next to it, and sank into a nearby chair. Ready or not, Allison was heading out on a ten-day trip with Wolf Johannsen.

# CHAPTER TEN

The Blue Wind Casino was, in Frank's humble opinion, a first-class joint. Covering over five hundred acres, the casino grounds featured an 18-hole golf course, a high-rise hotel with over 200 hundred rooms, an outdoor pool that was only a tad smaller than a large pond, and a full-service casino with three restaurants.

"Mr. Martin, can I interest you in an upgrade?" the obsequious desk clerk inquired. "Our junior suites are quite luxurious."

Frank considered the question. Normally, the P.I. kept his travel expenses as low as possible for his clients, but in this instance since the casino was his client, in a manner of speaking, Frank thought an upgrade sounded pretty darn good. "Yeh, whatever." Frank slid his credit card across the counter. "I paid online. You can put the extra charge on this."

"Oh, no sir," the clerk replied. "There's a note on your reservation to give you an upgrade. I just wanted to make certain that was agreeable to you."

Frank frowned. Allison must have told the casino to expect him. Frank didn't like that at all. He hadn't decided how he would attack this job, and the less the casino employees knew about him the better. "Why is there a note on my reservation?"

The hostility in Frank's voice caused the desk clerk an inadvertent shudder. Backing away from the counter, the confused clerk stammered, "Uh, I don't know sir. Usually, upgrades are reserved for high-rollers. Have you stayed with us previously?"

The clerk's question gave Frank an idea. Glaring at the now clearly frightened clerk, Frank growled, "I don't like people knowing my business, especially nosy reservations clerks." Snatching his credit card from the countertop, Frank continued, "and how much I win is none of your business."

"No sir, you are correct, sir. I didn't mean to pry, sir." Beads of sweat glistened on the clerk's forehead as he tried to mollify Frank. The customer was always right, that much had been drilled into the clerk's brain during job orientation. He'd already had one customer complaint this month. He didn't want another. "Let me start over, Mr. Martin. Blue Wind Casino respects all of its customers' privacy, and I deeply apologize for any impression I may have given you otherwise. As a gesture of good faith, I'm adding a free dinner for you at the casino's finest restaurant for the two nights you are staying with us."

This was working out better than Frank had expected. The private investigator was a keen student of human nature. No matter what protestations the clerk made, Frank knew the rumor mill would have Frank tagged as one of the casino's repeat high-rollers before he made it to the craps table. Staff would be friendly to him, making his job of obtaining information about Mona Phillips easier than he had initially feared.

"Well, I guess that's alright" Frank huffed, playing into the role of a rich and spoiled gambler. "Have the bar send up a bottle of Scotch as well. Macallan, not any of that cheap stuff."

"Certainly, Mr. Martin," The clerk nervously wiped his brow. He had barely avoided a catastrophe with whoever this Martin guy was. "Here is the key to the Yellow Tail Suite. The bellman will bring up your luggage shortly."

A few minutes later Frank took in the view from suite's large plate glass windows. No concrete parking lot marred the vista that lay before him. All that he could see were trees, grass and one of the fairways for the casino's golf course. "Definitely not the cheap seats," Frank thought with a smile. Pulling a chair in front of the window, Frank opened his laptop and called up the electronic file Allison had provided him on the Mona Phillips case. The information contained in the e-file was a condensed version of the paper file Frank had brought with him. Attention to detail was important, though, so Frank took the necessary time to compare the information in the two files, making certain nothing additional had been added since the last time he reviewed the information.

According to the information the casino's human resources director had provided, several of the employees who worked the night shift with Mona Phillips would be working tonight. Benji Smith, the alleged harasser, was also working this evening. Frank knew from the investigation made by the casino's HR director that Smith had not been suspended or fired because the HR director couldn't decide who was telling the truth, Mona Phillips or Benji Smith. The two employees had been reminded about the casino's sexual harassment policies and nothing more, prompting Ms. Phillips' charge of discrimination filed with the EEOC and her subsequent lawsuit.

Someone knew something. Someone had seen something. Someone had heard something. Working in a casino was like working in a restaurant. Everyone talked, just not to management. If the rest of his time turned out as well as the first few hours had, Frank would get all the information he desired.

Now to dress the part. Frank knew that no matter what clothes he wore, the rough edges of his personality couldn't be hidden. But there were plenty of men with tons of money and rough edges who liked to gamble.

Glad that he had thrown his Stetson in the back seat of his truck before he left Ft. Charles, Frank decided he could easily play the role of Texas oil man. The evening was looking up. A nice dinner on the house, a couple of hours at the Blackjack table, and some casual conversation with a few employees. Yep, this assignment was starting out much better than the P.I. had anticipated.

# CHAPTER ELEVEN

"It's more beautiful than I remembered." Allison pressed her face against the small window and soaked in the historic scenery passing beneath the Delta flight as the plane traveled over the Thames River in its approach to London's Heathrow Airport. "Look, Wolf. There's Big Ben."

Wolf laughed at his traveling companion's excitement. "There's more to see in this town than we can possibly pack into the three days we have here. If you can hold off jet lag, I want to spend some time at the British Museum today. It's one of my favorite places, and I always try to fit in a visit when I'm in town."

"I think I got enough snooze time on the flight over to make it until at least 8:00 tonight," Allison grinned. "After that, I make zero guarantees."

Deplaning and getting through Customs had taken almost an hour, reminding Allison of why she didn't like to travel. Flying first class had been more than comfortable, but the hassle of the baggage claim and Customs lines had just about done in the weary young woman. When Allison and Wolf slid into the back seat of the hired sedan that was waiting for them in the arrivals area, Allison was fighting to keep her eyes open.

"Don't you dare go to sleep," Wolf cautioned Allison. Addressing the car's driver, Wolf instructed the chauffeur to find the nearest café. "We'll get some caffeine in you and you'll perk right up."

A large cup of strong coffee had done the trick. By the time the Savoy's doorman greeted Allison with a cheery "g'day, Madame," the young woman had found her second wind.

The Savoy Hotel stood proudly on the north bank of the Thames River. Allison knew from the research she had done about the trip and the hotels where she and Wolf would be staying that the Savoy's location was convenient to the ballet, opera, and Covent Gardens. Shopping in the designer stores might be out of her reach, but the young woman, nevertheless, hoped she would have time, to at least, take a look at some of the high-fashion shops located in nearby Knightsbridge and Mayfair.

As promised, Wolf had booked separate sleeping accommodations, but instead of separate rooms, Wolf had booked a two-bedroom suite. "I thought it would be nice to share breakfast together without having to go down to one of the restaurants," Wolf explained. "Plus, with the suite we'll get our own English tea service each afternoon."

The Queen Victoria Suite was a statement in Edwardian design. Expensive fabrics covered the upholstered furniture in the suite's sitting room. The heavy, velvet draperies offered a thick yet elegant shield against the damp and rainy weather that, more often than not, inhabited the town. The king-size bed in Allison's bedroom – a luxury not found in most Continental hotels where tiny rooms and tinier bathrooms were the norm – beckoned with its many pillows and sumptuous looking duvet. The adjoining bath, complete with every bathing accessory imaginable, added to the suite's welcoming demeanor.

"Wolf, this is just fabulous. It must be costing you a fortune." Allison rewarded Wolf with a gentle kiss. "It's almost too nice to leave."

"That can certainly be arranged." A wicked grin accompanied Wolf's reply. "I'm sure room service can send up a nice luncheon repast."

Allison felt her belly respond with the low tingle of sexual excitement as Wolf's arms pulled her into a warm embrace. Strong, slim fingers cupped Allison's face as Wolf covered Allison's mouth with his own. A soft moan escaped Allison's lips. Her body was on fire, a response to the sexual attraction that she could no longer deny.

"This isn't the time," Wolf's voice was soft.

A deep red blush crept up Allison's chest and neck. Had she misread Wolf's intentions? "Oh, I'm sorry," she mumbled, embarrassment robbing her of a coherent response.

"Allison, look at me," Wolf commanded gently. "I want to make love to you. It's all I can do to stop myself right now. But our first time shouldn't be when you are so tired you can barely stand up."

Relief flooded Allison. Whether this was relief at not being wrong about Wolf's intentions or relief at being stopped before she took the next step in the relationship was a distinction that didn't matter to her at the moment. As much as she wanted to feel Wolf Johannsen's naked body next to hers, Allison was glad that decision had been postponed.

"I know," Allison squeezed Wolf's hand. "I feel the same way about you, and it terrifies me."

"There's nothing to be afraid of. When the time is right, there will be no hesitation. For either of us," Wolf smiled. "For now, let's enjoy a leisurely lunch. After that, we'll run by my office. There're a few things I need to check on before my meeting tomorrow with the new client. It won't take long. If you're still on your feet, after that, we'll head for the museum."

A short walk found the pair at The Coal Hole, an English pub located in what used to be one of the Savoy's coal cellars. With checkerboard tile floors, large mahogany bar, and frescoed walls, the Coal Hole regaled its customers with tales of a colorful past. Allison's order of fish and chips was superb, as was the large portion of bangers and mash placed before Wolf by the cheery waiter.

"For something with as unappetizing a name as bangers and mash, this dish is really quite yummy," Allison remarked, sampling the sausage and mashed potatoes from Wolf's plate.

"It's no weirder than that breakfast food you Southerners call 'grits'," Wolf replied.

"I guess that's so," Allison agreed. "But I'm fortified now with great food and ready to take in the sights."

"Then, by all means, let's get to it."

# CHAPTER TWELVE

"If it wasn't for the gray skies, I'd swear we were in Greece!" Allison exclaimed, gazing at the imposing façade of the British Museum. "The entrance reminds me of a Greek temple, with all these enormous columns and pediments."

"When the museum was designed in 1823, Greek Revival was all the rage," Wolf replied. "You'll see, as we explore the museum, that the wings which were added later have a different architecture."

Walking up the wide steps to the museum, Allison grew excited at the prospect of the ancient treasures she would see inside. "You said you've been here many times. What gallery should we look at first?"

"That's a hard question to answer," Wolf replied. "This museum houses some of the finest sculpture and artifacts from ancient civilizations. During its Empire years, the Brits basically stole whatever they wanted from the lands they ruled or invaded."

Allison was puzzled, "What do you mean?"

"You know what the Rosetta Stone is, right?" Wolf cast a curious eye towards Allison.

"Yes, of course," Allison nodded. "The Rosetta stone is a granite tablet that gave archeologists the key to deciphering hieroglyphics."

"Correct. That discovery allowed modern archeologists to begin unlocking the secrets of ancient Egypt and her Pharoahs." Wolf paused for effect. "The British Museum houses the largest and most extensive collection of Egyptian artifacts in the entire world other than the Egyptian Museum in Cairo. The Rosetta Stone has been in the possession of the Brits for over 200 years. The Egyptians have been trying to get it back since 2003. Unsuccessfully, I might add."

"That's terrible!" Allison exclaimed.

"Depends on your point of view," Wolf countered. "When Britain acquired many of the artifacts in the museum, they ruled the land where the artifacts were found. I think some of the Greek artifacts have been returned, but most of the really important finds are still here. You, of all people, ought to understand. Isn't possession nine-tenths of the law?"

Allison laughed, "I've certainly heard that expression more than once, but in my line of work, the courts usually make the final decision."

"Yes, but which court?" Wolf queried. "An Egyptian court will likely side with Egypt and an English court with the British Museum."

Leaving the ownership question to others, Wolf and Allison headed up the wide steps of the museum's south entrance. They wouldn't have time to see all of the seven permanent galleries containing the Egyptian exhibits, but the couple intended to see as much as they could.

"I think my mind is on overload," Allison remarked, resting her head against Wolf's shoulder as they walked through Trafalger Square. "That giant red granite statue of Amenhotep III was stunning."

"No telling how long it took for the craftsmen to carve something that size," Wolf remarked. "I knew you would be impressed with the museum's collection."

"And all those mummies," Allison shook her head at the memory. "It's really sort of freaky to me to think about how those people were embalmed and preserved for thousands of years. They even embalmed their cats."

Wolf laughed, "Yeah, the cat mummies are pretty freaky, to use your term, but cats had special status in Egyptian culture. In a religion that believed what was buried with the body would reappear in the afterlife, it's not so unexpected to see an animal with supernatural powers buried, as well."

The brightly lit façade of the Savoy Hotel beckoned as the couple approached their destination. "How about a drink in the bar?" Wolf asked. "We can eat something light and then turn in early."

"That sounds perfect," Allison agreed. "I'm on my last leg. It's almost five London time. If I can make it until seven, I'll be down for the count until sometime tomorrow."

"This is the only way to get your body adjusted to the time change," Wolf reminded Allison. "You'll be fine by tomorrow. You can lounge around the suite in the morning while I meet with the firm's new client. We'll continue our sightseeing after lunch."

The plush velvet booth offered both comfort and privacy. After perusing the bar's alcoholic offerings, Allison decided on a simple pinot noir and a small plate of various charcuteries.

"To us," Wolf raised his beer to toast Allison's glass of wine.

"To us," Allison agreed.

# CHAPTER THIRTEEN

Frank hadn't played Blackjack in a while, mainly because he hated losing. Poker was more Frank's kind of game, but the P.I. thought he might have more luck getting information from the dealer at the Blackjack table than playing video poker. The added benefit of his "sort of" disguise was the accommodating attitude of the pit boss and the waitress assigned to the table where Frank was trying his best to win.

Frank's first card was an eight of Hearts, followed on the dealer's second pass with a four of Clubs. Responding to the dealer's inquiry, Frank barked, "Hit me!" and watched as his third card was dealt face down.

Two of the other four players at the table had declined a third card, instead replying to the dealer with "stand," indicating they would take a chance that their combined cards would be higher in value than those held unseen by the dealer. The man and woman to Frank's left each took a third card and waited.

The dealer turned over his cards and counted them. "Seventeen," he announced. With trepidation, Frank flipped his third card.

"Eight of Spades," Frank announced, his winning combination of twenty points clearly crowning the P.I. as the winner of the current game, much to the chagrin of the other players. "I think I'll cash in for the evening." Reaching across the table, Frank gathered the chips stacked on the table with a smile. With so many other players at the table, there hadn't been a good opportunity to talk to the dealer about Mona Phillips. Maybe he'd have better luck elsewhere.

Winnings converted to cash, Frank ambled into the casino's well-appointed bar, heaved his considerable girth onto a seat at the end of the polished bar, and signaled for the bartender. "Budweiser."

Sipping a cold brew, Frank surveyed the bar area. It was still fairly early in the evening, so the crowd was sparse and the bartender wasn't overly-occupied fixing drinks or chatting with his customers. Frank decided to see what he could wrangle from the young man behind the bar.

"Hey, how about some nuts to go with this beer?" Frank gestured at the bartender. "Don't want to get plastered too early."

The barkeep placed a large bowl of assorted nuts in

front of Frank. "We've got a good bar menu, if you want something more than this."

"Nah, I've got a meal on the house at the Painted Horse Restaurant," Frank replied, dropping the name of the casino's most expensive restaurant. "Just need a little somethin' to take the edge off before my 8:30 reservation." Frank downed the last of his beer. "How 'bout one more?"

"You must be a frequent guest at the casino to merit a meal at the Painted Horse," the bartender commented, as he placed a second icy brew on the polished bar top in front of the P.I. "I've haven't been working here all that long, so there's a lot of players I don't know by sight yet."

"Perfect," Frank thought. "Well, I do most of my gambling over at the Blue Moon Casino in Mississippi. Got friends there, but I'd heard about this place and decided to give it a try a few months back." Frank took a slow sip of his beer. "Met one of the waitresses, a good lookin' gal named Mona somethin' or other, but I haven't seen her this trip. She still work here?"

In an instant, the expression on the bartender's face went from friendly to suspicious. Pulling a white rag from his back pocket, the young man began to polish the already-pristine surface of the bar top. Frank knew from experience that the young man was trying to decide what, if anything, he would say. And Frank knew better than to push, at least not yet. Casually, the P.I. grabbed a handful of nuts and waited.

"Mona isn't working here right now." The bartender

continued to polish the bar top, refusing to meet Frank's eyes. "Not sure if she'll be back."

"Sorry to hear that," Frank commented. "She sure was a friendly gal." Frank wondered if the bartender was old enough to understand the P.I.'s use of the word 'friendly'. No telling what word the twenty-somethings used nowadays to describe a man, or woman, who was casual about certain parts of his or her life.

"That woman is a piece of work - and trouble." The young man gave Frank a sharp look. "Lies like a dog, and gets away with it, too."

Frank decided to play along. "I thought she might have been comin' on to me last time I was here. What's her story?"

The bartender laughed, "What's her story? Rumor here is she's filed some sort of claim against one of the casino supervisors, says the guy has sexually harassed her. I don't believe it for a minute."

Frank leaned closer to the bartender and lowered his voice, "Really? Boy am I glad I didn't take her up to my room or anything. But why don't you believe her? You got something on her?"

"Nothing that's not common knowledge," the bartender laughed again. "Mona strips down at the Magic Lounge a couple of nights a week. The guy she's charged with sexual harassment is a damn choir boy. No way Benje would have done what Mona claims, and frankly, I doubt there's anything anyone could say or do to Mona Phillips that would offend her."

Part of Frank wanted to break his cover and ask the young man if he'd put what he had just told Frank into a written statement. The other part, the more rational part of the private investigator, knew that keeping his disguise in place might yet garner further information. Either way, Frank's gut told him the bartender wouldn't back off his story. In the meantime, Frank planned to enjoy a nice repast in the Painted Horse Restaurant. Maybe he'd get some other tidbit from whoever waited his table.

# CHAPTER FOURTEEN

Gyuri Vargha tied the scarlet ascot with a slight flourish. Admiring himself in the long mirror, Gyuri noted with satisfaction the figure that peered back at him. The expensive, European-cut navy suit barely concealed the compact muscle that covered his 5'10" frame. His longish hair curled along the back of his neck, a hairstyle intended to suggest to the casual observer that the man wasn't as old as the gray specks in the dark hair would indicate. The face work that Gyuri had paid for six months earlier had been purchased for vanity rather than disguise. The procedure had shaved a good ten years from the heavily lined face that the cosmetic surgeon had started with. Now, the man standing in front of the mirror looked rested, fit and ready for whatever the evening might bring.

Running into Charlene Jacobs a couple of weeks back had planted the seed of an idea in the Russian spy's mind. When Gyuri had shared his idea with his old KGB friend, his ex-handler had argued, "No one in the business knows you're alive, Gyuri. Why don't you leave it that way? Moscow has retired you. Stay on the island your money bought and enjoy life."

Gyuri hadn't bothered to tell Mika that he had already been recognized by the wealthy ex-pat American who lived in Rome. "Calm yourself, Mika. My plan is foolproof. If anyone questions where I've been for the past five years, I'll tell them I've been away working on a book. The civilians who knew me in Rome before will believe me now. To them, I'm just a rich and eccentric writer who has developed a passion for collecting art."

Gyuri turned off several table lamps as he walked to the apartment's front door. The spacious flat had been offered at an exorbitant rate for a two year lease, but Gyuri hadn't blinked at the price. Furnished with high-end pieces, oriental rugs and exquisite artwork, the flat offered Gyuri a comfortable abode in Rome's art district while, at the same time, adding to his cover. If his plan was successful, Gyuri hoped to be able to keep the apartment indefinitely. If not, well, it wouldn't matter.

Dusk was drawing to a beautiful conclusion as Gyuri left the apartment building and headed towards Via de Monserrato. The pinkish tinge of the sun's last gasp washed the buildings in a hue that human painters could only dream of achieving. Gyuri doubted that any of the paintings displayed at tonight's gala at Il Piccolo Parisdiso would compare with the majesty that covered the Rome sky as day slipped quickly into night.

Charlene Jacobs was standing just outside the gallery doorway. "Ciao, Bella" Gyuri smiled, greeting Charlene with kisses to both sides of the woman's aging but still attractive face. "I hope I have not kept you waiting."

"I've just arrived. Your timing is perfect." Charlene picked nervously at the double strand of Akoya pearls that encircled her neck. Gyuri Vargha had never shown a bit of interest in her when he had been part of the Rome art scene five years earlier. Charlene knew the man who had asked to meet her at the gallery opening could have had his pick of much younger and more attractive companions. Gyuri's purported interest in her had made Charlene more than a little anxious about the evening's date. She didn't think he was after her money, so what was he after?

The sound of multiple conversations floated from the gallery's open doorway. "Sounds like the party has already started," Gyuri remarked offering Charlene his arm. "Shall we?"

Il Piccolo Paridiso was a small gallery, but its main room was larger than the gallery's street frontage suggested. Twenty-foot ceilings and bright white walls reflected the overhead lighting perfectly, aided by smaller lighting effects which showcased the various canvases hanging on the gallery walls. In the center of the room stood two long wooden tables laden with all sorts of finger food and accented with enormous, but tasteful, floral arrangements, and in an alcove to the left of the main space, a bartender filled patrons' crystal flutes with French champagne.

"Charlene, darling." Rebecca Molinere rushed to greet her friend. "I was afraid you weren't coming." Purposely, Rebecca ignored Gyuri Vargha.

"You know I never miss your openings," Charlene laughed. "This time you may have outdone yourself. It looks spectacular. Gyuri and I were just heading to the bar for a libation before we toured the exhibit."

Rebecca allowed Gyuri a slight smile, "I don't believe we've met. I'm Rebecca Molinere."

"Renee Depeche's granddaughter," Gyuri gave Rebecca a short bow. "It's a pleasure to meet you. I'm Gyuri Vargha."

Rebecca struggled to keep her expression neutral, "Were you a friend of my grandfather?"

"Only peripherally," Gyuri replied. "I was an admirer of his work, and included him in a book on 20$^{th}$ century watercolorists that I published ten years ago."

Rebecca feigned confusion. "What did you say your name is? I thought I was familiar with most of the authors who wrote about my grandfather during his lifetime."

The Russian chuckled, "Gyuri Vargha. My books, unfortunately for me, have never been best sellers in the serious art world. It's unlikely you would have even heard of me, and I'm sure your grandfather wouldn't have remembered me either."

"Well, I hope you and Charlene will enjoy the exhibit, Mr. Vargha. There are some remarkable pieces that will most certainly double in value over the next decade. If you like what you see, tonight would be the time to buy." Rebecca brushed a light kiss over Charlene's cheek. "I've got to attend to other guests. Call me for lunch later in the week."

Rebecca Molinere watched her friend and the Russian spy who should have been dead merge with the crowd of gallery patrons. A call to one of her grandfather's old agents in Paris might confirm Gyuri's claim of knowing Papa Depeche. Certainly Vargha's story, true or not, had given her an excuse for calling him. More was to be discovered.

# CHAPTER FIFTEEN

The two days spent in London were barely enough for Allison. Wolf had suggested a Grey Line tour for their second and only full day in Britain's capitol. "It's the best way to see the most famous landmarks in the short time we have." Westminster Abby, Parliament, the Tower of London, Buckingham Palace – the brief excursions the tour had offered served only to pique Allison's desire for a return trip at some point in the future.

As Allison and Wolf settled into their seats for the two hour and twenty minute Eurostar train trip via the Chunnel from London to Paris, the Swede asked Allison which of the London sights had been her favorite.

"The Tower of London, definitely," Allison replied without hesitation. "Seeing the exhibit of the Crown

Jewels was amazing, but the tower's bloody history was a glimpse into Britain's past that I wasn't all that familiar with."

Wolf raised his eyebrows in mock surprise. "Do I detect a bit of bloodthirsty voyeurism?"

"Of course not," Allison retorted. "But seeing the chopping block where so many lost their heads and the actual axe that did the deed brought the words in my Western Civ textbook to life. I can't imagine the terror Anne Boleyn must have felt when they imprisoned her there. She had to know what was coming."

The English countryside passed quickly outside the train window. Most people unfamiliar with the area between London and the English Channel were always surprised to find themselves in a mostly bucolic area. Glancing at his watch, Wolf noted the train was almost at the British portal to the Chunnel.

"We're getting ready to head under the channel," Wolf advised. "You still nervous about going under the water?"

Allison forced a smile, "I know it only takes about twenty minutes to make the crossing at the speed we're going, but a lot can happen in twenty minutes."

Wolf kissed the top of Allison's head. "Don't worry, Alskling. We'll be in France before you know it." Then, deciding that Allison needed something to distract her, Wolf started with a topic he hadn't planned to discuss just yet. "You know most of my covert work for the C.I.A. was on the Continent, right?"

The surprising inquiry pushed all thoughts of drowning from Allison's mind. "Uh, yes." Allison's tone made her answer a question rather than a statement. Was there something Wolf had neglected to share with her about this trip? Allison gave Wolf her full attention and waited.

"And you know I've been out of the business now for several years."

"Yes, you told me that night coming back from the restaurant in Auburn, after I called you out on who you really were," Allison frowned. Remembering Wolf's initial deception still irked the lawyer, even though she understood why he had hidden his real agenda for being in Ft. Charles. But time had passed now, and Wolf had made the commitment to stay in Ft. Charles and run Johannsen Consulting remotely. In fact, Wolf's consulting business was the reason they had gone to London. A chilling thought caused Allison to exclaim, "Don't tell me you've gone back in!"

"No, not at all," Wolf rushed to assure Allison. "But since we're going to be in Rome at the end of the week, I thought I'd stop by and see if one of my old contacts would have dinner with us."

Allison considered Wolf's explanation. It sounded totally bogus to the amateur sleuth, but she decided to play along. "Oh? A woman? Should I be jealous?"

Wolf laughed. His diversionary tactic had worked. The windows in the train car once again showed a rural countryside as the Eurostar sped towards Paris' Gard du Nord train station. "Yes, a woman, but no one you need to worry about. My relationship with Rebecca was always a professional one, and I intend to keep it that way."

Allison was intrigued. "Is she an agent?"

"Not in the terms you are probably thinking," Wolf replied. "Rebecca owns an art gallery in Rome. Her grandfather was a fairly famous painter in his day, and Rebecca's family was – and is - wealthy. Rebecca has contacts across the art world that have made her a useful asset for the Agency. Really more information gathering than anything else."

When Wolf realized he was getting serious about Allison, the ex-operative had shared, as honestly as he thought advisable, the details of his work for the C.I.A. Thinking back on their multiple conversations about Wolf's shadow career, Allison recalled a small, but important, detail. "Information gathering is how you started with the Agency wasn't it?"

"Yes," Wolf nodded, "just like Rebecca, I had international contacts that brought me to the Agency's attention."

"But you didn't stick to just information gathering, did you?" Allison watched Wolf's body language closely. The young lawyer had learned that sometimes the truth showed more clearly in how a person reacted to a question rather than what he or she actually said.

"You already know the answer to that question." A shadow flitted briefly across the Swede's face. The conversation that Wolf had intended as a distraction had suddenly moved to a serious discussion. "I'm not ashamed of what I did for the C.I.A. But that part of my life is over."

Allison gathered Wolf's strong hands in her smaller, softer ones. "Wolf, I'm not angry with you, or ashamed of you. If that's how you heard my question, I apologize. I was thinking about the similarities in how you and your friend Rebecca started your hidden careers with the Agency."

"And you wonder if Rebecca has become something other than an information gatherer?" Wolf paused to process both Allison's question and to consider the significance of the message that had been waiting for him at his London office. "It's a legitimate question. I don't think Rebecca would be suited for the type of work I ended up doing for the Agency, but I can see her becoming more proactive than when I last worked with her."

The Eurostar's public address system announced the train's imminent arrive at the Paris station. Allison didn't push the conversation further, and Wolf followed her cue. They wouldn't be in Rome before Friday. In the meantime, the George Cinq and all of Paris beckoned.

# CHAPTER SIXTEEN

Biting off the end of a fresh cigar, Frank Martin spat in the general direction of the overflowing trash can. Half hidden by the crap Frank had earlier tossed towards the container as the P.I. rummaged through envelopes, assorted papers, potato chip bags and candy wrappers that had accumulated on his large desk, the smallish silver wastebasket couldn't hold another item, even one as tiny as the butt end of a Cuban cigar.

"Sheila!" Frank bellowed. "I need you!" When his command failed to instantly materialize his secretary and Girl Friday, Sheila McMurray, the irritated man hollered, "NOW!"

The sound of running footsteps heralded the approach of an out-of-breath Sheila. "Mr. Martin," Sheila's exasperation accented her words. "all you have to do is press the intercom button on your phone. There's no need to shout."

"Harumph!" Frank's grumble was as close to an apology as his seasoned secretary was likely to receive. "I can't find my notes on the Blue Wind case."

"You mean the ones you gave me yesterday to type up?" Leaning against the door jam, Sheila crossed her arms and waited for a response.

Frank shuffled a few of the papers on his desk. He hated forgetting things. It made him feel old. Shaking his head, the P.I. gave Sheila a rueful smile. "Yes, the ones I gave you yesterday."

"Here you go." Sheila handed her boss a sheaf of typed pages and Frank's original hen-scratched notes. "If you need something else," Sheila moved to Frank's desk and uncovered his office phone, "just press this button and I'll answer right away."

Frank's trip to the Blue Wind Casino had turned out to be more profitable than he had anticipated. In addition to his winnings at Blackjack plus the two free dinners at the casino's high end eating establishments, Frank had uncovered a goldmine's worth of information about Mona Phillips from several of the casino's employees. The absolutely most interesting piece of Intel Frank had garnered was Mona's part-time job at the Magic Lounge. Making a visit to the strip club would be Frank's next step in the investigation.

Unfortunately, however, the Mona Phillips case wasn't Frank's only investigation. Frank turned his chair to face the credenza situated on the wall behind his massive desk. A coffee pot that had seen better days sat dangerously near the edge on the far left, flanked by a couple of chipped mugs. Stacks of investigative files relating to current matters offered a visual counterweight to the Mr. Coffee, the two kept apart by a large, old-fashioned, monthly calendar which commandeered a good two feet of space. Frank was old-school and he liked to actually see a calendar instead of trying to decipher the midget ones on his cell phone. Most of the calendar's black-edged squares denoting the days of the current month were covered in X's.

The P.I.'s calendar for the next couple of weeks was packed with obligations for other clients. He was scheduled to testify in a divorce proceeding starting the following Monday, and then in a criminal matter for another client at the end of that week. Frank didn't mind testifying about targets suspected of monetary crimes, but he hated testifying about cheating spouses. But, surveilling cheating spouses paid Frank's overhead and since that sort of behavior was likely to continue for the foreseeable future, Frank took the cases if he had the time to handle them.

Reluctantly, Frank laid aside the Phillips file and turned his attention to the McNamara case. Mark Lockridge's call to Frank earlier in the year had been a surprise. The last time Frank had spoken to the local attorney was during the Goodpasture divorce trial. Frank's testimony against Lockridge's client, Evelyn Goodpasture, had established Evelyn's guilt as an adulteress. The resulting judgment in favor of Evelyn's husband Miles and the wagging tongues of Ft. Charles' society gossips had set Evelyn on a murderous path. Frank still struggled with guilt, even though he knew Evelyn's own actions were what had ultimately caused the tragedy.

Frank also knew that his testimony in the Goodpasture case wasn't the only reason Lockridge had hired him to tail his client's husband. Frank was a damn good private investigator, with ethics that many in his trade didn't have. Frank dug, and dug deep, on a target, but he played by the rules. Mostly. Having contacts in various public and non-public records agencies often gave Frank information that would otherwise have been difficult to retrieve. In Frank's mind, he came close to the line but he never stepped over it.

Mark Lockridge was happy with Frank's report on Tim McNamara. Over the three months that Frank had surveilled his target the P.I. had been able to record several hours of motel rendezvous with a woman not Tim McNamara's wife. On one occasion, an open curtain had allowed the zoom on Frank's camera to snap pictures of the couple in flagrante delicto. Personally, Frank couldn't think of anything more embarrassing that seeing one's naked ass on the big screen in a Calhoun County courtroom. If Tim McNamara had a brain cell left in his head, he would settle a healthy sum of money on his wife and end the case before trial. If the case settled, the several days Frank had set aside to be in court would be wide-open giving him a last minute opportunity to take a trip to the Magic Lounge.

# CHAPTER SEVENTEEN

Rebecca Molinere considered her next move. Getting close to the alleged Russian spy might be easier than she had initially thought. The man's comment about knowing her grandfather offered a convenient and believable pretense for the gallery owner to reach out to the man calling himself Gyuri Vargha. Rebecca had asked Bastien Dubois to find out what Langley might have on the real Vargha's life as an art critic and author. Information was insurance in Rebecca's work as a deep cover agent. Sometimes, just the smallest and seemingly inconsequential fact ended up being the key that allowed the Agency to close a case. With sufficient background information on the real Guyri Vargha, Rebecca intended to sniff out whether the man she had met at the gallery's latest show was the real deal or an imposter.

If Gyuri Vargha was actually who the Agency thought he might be, Rebecca would have to be careful. A spy clever enough to get away with faking his own death and then bold enough to resurface under his own name, was a man to be very wary of. The question in Rebecca's mind was simple. If this was, indeed, Gyuri Vargha, where had he been for the past five years, and what was he doing in Rome? Shaking her head, Rebecca placed the question on a mental shelf. She needed more information from multiple sources before she would know the answer. In the meantime, Rebecca's reputation as one of Rome's most interesting hostesses would give her an excuse to invite Vargha to a cocktail party at her home. But not directly.

Retrieving Charlene Jacobs' number, Rebecca rang her friend. "Charlene, darling, how are you today?"

"Fit as a fiddle, as the Yanks say," Charlene replied. "At least, I will be after I have a little 'hair of the dog'."

"Late night and too much fun?"

"Lord, yes." A yawn reverberated across the phone line. "Gyuri and I were out until almost 2 in the morning. I'm not used to staying up that late."

"I hear you. I haven't seen midnight in longer than I want to admit." Rebecca sent a silent thank you to the Universe for the opening Charlene had given her. "I guess you and Gyuri are seeing each other some?"

"As amazing as that sounds, it seems that I've caught Gyuri's eye." The faint sound of liquid splashing over ice cubes followed by a gratified sigh prefaced Charlene's further reply. "He's going to Florence tomorrow for an overnight and he's asked me to go with him."

"And are you?" Rebecca knew all too well her friend's penchant for spur of the moment decisions that often backfired.

"I thought about it," Charlene admitted, "but I don't want Gyuri to think I'm an easy lay. I told him no."

Her friend's reply surprised Rebecca. "Charlene Jacobs!" Rebecca exclaimed. "Are you seriously interested in this man?"

"I know he's at least ten years younger than I am, and he's probably just interested in my money, but at this point in my life I don't care," Charlene paused. It was hard to admit the truth even to Rebecca. "If money can buy me happiness with Gyuri, then I'm willing to pay."

"You don't need to buy happiness," Rebecca assured her friend. "There's not a man out there who wouldn't be interested in you. But- playing a tad hard –to-get isn't a bad idea."

"I hope I haven't run him off, declining his invitation to Florence," Charlene worried. "Maybe I should call him back and tell him I've changed my mind."

"I have a better idea, and it's the reason for my call," Rebecca interjected. "I'm throwing a cocktail party this coming Friday. You can call Gyuri and invite him as your date."

The phone line was silent while Charlene considered Rebecca's suggestion and invitation. Just as Rebecca was getting ready to ask, "Are you still there?" her friend replied,

"That's a great idea. I'll ring him later this morning and let you know what he says."

The remainder of the morning passed quickly for Rebecca Molinere. A meeting with a young, new artist who was trying to break into the Rome art scene consumed several hours. Rebecca's trained eye thought Sergio Cantele's work showed promise. If the young artist's edgy style continued to improve, it was quite likely that even his early paintings would one day fetch a handsome price. By the time the meeting had concluded, Rebecca had agreed to show three of Sergio's paintings for a 50% commission. If the work sold, Rebecca would take the next few pieces at a lower rate.

As per her habit, Rebecca closed the gallery between noon and 3:00 to take riposo, the Italian equivalent of a siesta following a leisurely lunch. Today, however, she wanted to use part of that time to decide who to invite to her cocktail party. Most of the guests would be from her close-knit social group, but she would add one or two artists and authors for entertainment. Penning invitations on monogramed notecards, Rebecca asked for an RSVP by Thursday, noon. She would have the gallery's runner take the invitations around to the recipients later in the afternoon.

The last invitation would, by necessity, need to be made via telephone. When the answering machine beeped, Rebecca began, "Hello, Bastien? It's Rebecca. I've decided to host a cocktail party this Friday and would love for you to attend. That old friend we talked about should be there. 8 P.M. my flat."

# CHAPTER EIGHTEEN

The city views from the balcony of Gyuri's rented apartment were stunning. Situated in the Rioni Monti area of Rome, Palazzo Giorgioli offered its tenants close proximity to many of the city's most famous landmarks. Just a short half-mile walk from his apartment, Gyuri had considered the Coliseum for today's meet. The large crowds of tourists would provide excellent cover for him, but it had been a long time since the spy had seen his Rome contact. Better to be in an unobtrusive, out-of-the-way location for today's agenda.

At exactly 2 P.M., Gyuri Vargha descended the steps to the relic museum located underneath the Basilica de Maria Maggiore. Personally, Gyuri thought the contents of the small museum rivaled anything he had seen at the Vatican. Paintings, original gold-laden Papal garments, numerous gold and bejeweled chalices and crowns – the treasure trove belonging to the generations of men who ruled the Catholic Church as God's Voice and Emissary to mankind filled the small cavern space to overflowing. In all the times Gyuri had visited the museum, he had never encountered another soul. Hopefully, that fact would hold true today. If Franco Perelli had changed sides, the relic museum would be a fitting place to leave a body.

Hiding himself but with a clear view of the museum entrance, Gyuri didn't have to wait long. The man who entered had aged, but he was still recognizable. Gyuri waited until Perelli's back was to him, then moving quickly, placed a hand around Perelli's mouth and the barrel end of a silenced Ruger in his back.

"Move!" Gyuri ordered. "Hands on the wall. If you make a sound, you're dead."

Keeping the gun pressed firmly into Perelli's back, Gyuri conducted a fast but thorough pat-down. "I see you still favor the blade." Gyuri tucked the stiletto into his own waistband.

"And I see you're still the same ass-hole," Perelli muttered.

"Being an ass-hole is better than some alternatives I can think of." Gyuri removed the gun from Perelli's back. "Anyone follow you?"

"Of course not." Franco Perelli was insulted. "Besides, it's been quiet for a while now. Hacking has replaced boots on the ground." Perelli examined the man standing before him. The news that Gyuri Vargha was still alive had come as a shock to the experienced operative. "When I got your message, I was certain it was a trick. But I ran it up the line, and here you are. Hell, you don't even look like you've aged."

The ghost of a smile briefly crossed Gyuri's face. "You might say I've been on an extended vacation." Franco Perelli didn't need to know about the cosmetic surgery Gyuri's vanity had prompted him to undergo. "No stress. No worries. It's amazing how the simple life removes years from one's face."

Perelli leaned against a class cabinet displaying a collection of jewel-encrusted chalices. Gyuri Vargha had never been trustworthy, and Perelli doubted a so-called five-year vacation had brought about a change in the man in front of him. "Enough chit chat, Gyuri. Why did you reach out to me?"

"What do you know about the agent who tried to kill me?" Perelli had to strain to hear Gyuri's question. "What did you hear after it went down?"

"Just rumors," Perelli lied. "The hit could have been ordered by London or Washington. Maybe even Berlin. We never got any credible leads on your assassin."

Silence filled the cavern as Perelli studied Gyuri's face. Would the Russian catch the lie in his words? The operative had taken a chance coming without a gun, but he knew Gyuri would search for a weapon, so bringing it on his person would have served no purpose. "Why do you ask?" Perelli moved nearer to the small caliber backup piece he had secreted inside the museum earlier that day. If Gyuri made a move, Perelli would have only one chance to defend himself.

"Unfinished business," Gyuri's face was as blank and cold as stone. "Do you still have contacts in the underground?"

"Yes, although I haven't reached out to them in a while," Perelli replied. "Like I said, it's been quiet for a long time."

"I want to know the name of the man who tried to kill me,"Guyri stared at Perelli. "See what you can find out."

Perelli fought to keep a calm façade. Gyuri's request was bad news on a variety of levels. "Gyuri, it's been five years. No one is going to have that kind of information now if they didn't have it five years ago. Let it go. You're alive, and according to Moscow, out for retirement. Not many in our line of work get the luxury of retiring on the upside of the grass. Enjoy the gift you've gotten."

"Someone tried to kill me," Gyuri spat the words. "I lost years trying to heal from the damage the bullets and the drugs I took to mimic death inflicted on my body." Gyuri's eyes grew dark, "I will have my revenge."

Franco Perelli nodded. He would play along until those above him instructed otherwise. "I will see what I can find out. How can I contact you?"

"I'm staying at Palazzo Giorgioli."

"In plain sight and under your own name?" Perelli was surprised. This might be worse than he thought.

"Yes," Gyuri laughed. "I'm just an old art critic and author visiting Rome again. Whoever gave me up to the assassin five years ago may still be around. If so, becoming a part of the art scene again ought to make that person very nervous. And this time, I'll be watching."

Perelli waited in the museum for several minutes after Gyuri left. He felt confident no one had followed him to the meet, but in the slim chance that he had not noticed a tail, being seen leaving with Gyuri Vargha was not a good idea.

Gyuri's plan for revenge was more than dangerous. Not only was Wolf Johannsen possibly in danger, several other operatives in Rome and Paris might be as well. Given the fact that he was still alive, Perelli felt certain Gyuri was unaware of where Perelli's true loyalties lay. Hopefully, Rebecca Molinere had notified Langley about Gyuri's presence in Rome. The gallery owner had been as shocked as Perelli at Gyuri's reappearance.

"So much to do," Perelli thought as he hailed a cab. "Would there be enough time?"

# CHAPTER NINETEEN

"I loved that little patisserie on Rue des Opera. Maybe we can go back there this afternoon?"

Wolf grinned at his companion's request. For a woman as petite and slim as Allison, the amount of food she had consumed so far in Paris had been astounding. "I take it you like French cuisine a lot better than what we had in London?"

"There wasn't anything in London like La Tour D'Argent. I could eat there every day." Allison fingered the waistband of her slacks. "Except that I'd have to buy all new clothes. I'm just hoping all the walking we're doing is counter-acting the calories."

"Since we're leaving for Rome tomorrow, I thought we'd spend today at the Louvre. We can have an early dinner afterwards at the hotel. That 6:00 flight is going to mean an early wake-up call." Wolf reached for Allison's hand as the two continued their walk. "We can grab some pastries after the Louvre. They'll make a quick breakfast in the morning before we grab a cab to the airport."

The walk from the George Cinq Hotel to the Louvre down the Rue Francois took a good forty minutes, due in part to Allison's insistence on perusing the windows of the various small shops they passed. Normally not a big shopper, the delights of the Parisian merchants had caught her eye. The big-name stores like Louis Vuitton and Chanel that the couple had seen earlier in the Paris trip held no interest for the young woman from Alabama. Instead, Allison found herself drawn to the smaller boutiques where the shopkeepers didn't ignore Allison's attempts at the native language, and the items for sale were more unique and certainly more affordable.

"Did you know the Louvre was originally built as a fortress?" Allison had researched the museum the night before. "It was used as a royal palace for almost six hundred years before Louis XIV moved the royal household to Versailles."

Entering the museum through the glass pyramid designed by Chinese-American I.M.Pei, Wolf remarked, "And it's been added onto more than once. This latest addition," Wolf motioned with his hand, drawing Allison's attention to the enormous glass structure, "caused tons of uproar over the modernistic design."

"I can see why." Allison craned her neck to examine

the multi-paned glass building. "While the pyramid itself is an interesting design, I think it's out of place – really sort of incongruent with the rest of the Louvre's architecture."

"You're not alone," Wolf replied. "But whatever one's thoughts about it, the pyramid makes for an unusual entrance to the museum."

Wolf and Allison spent the next five hours taking in a portion of the treasures housed in the world famous museum. The Café Richelieu outside the apartments of Napolean III provided an infusion of caffeine and a much needed respite for the couple before they tackled as much as they could of the remaining 700,000 square foot museum. By late afternoon, the weary pair hailed a taxi and settled in for the ride back to their hotel, allowing just a brief detour for Allison's desired pastries.

"I can't get over how small the Mona Lisa is." Allison leaned against Wolf's shoulder in the back seat of the Citron. "Tiny, really, in comparison to so many of the other works in the Louvre."

"A little less than two feet by two and a half feet," Wolf replied. "Small indeed compared to what most of us imagine when we see a picture of that portrait in a book."

"And those enormous paintings that took up entire walls," Allison remarked. "The Wedding at Cana is over thirty-two feet wide. How can anyone paint something that large?"

"I guess that's why some painters are known as

the Masters? It takes a genius to paint something as magnificent as the works we saw today."

"Le George Cinq, Monsieur." The cab had stopped at the hotel's front entrance. "Nous sommes ici."

"Merci," Wolf replied, handing the driver his requested fare and a generous tip as he and Allison exited the car.

The lights of the several crystal and gold chandeliers beckoned as the couple traversed the hotel lobby, the reflected illumination softening the ornate trappings which marked the George Cinq as an expensive and select hotel. Instead of making Allison feel out of place by its extravagance, the George Cinq had, somehow, given just the opposite impression to the young woman. A part of her would be sorry to leave the comforts she had enjoyed for the past few days.

"Wolf, do mind if we take supper in our suite?" Allison gathered her courage and made the request. She had more than food on her mind.

A look of surprise crossed Wolf's face. "Are you tired?"

A slow blush crept up Allison's neck. "No." Allison forced herself to look Wolf squarely in the eye. "Paris is the city for lovers as much as the city for diners." Good lord, Allison, the young woman reprimanded herself. You sound like lines from a bad movie. Taking a deep breath, she continued. "I want to remember our first time here, in this city, in this fabulous old hotel, in this magical space we have created."

The elevators doors closed behind the couple. Wolf's strong arms gathered Allison's body to his own.

Hungry mouths sought one another, interrupted only by the ding of the opening elevator doors announcing their arrival at the hotel's penthouse floor.

Inside their suite, Wolf placed a "do not disturb" sign on the front of the door. Closing the short distance between him and Allison, Wolf's fingers caressed the young woman's face. "You don't know how long I have wanted this. Are you sure?"

"Absolutely." The increasing heat between Allison's legs made it hard for her to reply. With trembling hands, Allison began to unbutton Wolf's shirt. "I've never been more certain."

Wolf's lips crushed Allison's. Hands tore at clothing. Their first time would be fast, intense, and demanding. The thick pile of a Persian rug softened Allison's body as Wolf lowered her to the carpet. Instinct and desire consumed them. Nothing existed but the need to be joined as one.

Allison wrapped her legs around Wolf's back, opening herself to receive her lover. Slowly at first, and then with increasing intensity as passion overwhelmed him, Wolf thrust himself deep inside the wetness that surrounded his member.

Wolf fought to hold off the release his body demanded. Finally, when his cause seemed lost, he felt the walls of Allison's vagina pulse against his penis, signaling an orgasm which welcomed Wolf's own.

After their breath had calmed, Wolf rolled to Allison's side, their sweat-drenched bodies still touching. "That was something," he whispered, emotion still raw in his voice.

"It was more than something." Allison turned to face Wolf as a soft smile lit her face. "But I have one question."

"Which is?" Wolf ran his fingers across Allison's taut belly.

"Are you up for seconds?"

# CHAPTER TWENTY

The dossier that Bastien Dubois had Fedexed to the gallery lay discarded on Rebecca Molinere's desk. Bastien's research had been thorough. Gyuri Vargha had, indeed, been a member of her grandfather's social circle in the waning days of his career, before Parkinson's had robbed Rene Depeche of his ability and driven the artist to suicide. A tear rolled down Rebecca's cheek as the sad memories flooded back.

Bastien had included a copy of a biographical article Vargha had published about her grandfather in Art International Magazine the month after the artist's death. It was clear from the contents of the article that Vargha had known her grandfather much better than she had realized. Strange, Rebecca thought. She had met most of her grandfather's friends on her various trips to Paris over the years, yet she had no recollection of ever meeting or hearing about Gyuri Vargha from her grandfather.

Vargha's life as an art critic had been a good cover for the foreign agent. Gyuri had an actual degree in Art History from a reputable university, had spent time as an assistant curator at Museum Berggruen in Berlin, and had published extensively in critical art magazines. It had taken the C.I.A. almost a decade to discover Vargha's real job, spying for the K.G.B., and then only fortuitous circumstances had revealed the agent for who he was.

Gyuri Vargha had been Wolf Johannsen's last kill for the Agency. If the man now claiming to be Vargha was the Russian spy, Rebecca shuddered to think what the implications might be, not only for the Agency but possibly, for Wolf Johannsen as well.

Normally, Rebecca would not use a friend in the way she was considering, but Charlene Jacobs' access to Gyuri Vargha was an opportunity Rebecca couldn't refuse to ignore. Langley had ordered Rebecca to confirm or deny Vargha's true identity, and using Charlene was the best option currently available to the deep cover agent.

The small gray phone on Rebecca's desk buzzed announcing a visitor at the gallery's back entrance off a narrow alley. Activating a remote camera, Rebecca recognized the slight figure of Bastien Dubois standing close to the door.

"Bastien," Rebecca spoke using the security system's intercom. "Why are you at the back door?"

"Just let me in," Dubois replied, his furtive glances towards the back of the alley recorded by the security camera. "Now!"

Carefully navigating the smooth concrete steps that led from the back of the gallery to the lower basement level, Rebecca hurried to unlock the door on the gallery's small loading dock. The cylinders inside the locking mechanism sounded a soft "snick" as the door's deadbolt slid open. On alert from the tone in Bastien's voice, Rebecca peered tentatively around the partially opened door.

"What is going on?" she asked as Bastien Dubois bolted inside. "Why the cloak and dagger entrance?"

"Is anyone in the gallery?" Bastien motioned towards the stairs.

"No," Rebecca shook her head. "I closed today at noon. I didn't want to be rushed getting things ready for my party tonight."

Bastien retrieved a rumpled pack of Gauloises from his pocket. "Mind if I smoke?" he inquired, proceeding to light up without waiting for Rebecca's reply.

Rebecca had worked with her French handler long enough to recognize the man's stalling technique, as well as the probable reason. Bastien was worried about whatever bit of information he was getting ready to share with her. Pressing Bastien wouldn't work. Patiently, Rebecca waited. When the French cigarette had burned almost to Bastien's fingers, Rebecca asked, "Bastien, what is it that you need to tell me?"

"You've read the dossier I sent?"

"Yes, I was just taking a second look at it when you arrived."

"Did anything in particular grab your attention?" Bastien paused. "Anything seem odd to you?"

Rebecca considered Bastien's questions. They were the same questions she had earlier asked herself. "I was surprised that my grandfather knew Gyuri Vargha."

Bastien nodded, "So was I, so after I sent the dossier to you I continued to dig. I reached out to some old contacts, pulled in some favors, listened to some rumors."

"And?" Rebecca prodded.

Bastien wasn't sure how his next statement would be received, but he had to tell Rebecca, "I think your grandfather was working for the Russians."

"That's impossible!" Rebecca exclaimed.

"No," Bastien corrected his protégé, "it's the only explanation. It is highly unlikely, regardless of Vargha's cover as an art critic, that he would have had the kind of intimate access to Rene that he had. You knew all of Rene's close friends, yet you had never meet Vargha."

"This is all pure speculation," Rebecca was angry. "You've based this on rumor – you said so yourself – and information that is years old. How dare you accuse my grandfather of being a spy."

Bastien leaned against a long wooden table where several canvases were stacked. He withheld comment, instead allowing Rebecca the needed time to intellectually process what she had just heard after her initial emotional response had run its course. When the red color had faded from Rebecca's face, Bastien gently remarked, "You're a spy, Rebecca. Your grandfather being a spy isn't the issue here, and you know it."

"Grand-Pere would never have worked for the Russians. He hated the communists almost as much as he hated the Nazis. If he was a spy, his loyalties would have been with the west." Rebecca pulled a rickety chair from the corner and sat down. "But, I wondered, myself, why I had never heard about Vargha from my grandfather, especially if they were close enough for Vargha to be able to write that in-depth article about him after Grand-Pere died." A deep sigh escaped Rebecca's lips, "Let's start over. Tell me exactly what you found out."

# CHAPTER TWENTY-ONE

Frank lit a cigar to celebrate. The McNamara case had settled late the day before, freeing the P.I. from testifying in the nasty divorce case. Mark Lockridge's call giving Frank the good news also included an unexpected boon. Lockridge's client was so thrilled at the settlement amount, which was due in no large part to the surveillance Frank had provided on Mrs. McNamara's cheating spouse, that she insisted on paying Frank a bonus over and above the healthy fee he had charged.

"Sheila!" Frank's voice boomed through his office doorway and down the hall. "Bring me the Blue Wind file, will ya?" Having a clear calendar for the next three days meant the detective could return his attention to the case Allison had asked him to take.

"Here you go, Mr. Martin," Sheila placed a thick folder in front of her boss. "Can I get you anything else? Maybe a lesson in how to use the intercom on that phone sitting on your desk?"

The scowl that appeared on Frank's face was so deep that his bushy eyebrows practically touched. But the P.I. couldn't stay mad at his Girl Friday for long, especially when she was right. Removing the cigar from his mouth and laying it in an overflowing ashtray, Frank grumbled, "Sorry. It's just easier to holler."

"Old habits are hard to break," Sheila replied. "And I shouldn't have said anything. Wasn't my place."

Now Frank felt really bad. Sheila McMurray was the best secretary he had ever had, and on top of that important fact, Frank had become fond of the young woman who was working a full-time job and taking night classes at the local community college so she could obtain her degree. "You can say anything you want to me. I know I'm a crotchety old bastard sometimes."

"Sometimes?" Sheila teased.

Frank laughed, "Point taken, as my friend Allison would say. I'll try to do better." Satisfied that peace had returned to the small office, Frank turned his attention to the Blue Wind file, motioning to Sheila that their mutual apologies had served their purpose.

A quick rummage through the Blue Wind casefile produced the field notes Frank had made during his visit to the Blue Wind Casino. Flipping through the several pages, Frank found what he was looking for. The bartender Frank had spoken with had mentioned the club where Mona Phillips supposedly held down a job of different sorts.

A Google search located the Magic Lounge and offered a link to the club's website. Exclusive Members Only Gentlemen's Club. Frank recognized the euphemism for strip club. "Members Only" afforded the private club some protection from the local constabulary, along with the delusion that the "members" would remain anonymous. Frank was willing to bet the membership list included more than a sprinkling of prominent businessmen. The "Members Only" designation didn't worry Frank. Membership was easily purchased at the door.

A few clicks of the keyboard and Frank had pulled up the link to the Blue Wind Casino. It could take a few visits to the Magic Lounge to surveille Mona Phillips. Frank might as well have a comfortable place to stay for the duration. The P.I.'s stomach growled, remembering the 20 ounce steak he had enjoyed at the casino's restaurant on his last visit.

Before closing the file, Frank decided to send a quick email to Allison, giving her an update on the investigation. The information he had gathered so far would be advantageous to Allison's defense of the sexual harassment claim Mona had filed against Allison's client. If Frank was able to add first-hand evidence of Mona working in a strip club, Allison would have ammunition to attack Mona's credibility. It might not totally negate a claim of sexual harassment, but the evidence would certainly impact Mona's claim that mere words had offended her, thus diminishing the value of any damages that might be awarded by a jury.

It didn't take long for Frank to summarize his progress to-date. "I hope to have the investigation concluded by the time you and Wolf are back," he typed after detailing the information he had so far uncovered. "Y'all enjoy yourselves. See you next week."

Frank stuffed the Blue Wind file inside a battered briefcase. Maybe he'd splurge and spend part of the McNamara bonus on one of those expensive Italian leather briefcases he had seen online. Frank had more than gotten his money's worth out of the poor contraption that required a heavy rubber band to keep the latch closed. He'd send it to a well-earned burial at the local thrift store.

"I'll be out for the next couple of days," Frank informed Sheila as he headed through the firm's reception area. "I'll be at the Blue Wind Casino working the Phillips case for Allison."

"Do you want me to forward your calls to your cell or just take messages?" Sheila figured the latter, but she wanted to make certain.

"Unless it's the Sheriff or an emergency, tell them I'll call when I'm back in town." Frank stopped at the front door. "Or if Allison calls," he added, "not that I expect to hear from her."

"I seriously doubt that Ms. Parker has work on her

mind right now," Sheila observed. "I hope she's having a wonderful time with Mr. Johannsen. I think they make a great couple. Don't you?"

Heading to his truck, Frank thought about Sheila's words. His secretary was right. Allison and Wolf did make a great couple. The trip to Europe was just what his friend needed – rest, relaxation and a respite from the personal trials and dangers that had come Allison's way over the past few years. Nothing like a carefree vacation, Frank thought. He hoped Allison had taken plenty of pictures.

# CHAPTER TWENTY-TWO

The two-hour, non-stop flight from Paris' Orly Airport to the Leonardo da Vinci-Fiumicino Airport would give Allison just enough time for a much needed cat nap after a long night of lovemaking. Not that she was complaining about being tired. Remembering Wolf's hands on her naked body, Allison felt a rush of heat between her legs as she buckled the seatbelt and settled into her first class seat for the short flight.

"Un café, madame?" the Air France attendant inquired, bringing Allison's x-rated thoughts to a stop. "Or a juice?"

"Non, Merci" Allison smiled at the young woman standing next to her. "But I'd love a glass of water."

"Bien sur, madame. And pour vous, monsieur?"

"Café Americano, s'il vous plait," Wolf replied, then

continuing in French, advised the attendant to bring double cream and some pastries.

"First class has its perks," Allison remarked. "In fact, you can be my travel agent any time," Allison grinned, "especially if you book us into a penthouse wherever we go."

Wolf leaned close to his seat mate, "And might there be another evening awaiting us like last night?"

"I certainly hope so," Allison laughed. "Last night was wonderful."

Further conversation was halted by the arrival of Wolf's coffee, Allison's water and a small plate of sinful pastries which Wolf consumed. By the time the passengers were asked to return their seat trays to a locked position in preparation for take-off, Allison had succumbed to Morpheus' ministrations. Even the jet's take-off failed to rouse the sleeping woman. Catching the attendant's eye, Wolf motioned for a blanket to cover Allison. A few Z's was a good idea, Wolf realized. Closing his eyes, the Swede relaxed into a light doze.

Allison and Wolf awoke to the ding of the airplane's PA system announcing their approach to Rome. "Thanks for letting me sleep," Allison retrieved her purse from beneath her seat. "I know I've got a hairbrush in here somewhere," she muttered digging through the large bag. "Aha!" Allison withdrew a small brush and set about bringing order to her sleep tossed blond hair.

Fifteen minutes later the plane landed with just a slight bump as the wheels touched the runway. A second ding notified passengers that they could use their electronic devices while the plane was taxiing to the gate. Wolf turned on his cell phone and checked for messages. Two were from his Atlanta office, one from the London office, and one from a Rome number that he didn't recognize. Pressing "play," Wolf listened to the voice mail from the unknown number.

"Wolf, it's Rebecca Molinere. I got your message that you would be coming to town today. I'm having a small party at my flat tonight. The person I messaged you about in London will be there. Give me a call at this number, it's my private line, and let me know if I can expect you. Ciao."

"Who was that?" Allison had caught the sound of a woman's voice as Wolf listened to the voice message.

Making their way off the crowded plane, Wolf waited until he and Allison were headed towards the baggage claim to reply. "Remember I told you about an old contact in Rome? That was Rebecca on the phone. She's invited us to a party at her flat tonight."

A small frown marred Allison's features, "Invited us or invited you?" Allison didn't want to be jealous, but the feeling that Wolf's comment had generated was one Allison unfortunately recognized.

Pulling Allison out of the stream of passengers hurrying to their various destinations inside the terminal, Wolf cupped Allison's face in his hands. "I'm not going anywhere without you," he whispered before planting a soft kiss on the woman's lips. "My relationship with

Rebecca was purely professional. Actually, I'm a little concerned about the reason for the invitation."

Reassured by Wolf's actions more than his words, Allison asked, "Why? It's just a party, isn't it?"

"I haven't heard from Rebecca since I left the Agency. The message she left for me a few days ago was disturbing. She never had this cell number, so she's been in contact with someone close enough to me to know the number."

"So?" Allison was confused.

"My last assignment was in Rome. Rebecca was involved peripherally," Wolf paused. He wasn't sure he ought to share the next bit of information with Allison. But the Swede knew that information was a good defensive weapon, and if Rebecca's information was correct, Allison needed to have all the facts. "The message Rebecca left for me at my London office used a code. If she hadn't reached out to me with this latest call, I would still have contacted her once we arrived here in Rome."

Years of reading body language during depositions and trial had honed Allison's instincts and abilities. The slight changes in Wolf's tone and demeanor had not gone unnoticed. Whatever was going on was, at least in Wolf's estimation, something quite serious. "What is it, Wolf? And be completely honest. No holding back," Allison commanded.

"My last assignment was a Russian spy by the name of Guyri Vargha who had caused the deaths of several American and British operatives. The kill was confirmed by a contact in the medical examiner's office." A fleeting thought caused Wolf to pause as an unwelcome possibility formed in his mind. "But recently a man claiming to be Vargha has resurfaced in Rome. He looks like Vargha, acts like Vargha, and has historical knowledge that only Vargha would have."

"Wait a minute," Allison interrupted with a wave of her hands. "I thought you said this Vargha guy was a spy. How is he going around acting like a normal person?"

"Gyuri Vargha's cover was as an art critic. Lots of people knew him, they just weren't aware of his covert life," Wolf explained. "Rebecca believes this is the real man, not an imposter, and if she's right .... Well, I don't want to think about what that means."

Allison considered what Wolf told her as they grabbed their luggage from the baggage claim conveyor belt. Wolf could be walking into a very dangerous situation – and so could she for that matter – if this Rebecca woman was correct about the man Wolf thought he had killed. But not knowing the truth could be just as dangerous, a reality Allison had learned in the past few years. By the time the pair had settled into a cab for the drive to their hotel, Allison had reached a decision. "Give Rebecca a call back. Let her know we will be coming tonight."

"Until I know more about this situation I'd be much more comfortable if you'd stay at the hotel," Wolf replied. "I'll go to Rebecca's alone."

Allison's temper flared. Turning her body so she could confront Wolf both physically and verbally the young woman began, "Don't start that crap with me Wolf Johannsen. There is no way you are going to that party alone." Allison put her hand up, cutting off Wolf's interruption. "No. End of discussion. If this man is who Rebecca thinks he is and you come by yourself, he may realize you or Rebecca are onto him. If he is as dangerous as you make him out to be, you don't need to go in unprepared. If you come with me, we can play this as your introducing me to your Rome friends – which you are, actually. See if he's who you think he is, we'll leave and then you can plan."

"Here we are, signore. The St. Regis Hotel." The driver's announcement offered Wolf a reprieve from an immediate reply, buying the Swede time to fashion a counter-argument to Allison's declaration.

# CHAPTER TWENTY-THREE

"This is the life," Frank commented to no one, seeing as how he was alone in the deluxe room he had reserved at the Blue Wind Casino. It took Frank a few minutes to relieve himself of the alligator cowboy boots he had worn as part of his disguise. Sure, the boots belonged to Frank, but they also enhanced the look he wanted to project – a rich, slightly over-the-hill cowboy in town for a good time and to spend some money.

Earlier in the evening Frank had made his way to the Blackjack table to play up his role and see if he could find out whether Mona Phillips had returned to work. The P.I. could have gotten that information directly from the casino, but after his last visit, Frank had decided being completely undercover was the wiser route. Loose lips from HR would be all it took to put the kibosh on

Frank's plan.

It hadn't taken long for Frank to discover that Mona had, indeed, come back to work, but was off that evening. If he couldn't catch her working in the casino, Frank hoped he'd find her working the poles at the Magic Lounge. Frank had two nights to devote to the investigation before his other commitments again took center stage. The comforts afforded a high-roller at the Blue Wind were pretty darn nice, but Frank knew he needed to produce more results this time. Setting the bedside clock for a 45 minute nap, Frank planted his considerable bulk on top of the fancy bedding and dropped off to sleep.

The Magic Lounge was rocking when Frank walked through the business' front door at ten after eleven. Disco music roared from 80's era speakers hanging from the four corners of the smoke-filled room. Frank enjoyed his cigar, but this amount of cigarette smoke was a bit much in the P.I.'s mind. Hopefully he would get what he needed on his target and not have to spend too much time in the joint, even with the allure of semi-naked women urging him to stay a while.

A large stage illuminated by multi-colored lights drew Frank's attention. The scantily clad girl prancing about to a Bee Gees tune was not Mona Phillips. Neither were any of the waitresses carrying drinks to the men who were seemingly enthralled by the current performer. Settling into a two-top near the corner of the stage Frank ordered a beer and waited.

He didn't have to wait long.

A loud, crackling sound followed by a shrill squeal caused Frank to wince as the Magic Lounge's PA system roared into operation. "And now, back by popular demand, the evening's star – Misty Majesty," a loud voice announced. "Let's give her a big Magic Lounge round of applause."

The stage lights lowered as Ravel's Bolero poured out over the club's ancient speakers. A single spotlight fixed on a split in the dark curtains that covered the back portion of the stage. Slowly the barrier parted, allowing Mona Phillips, a/k/a Misty Majesty, to present herself to the cheers and whistles of the crowd.

Mona Phillips was beautiful. Thinking back to the photograph in Phillips' personnel file, Frank had to admit the picture hadn't done his target justice. Adjusting the lariat tie that he had added to his disguise, the P.I. switched on the tiny camera that looked for all the world like a harmless clip holding the tie together at his neck.

The music Mona Phillips had selected for her act was the perfect accompaniment to the sensuous dance she was performing. Frank wondered how much of her attire would find its way to the stage floor by the time Bolero reached its climax. If what he had heard about Mona from the Blue Wind Casino's bartender was correct, Frank was betting on 100%.

Sporting nothing but a G-string and pasties Mona began to make her way across the front of the stage, allowing her slathering fans to slip five and ten dollar bills inside what remained of her clothing. When the stripper ended up close enough for Frank to touch, the P.I. knew his evening at the Magic Lounge had been worth every penny he'd spent on the watered down beers. Frank slipped a folded bill inside Mona's G-string, bending close enough for his hidden camera to record the barely concealed honey pot that peeked out as Frank crammed the ten dollar tribute into the overflowing scrap of cloth.

The music reached its ending crescendo as Mona peeled the pasties from her nipples. Cries of "Take it off! Take it all off!" urged the stripper to discard the remaining covering that left little, if anything, to the imagination. Blowing a kiss to her admirers, Mona Phillips left the stage, and Frank lost the bet he had made with himself.

Later, back in his room at the Blue Wind Casino, Frank placed the tiny camera in the specially made device that allowed Frank to upload the recorded video to his computer. There he saved the file, made several copies, and emailed one to Allison. Frank doubted the lawyer would look at her business email while she was in Europe, but just in case, Frank wanted her to see the results of the evening's work.

# CHAPTER TWENTY-FOUR

Wolf's return call had not surprised Rebecca, but his information certainly had. Wolf Johannsen was, to use a trite expression, in a relationship. At one point in her life the news would have made Rebecca jealous. Wolf Johannsen was a sexy, intelligent, and brave intelligence agent, and Rebecca had been strongly attracted to him when the pair had worked together. But Wolf, the consummate professional, had never responded to Rebecca's lightly veiled suggestions of more. At the time, the gentle rebuff had embarrassed her, but from her current perspective and with more life experience, Rebecca had to admit the Swede had been right. Becoming involved with another agent could compromise the mission for any number of reasons, and Wolf Johannsen was not a man who took unnecessary chances.

Still, Rebecca thought Wolf would remain a bachelor. Wolf hadn't been a choirboy, and he certainly hadn't led a celibate life, but as far as Rebecca knew, Wolf had never been in a serious relationship. Remembering the man she had worked with over the years, Rebecca realized she was happy for Wolf, happy that he had found a woman he loved, happy that her friend had been able to leave the shadow world behind him.

Except, maybe, that shadow world was closer than Wolf or Rebecca thought. Had she made a mistake inviting Wolf to a party where Gyuri Vargha would be? No, information was power. So long as Vargha didn't know who Wolf was, or rather, who Wolf had been, Rebecca believed Wolf Johannsen would be the best person to tell Langley whether the man claiming to be Gyuri Vargha was the man Wolf thought he had killed.

The sound of loud knocking coming from the gallery's front door caught Rebecca's attention. The sign at the entrance of Il Piccolo Paridiso clearly stated that the gallery was closed to the public for the remainder of the day due to a private event. The caterers weren't due at her flat for another two hours and they wouldn't be coming to the gallery anyway. Curious, Rebecca left her office and headed towards the front of the gallery.

The hooded figure standing by the gallery's glass front doors had its back to Rebecca. Odd, she thought. Instead of peering inside to see if the knocking would bring anyone to the door, whoever was standing there seemed more concerned about the street in front of the gallery. With its back to the door and head concealed, Rebecca wasn't certain whether the figure was that of a man or a woman. Instinctively, Rebecca slowed her approach and moved to the side of the glass doors to depress the external intercom button.

"The gallery is closed until tomorrow," Rebecca spoke authoritatively.

The figure turned, revealing a face Rebecca had not seen in several years, but knew well. Franco Perelli's appearance at her gallery door, coupled with his obvious attempt to hide his identity, did not bode well. Quickly, Rebecca unlocked the door and motioned for Perelli to come inside.

"What is going on?" she hissed. "First, Bastien this morning, and now you."

Perelli pulled back the hood, revealing the signature salt and pepper hair that caused people to sometimes notice him when he would rather remain unseen. Nodding towards the back of the gallery, Perelli moved away from the front windows. "Not here," he replied, "I can't risk being seen with you."

Safe from prying eyes in the gallery's back office, Rebecca settled into the nearest chair. "Franco, why the cloak and dagger act?"

"Did you talk to Langley about Gyuri Vargha?"

Perelli answered Rebecca's question with one of his own.

"Yes. And fortunately I reached out directly to Wolf Johannsen. No one at the Agency had contacted him." Rebecca frowned thinking about Langley's decision not to give Wolf a heads-up on what could be a very dangerous situation.

"Interesting," Perelli replied, "and disturbing. Protocol would have required Wolf being put on notice. I'm not sure if we're looking at a deliberate act or just a negligent one."

"Gyuri Vargha was a top target and sanctioned removal. I find it hard to believe anyone at the need-to-know level wouldn't have notified Wolf once Vargha's possible existence became known," Rebecca mused.

Franco Perelli paced nervously. "That's my thinking as well. And if not notifying Wolf was deliberate, the next question is why and who."

Rebecca poured a coffee for herself while she considered the implications of Perelli's assessment. None of the scenarios her mind called forth were encouraging.

"But that's not why you're here, is it?" Rebecca returned to her seat and sipped the hot beverage.

"Vargha set up a meet with me, two days ago." Perelli ran his hand through his hair, obviously agitated. "He ordered me to find out who tried to take him out five years ago."

"What did you tell him?" Rebecca asked.

"I tried to discourage him, told him no one had been able to figure out who the assassin was five years ago and there was no way anyone would know that now." Perelli's expression was grim, "He wouldn't let it go. He's determined to have his revenge."

A bad feeling arose in the pit of Rebecca's stomach. Just how much did Gyuri Vargha really know? Would Wolf be in danger tonight at her party? Did Langley have an agenda that hadn't been shared with Rebecca, or Wolf, or Perelli? It wouldn't be the first time Langley had sacrificed a retired agent for what the Agency deemed the greater good. Thinking about Langley's periodic disdain for individual life, anger began to replace fear.

"I'm having a cocktail party at my flat tonight. Guyri Vargha is coming with a friend of mine. Wolf just got in town, and I've invited him as well, hoping he can determine whether the man claiming to be Gyuri Vargha is the real deal or an imposter." Rebecca paused to allow Perelli a minute to digest the information she had just imparted. "I know you can't be there, but Bastien will be, and he'll be armed. So will I. If there's trouble we'll be prepared."

# CHAPTER TWENTY-FIVE

The junior suite Wolf had booked at the St. Regis was stunning. Decorated in a tasteful mixture of Empire, Regency and Louis XV styles, the rooms offered a magnificent view of Bernini's church of St. Maria della Vittoria. Comfortable yet upscale, the St. Regis was quickly becoming Allison's favorite hotel of the trip.

"I wonder if all the rooms have frescoes?" Allison examined the detailed painting which covered most of the wall above the large king bed. "This is lovely."

"Indeed they do," Wolf replied. "Even the least expensive rooms, although maybe not as large as the frescoes in the suites. It's the St. Regis touch."

"Too bad it isn't winter," Allison pointed at the ornate fireplace flanking one of the bedroom walls. "A crackling fire, a glass of wine, and us snuggled under the covers…," Allison raised her eyebrows suggestively.

"Maybe we should give the bed a try anyway," Wolf's grin spoke more than his words. "It looks pretty comfortable, but you never know."

A slow moan escaped Allison's lips as Wolf's fingers gently traced the outline her breasts made in the thin cotton shirt she had donned for the planned afternoon of sight-seeing. Pressing her body closer, Allison reached for Wolf's belt. "This is in the way."

Naked, Wolf and Allison fell upon the silk covered-bed, hands frantic to touch the other, lips stoking the rising heat that threatened to consume the lovers. Deftly, Wolf caressed the folds of Allison's most private parts. Wetness covered his hands as Allison's body responded to the increasing pleasure. Moving to straddle Wolf, Allison lowered her body onto her lover's hard penis. Desire and instinct overwhelmed Allison as she rode Wolf's erection, moving up and down his shaft, until the intensity of the friction could no longer be denied.

Afterwards, their bodies glistening with sweat, Allison and Wolf lay quietly for several minutes as their breathing returned to normal. Allison rested her head on Wolf's chest, content to feel Wolf's hands gently stroking her hair. How had she been so lucky to find love a second time?

"Are you hungry?" Wolf raised himself to one elbow and admired the woman lying next to him. "Rebecca's soiree won't start until 8:00. We've got time to grab a bite to eat before we head over to her flat."

"You certainly know the way to a woman's heart," Allison teased. "Sex and food – what more could I want?"

\#

The lighted dials on Wolf's watch displayed 8:45 by the time he and Allison approached Rebecca Molinere's flat. Their early dinner had been delayed by a lengthy interlude of shower sex, coupled with Allison's indecision about what to wear to Rebecca's party. From experience, Wolf knew half of the guests would not yet have arrived - Rome was a late-night town – but the ex-agent had hoped for time with his hostess before the crowd made private conversation impossible. If he knew anything about Rebecca Molinere, it was that she would have garnered more information about Gyuri Vargha since they had last spoken.

The sounds of merriment and music floated above Wolf and Allison as they approached the building where Rebecca lived. "Rebecca has the top flat," Wolf explained, "with a large terrace. In weather like this most of the guests will be outside before the evening's over."

To the left of the building's front door, Wolf noticed a display of brass nameplates. Depressing the button next to "Molinere," Wolf waited.

"Ciao, chi va la?" A woman's voice inquired.

"Wolf Johannsen and Allison Parker." Wolf recognized his host's voice. "You going to let us join the party, Rebecca?"

"Of course." A peel of laughter accompanied the buzz

indicating admittance to the lobby's tastefully decorated interior. "Come on up."

An ancient caged elevator groaned as it slowly carried Wolf and Allison to the building's fifth floor. Nervously Allison reached for Wolf's hand. "I hate these old elevators."

"It's perfectly safe," Wolf assured Allison. "And remember what we talked about. If the man claiming to be Gyuri Vargha is here and you are introduced to him you cannot give any indication that the name is familiar to you."

"Do you take me for an idiot?" Peeved by Wolf's admonition Allison jerked her hand from her lover's larger one. "I understand exactly what is at stake here. And I know exactly what role I need to play under the circumstances."

With strong arms, Wolf pulled Allison close. "No offense intended, but if this is the man I thought I killed five years ago, there is every need for extreme caution. Even a small slip could be deadly." Brushing an errant strand of blond hair from Allison's face, he continued, "I don't want to lose you."

"Nor I you," Allison whispered as the elevator jerked to a stop and the iron gates opened. "I'll be careful."

Although Rebecca's flat encompassed the entire fifth floor, the elevator opened onto a medium-sized foyer instead of directly inside the flat itself. Large, ornate concrete urns overflowing with a colorful assortment of tropical plants covered the tiled floor, gracing the area with a welcoming tone. An intricately carved and massive wooden door stood partially open, giving Wolf and Allison a narrow line of sight to the crowd inside.

"Looks like there's no need to knock," Allison observed.

A raucous combination of laughter, conversation and the clinking of glasses greeted the pair as they made their way into the party. With surprise, Allison realized she was both frightened and exhilarated by the thought of what might transpire if this Vargha fellow was actually who he claimed to be. Pushing her trepidation aside, Allison silently reminded herself she'd escaped a serial killer and a group of terrorists. Surely she could deal with one Russian spy.

# CHAPTER TWENTY-SIX

Gyuri Vargha was tempted to back out of his date with Charlene Jacobs. The woman was a pain in Gyuri's ass, no doubt about it. Vapid, overweight, and with horrendous taste in just about everything, the American ex-pat was someone Gyuri Vargha would never have associated with under normal circumstances.

But circumstances weren't normal. In fact, they were far from it.

The past five years, or at least the first three of the five, had been almost unendurable, both physically and mentally, for the spy. The multiple surgeries needed to correct the damage the assassin's bullets had done to his internal organs had been nothing compared to the damage from the drugs that had feigned his death. Gyuri didn't remember his "death," of course – he was in a deep coma-like state – but he remembered with excruciating clarity the long period of time during which his body made a slow and painful recovery. Only the desire for revenge had kept Gyuri from taking his own life when it seemed that health and vitality would never return.

His death. Had it not been for the mole at the C.I.A., Gyuri would have been truly dead from the assassin's bullets. The extraordinary sums that Gyuri had paid the American traitor had been well spent, for it was through him that Gyuri had learned that Rene Depeche, the man Gyuri had actually considered a friend, had instead given him up for assassination. Thinking about Depeche, Gyuri felt a fleeting regret over his current plans, but business was business, and Gyuri believed that had the circumstances been reversed, the Frenchman would have been planning his own revenge, just as Gyuri was now planning his. Still, he thought, it was a shame that he might need to eventually kill Depeche's granddaughter.

Gyuri wasn't yet certain what Rebecca's role had been in the attempt to kill him, if, indeed, she had been involved at all. The facts tying her to the attempt on his life were slim and circumstantial. The hit had taken place in Rome, not Paris. Rebecca lived in Rome. So did a lot of other people, including Franco Perelli. Gyuri placed his suspicions about Perelli on a mental shelf as he continued to think about Rebecca Molinere. Although unusual, it was not unheard of to have two members of the same family working for one of the world's intelligence agencies. In his business, collateral damage was always a possibility, but given the uncertainty of exactly who and what agency tried to kill him, Gyuri was somewhat reluctant to kill Rebecca without further evidence of her involvement.

As he had planned his return to Rome, Gyuri had remembered Charlene Jacobs and her friendship with Rebecca Molinere. All it had taken to sucker-in Charlene had been a couple of dates and a roll in the sack. Fucking the woman had been distasteful – she wouldn't shut up, even in bed – but Gyuri needed the cover and access Charlene provided. Thinking about the evening ahead, Gyuri figured he'd have to screw the fat pig one more time, but if he was able to determine Rebecca Molinere's role in the attempt on his life, he would be one step closer to the identity of the man who tried to kill him. To Gyuri's mind, no act was too distasteful if it led him to his assassin.

Considering where Rebecca Molinere's allegiance might lie brought Gyuri to another unpleasant question. What was he going to do about Franco Perelli? The temptation to kill Perelli had been strong when the two men had met in the museum underneath Maggiore. But Gyuri was certain that Perelli knew the identity of the assassin, or knew someone who did. Maybe Perelli had even been involved in the botched attempt. The more Gyuri thought about how evasive Perelli had been that day, the more convinced he became of Perelli's betrayal.

The antique mantle clock struck eight times, interrupting Gyuri's half-formed plans for interrogating

Perelli and reminding him that he was late picking up Charlene. Throwing on his jacket, Gyuri slipped an expensive-looking silver cigarette lighter into an interior pocket and a pack of Gauloises into an exterior one. Gyuri didn't smoke, but he needed an excuse for carrying the camera which looked for all-the-world like an old-fashioned cigarette lighter. The lighter worked for the purpose for which it appeared intended, of course, but by depressing a small indentation on the side of the case, a tiny eye recorded and transmitted the image on which the lighter-turned-camera focused. Tonight, absent unforeseen circumstances, Gyuri hoped to have the opportunity to slip into Rebecca Molinere's home office and record any incriminating evidence he found there.

Charlene's flat was not far, so that, even walking, Gyuri's tardiness was well within the expected norm of Rome society. Depressing the bell, Gyrui donned the necessary persona, greeting his date with a "Ciao, Bella. How lovely you look tonight."

Flagging a taxi, Gyuri ushered his date into the vehicle's back seat and, settling in beside the garishly dressed woman, steeled himself for Charlene's inane chatter. Responding with nods, grunts, and non-committal responses, Gyuri almost missed Charlene's mention of party guests from America.

"What did you just say?" Gyuri interrupted.

Well into another topic, it took a minute for Charlene to grasp Gyuri's question. "You mean about Rebecca's friends from America?" Seeing Gyuri's nod,

Charlene continued, "Oh, it's an old friend of hers, Wolf Johannsen. He used to travel a good bit in Europe for some sort of business. Rebecca said it had been five years since she'd seen him. I've never met the man. He's bringing some woman he's been dating."

The taxi pulled to the curb in front of Rebecca's flat. Paying the driver, Gyuri considered what Charlene had just told him. Five years. Was it possible? Surely the odds were astronomical that this Johannsen man would be the man who had tried to kill him. But…. Making a mental note to give Franco Perelli Johannsen's name, Gyuri offered Charlene Jacobs his arm. "I look forward to meeting Rebecca's friends from America."

# CHAPTER TWENTY-SEVEN

Rebecca's party was in full swing when Gyuri and Charlene stepped off the elevator. A glance through the flat's open door revealed a mass of gaily attired guests. Given the propensity of Italians to talk with their hands as much as with words, Gyuri reminded himself to watch out for spilled drinks as he guided Charlene into the welcoming fray.

"There's Rebecca." Charlene didn't know the man and woman her hostess was talking with. "I bet that's Wolf and his girlfriend," she remarked.

"Let's find out." Gyuri urged his date towards the trio. The tall, blond man engaged in conversation with Rebecca Molinere was not familiar to the Russian. But Gyuri had never seen the man who tried to kill him, so it was still possible this was the assassin. "Remotely possible," Gyuri thought, considering again the long odds that this particular American would actually be his killer.

"Charlene, Gyuri," Rebecca turned to welcome her friend and her date. "I was hoping you'd be here before Wolf and Allison headed back to their hotel. I want Charlene to meet some of her countrymen," Rebecca laughed. "And you too, Gyuri."

Flattered by the attention directed her way, Charlene gushed, "It's so nice to meet you, Mr. Johannsen. Welcome to Rome. And who is your lovely companion?"

Instinctively, Wolf placed a protective arm around Allison. The conversation might be light, but he had recognized Guyri Vargha the minute the man walked into the party. "Thank you, Ms. Jacobs. It's nice to visit this lovely city again. Let me introduce Allison Parker."

Gyuri listened to the repartee between Charlene and the Parker woman closely. The American was clearly from one of the Southern states. One-syllable words became two, all with a pleasant slow-paced and lyrical overtone. In response to Charlene's question of how Allison and Wolf met, Gyuri learned that the woman was an attorney and had met Wolf Johannsen when he bought an inn in some place called Ft. Charles, Alabama. Storing the information, Gyuri turned to Wolf Johannsen.

"I guess Rebecca considers me an unnecessary appendage." Gyuri offered Wolf his hand and introduced himself. "Charlene said you and Ms. Parker are Americans, yet your accent sounds Scandinavian."

Wolf nodded. "You've got an ear for accents. I was born in Sweden but my business interests eventually landed me in the States. Several years ago I decided to make the U.S. my permanent home, and I became a citizen." Wolf knew there was no harm in giving Gyuri this information. An internet search would have turned up the same data.

Gyuri smiled, "I've never been to America. Perhaps I'll make a trip there some time." When Wolf declined to comment Gyuri probed, "Charlene said you used to travel to the Continent frequently for business. What sort of business do you have?"

Wolf hesitated. He would need to be very careful how he answered this question. His cover had been a good one. To his knowledge, the only people In Europe who had known about the work he did for the Agency were Rebecca in Rome and Bastien Dubois in France. Still, Wolf was painfully aware that mistakes had gotten better agents than he killed. "I have a consulting business. Some of my clients are in Europe, of course, given that I started my business in Sweden."

"So you would visit your various clients?" Gyuri pressed.

"Yes," Wolf smiled.

"When were you last in Rome?" Gyuri desperately wanted to know the answer to this question, but before Wolf could reply the men were interrupted by their hostess.

"That's enough of the inquisition," Rebecca admonished Gyuri. "You and Charlene can't monopolize Wolf and Allison all evening. I want to introduce them to some of my other guests."

When Rebecca, Wolf, and Allison were far enough away from Gyuri and Charlene for a private conversation, Rebecca asked, "Well? Is he who he claims to be?"

Wolf nodded. "His voice is as I remembered, and he certainly looks like the man I targeted. But what is more convincing to me than his voice and appearance are the questions he was asking me."

"What do you mean?" Allison interjected. "I couldn't tell what y'all were talking about for trying to be polite and pay attention to Charlene's patter. I swear that woman would try the patience of a saint."

"The man's smooth," Wolf admitted, "and his tone was casual, but his questions were pointed. Who was I? Where did I come from? What kind of business did I run? Why did I travel to Europe? He had just asked me when I was last in Rome when you grabbed Allison and me – and thanks, by the way, for that save."

"One more thing," Rebecca spoke quietly. "I have it from a good source that Gyuri has feelers out for the identity of his assassin. For your own safety, I think you and Allison should cut short your trip."

Wolf considered Rebecca's warning and suggestion. If it were just him, there would be no way Wolf would leave. Gyuri Vargha had been his last assignment. If he had failed the first time, he certainly would not the second. But Allison's presence was another issue all together. Wolf Johannsen was not willing to expose the woman he loved to danger.

"We'll head back to the hotel shortly. It's time for me to have a talk with my old handler," Wolf replied. "I shouldn't have learned about Vargha from you, but I'll deal with that later. Right now Gyuri Vargha has to be the number one priority. I'll put Allison on a plane tomorrow and then coordinate with Langley over the next steps."

"Don't even think about it," Allison argued. "You've been out of the business for a long time. Contact your man, tell him what you think, and let someone else deal with this. We can stay here for a few more days, together, or we can get on a plane back to the states tomorrow, together." Allison eyed Wolf to make certain he had understood the emphasis she had placed on the word "together."

"Smart woman you have here," Rebecca informed her friend. "Take her advice, and mine. Let Langley handle this. Now, let's look like you're having a great time meeting more of my friends. I'm sure Gyuri is watching."

# CHAPTER TWENTY-EIGHT

Wolf and Allison had argued the entire way back to their hotel. The Swede was insistent that Allison return to the States without him, while she was equally adamant that they would not be separated. Now back in their suite at the St. Regis where they had the protection of privacy, the argument continued unabated.

"This is nothing compared to some of the situations I've been in," Allison argued. "This Vargha guy has no idea who you are, and if you have a brain in your head, you'll leave it that way. I don't care how good you think your skills are, you've been away from that life for a long time. You don't need to get back in it now."

"Gyuri Vargha was my assignment. Cleaning up my mess is on me, not some other agent," Wolf explained.

"And you completed your assignment. You took

him out, he was declared dead by the Medical Examiner, and his body sent for burial." A frustrated sigh escaped Allison's lips, "I know you think this is the same man, but his identity has not been 100% confirmed."

A heavy silence filled the room as Wolf considered his reply. Pouring himself a splash of Scotch from the suite's well-stocked bar, Wolf turned to address Allison. "In all my years as an operative, I never failed in an assignment. Maybe it seems cold to think of killing someone as an assignment," Wolf paused to see Allison's reaction to that last statement, "but that was my job. I knew the risks going in, and I accepted them. It is very difficult for me to let another agent finish a job I didn't complete – to put someone else in harm's way because I failed."

"I understand better than you think." Allison patted the plush sofa, indicating a spot for Wolf. "Come and sit by me."

Patiently, Allison waited. She could tell Wolf was struggling with conflicting emotions. After a few seemingly interminable minutes, Wolf settled on the couch and reached for Allison's hand. Now she could continue.

"I've never been in your line of work," Allison acknowledged, "but I've been in mortal danger more than once because I took it upon myself to stop an injustice or to protect innocent lives. Believe me, Wolf, I understand, at least partly, why you feel so strongly that dealing with Gyuri Vargha is your responsibility. My late husband worried constantly about the danger I put myself in, but he never stopped me because he knew how important the work was to me."

"So you understand why I have to handle this myself," Wolf interjected.

"Yes, I do. But I'm asking you not to do anything." Allison let her words hang in the air. Wolf's response to what she said next would determine the course of their relationship. "Jim always worried that my amateur investigatory work would get me killed. And then, out of the blue, it was his own work as a judge that caused an angry and vindictive litigant to take my husband's life." Allison drew Wolf's face close, kissing him. "I absolutely refuse to lose you, Wolf Johannsen. I am begging you, let another agent deal with this. If this is the real Gyuri Vargha, let someone else remove him. Please, please, come back to Ft. Charles with me and leave this alone."

Rebecca's words echoed in Wolf's mind. "Smart woman you have here. Take her advice and mine. Let Langley handle this." Wolf looked at the woman he loved, a love he had never expected to have, a love he would never have had if he had stayed active with the Agency. Was he willing to risk what had come to him so unexpectedly? No, he was not. Gently, Wolf caressed Allison face, telegraphing his decision before he spoke. "It's late afternoon in the States. I'll make the call now."

"Thank you." A tear slipped from Allison's eye. "I know how hard this must be for you, but I am so grateful for your decision."

Wolf wiped the errant tear from Allison's face. "Don't

cry, my love. I made my decision five years ago. Wanting to go after this man, whoever he is, was a momentary slip, old habits finding it hard to die."

Retrieving his cell phone, Wolf punched in multiple numbers, giving several cryptic responses to questions apparently posed, either electronically or by a living person, once the call connected. Given the nonsensical words Wolf was using, Allison figured there was some sort of vetting process going on at Langley's end. Finally, Wolf began to speak in coherent sentences.

"Ned, it's Wolf Johannsen. I'm in Rome and I've met the man claiming to be Gyuri Vargha. I believe there is a better than 90% probability that this is the same man I thought I killed five years ago. How he survived is unknown. Rebecca Molinere is aware of my assessment. I'm leaving Rome tomorrow. If you need me you can reach me on my cell. Same number. And by the way, I want to know why I had to find out about Vargha from someone other than you."

Allison was surprised at the brief conversation, "What did he say?"

"I left the message on Ned Bakke's secured line." Glancing at his watch, Wolf frowned. "He should still have been in the office, but no matter, he'll get my information. Agency personnel are required to check secure messaging frequently."

"Do you think we'll have a problem getting a flight out tomorrow?" Allison worried. Now that Wolf had agreed to leave, Allison knew the sooner she got him on a plane the less opportunity there would be for him to change his mind.

"I've already thought about that," Wolf replied. "I'll have London send the corporate jet for us."

"You have a jet?" Surprised words stumbled out of Allison's mouth. "For real?"

Wolf grinned at Allison's question. "We'll have to stop in London before heading home. I'll need to actually do some work to justify the flight. That will give us time to get a booking from London to Atlanta in a day or two. Is that an acceptable compromise?"

"More than acceptable," Allison smiled, the relief over Wolf's decision washing over her. "Now that I know you're not going to go off and do something dangerous, I think I can get a few restful hours of sleep."

"Sleep?" Wolf asked. "Are you sure I can't talk you into something else? Something to reinforce the rightness of my decision not to engage with Gyuri Vargha?"

"Normally, I would say yes." The hint of a smile creased Allison's face. "But tonight I just want to hold you, to feel your skin next to mine, to listen to you breathe. I love you, Wolf Johannsen, and I don't want anything to happen to you."

"And nothing will," the Swede assured Allison as they moved towards the bedroom. "Nothing will."

# CHAPTER TWENTY-NINE

Two days in London and a long flight back to the States had proved to be blessedly uneventful. Another couple of days to get over jet lag would have been nice, but almost two weeks away from the office was all Allison could realistically justify. So, with a stretch and a big yawn, Allison rolled herself from her comfortable bed and headed towards the shower.

Waiting for the water to heat to her preferred just-short-of-scalding temp, Allison replayed the events of the prior evening. By the time Wolf and Allison had navigated Atlanta traffic and made the drive to Ft. Charles, Charlotte and Mack's bed time had long since passed, but Allison knew full well that her children would have stayed up to welcome her home. Charlotte, in particular, had inherited her parents' talent for persuasive argument, and Sharon, the children's longtime sitter, had become adept at deciphering when to give in to Charlotte's demands. Added to the late hour of her arrival was the opening of many presents purchased in London, Paris and Rome. Frankly, Allison mused as she dried off from the morning's shower, it was a miracle that her children had gone to sleep at all.

Hands on hips, Allison surveyed her closet. Today would be a catch-up day at the office, with no need to wear a suit and heels. A pair of medium-green cargo pants and a striped tee would be just fine. Slipping her feet into her most comfortable pair of sandals, Allison applied a bare amount of makeup, pulled her long hair into a stylish chignon, and headed for the kitchen and an eye-opening cup of coffee.

Allison was on her second cup of coffee and halfway through several messages left on her phone when a sleepy Mack stumbled into the room.

"Do you have to go to work today?" Mack rubbed sleep from his eyes. "Can't you stay home?"

Allison grabbed her son in a warm embrace. "I'm waiting to fix breakfast for you and Charlotte before I leave." Allison brushed Mack's tousled hair with her hands. "Sharon isn't coming until around 10:00. I'll go into the office after she gets here, and I promise to try to be home before supper." Giving her son a kiss, Allison instructed Mack to wake his sister. "Tell Charlotte I'm making blueberry pancakes."

#

Two hours later, Allison pulled into the parking lot next to the law offices of Parker & Jackson that the firm shared with Martin Investigations. Noting that Frank's behemoth pickup truck wasn't in its usual spot under the shade of a large oak, Allison cut the engine and headed for her firm's employee entrance. Allison was anxious to hear and see what Frank had uncovered on the Blue Wind Casino case in her absence.

"Welcome back." Donna Peavey hugged her boss. "I want to hear all about your trip."

"And you shall," Allison laughed, "but not today. I'm sure there's a mountain of calls, emails, and work waiting for me."

Refusing to be put off, Donna pressed, "Did you enjoy being with Mr. Johanansen?"

Allison paused at the entrance to her private office. "Yes, and we're not discussing that right now, either," she replied, unable to repress an accompanying smile.

"Uh-hum," Donna replied. "Well, you're right about a pile of work waiting on you. I've got it organized chronologically so you can start with what came in right after you left and work your way current." Seeing a slight look of distress on Allison's face, Donna continued, "No fires, just regular stuff. Oh, and by the way, Frank Martin wants you to call him as soon as you are in the office."

Allison wanted to talk to Frank, too, but first, she needed to look at the video Frank had emailed to her while she was in Europe. She should have looked at the video when Frank sent it to her, but part of the reason for the trip with Wolf was for a real vacation, not one where she was constantly being reminded of her day job. Allison knew Donna or David Jackson would have contacted her if there had been a matter of real urgency, so when Frank's email showed up she had simply ignored it.

Scrolling quickly through her emails, Allison spied the one Frank had sent to her. A couple of clicks and an almost-naked Mona Phillips filled Allison's computer screen. "My word," Allison gasped watching the plaintiff in the Blue Moon Casino case bump and grind across a brightly lit stage. The video quality was excellent, so excellent in fact, that Allison expected to see Mona Phillip's private parts each time one of the patrons stuffed a dollar bill inside the dancer's g-string. When the proximity of one particular hand pressing a bill inside Mona's "attire" appeared onscreen, Allison started laughing. "Oh Frank," she murmured, "you didn't…."

Allison was still laughing as she punched in the numbers for Frank's office.

"Martin Investigations," Sheila McMurray's soft voice announced. "How may I help you?"

"Hey, Sheila, it's Allison Parker. Is Frank around?" Allison hoped Frank had returned to the office.

"Welcome back, Ms. Parker. How was your trip?" Without giving Allison an opportunity to reply, Sheila answered Allison's question, "No, Mr. Martin is out right now. I don't expect him until later today. Can I have him call you?"

"Please," Allison replied, "and my trip was great, thanks for asking."

"Is there a message for Mr. Martin?" Sheila knew her boss would ask.

"Just tell Frank I'm ready to talk about the casino case he's working for me." Allison knew Sheila was discreet. Anyone working in a P.I.'s office had to be, but Allison was careful about what information she shared, and with whom, when she was working a case. "I'll be in until around five. If he comes in after you leave for the day, leave him a note to call me at home."

# CHAPTER THIRTY

Franco Perelli was worried. The conversation he had just had with Gyuri Vargha had warning signs all over it. What had Rebecca been thinking, inviting Wolf Johannsen to her party? Surely there could have been another way to let Wolf evaluate Gyuri Vargha, one that didn't put suspicion in the Russian's mind. It was all Perelli had been able to do to conceal his concern when Vargha told him he thought Wolf Johannsen might have been the man who tried to kill him.

"There are no such things as coincidences," Vargha had argued. "Johannsen had the type of cover that made his travel to Europe believable."

"Lots of people have business that requires them to travel in Europe," Perelli had countered. "Are all of them potential assassins?"

"Charlene told me Rebecca hadn't seen Johannsen in over five years. Why now? And at a party where she knew I would be?" Vargha's arguments had hit too close to the truth. "It's all too convenient. I'm going to take a harder look at that man. And at Rebecca Molinere."

Vargha's closing comment echoed in Perelli's head. Wolf Johannsen could take care of himself. The man was a trained operative, no matter how long he'd been out of the business. The kind of training and instincts Wolf Johannsen had were never forgotten. In addition, the man had returned to the States. Distance would give Johannsen a measure of protection.

Rebecca Molinere, however, was a different matter altogether. Agents like Rebecca, men and women who only gathered information, were rarely, if ever, put in harm's way. The fact that Rebecca's grandfather had been a friend of Gyuri's wouldn't stop the Russian from pursuing the man's granddaughter.

Franco Perelli considered his options, self-preservation coloring the choices he might have available. Perelli was old for his line of work. He should have retired years earlier, but every time he thought about that, all he could envision were empty days of absolute boredom stretching as far as his imagination could conceive. But Perelli was also a realist. The odds caught up with agents who stayed in the spy business after a certain age, after their reflexes slowed, after they got lazy.

Perelli knew all of this, but he just couldn't leave work that invigorated him more than anything else he had ever experienced. So, whatever he decided to do about Rebecca Molinere and her safety, Franco Perelli intended to make certain that Gyuri Vargha never knew of his duplicity. As long as Gyuri Vargha remained in Rome, Franco Perelli would have to be very, very careful.

Over the next few days, Franco Perelli considered, and discarded, a number of scenarios that might be believable enough for him to pitch to Vargha. The solution, when it came to him, was so simple that Perelli chided himself for not thinking of it in the first place. Gyuri Vargha couldn't get revenge on a dead man. Surely one of Perelli's contacts could provide the name of an agent who had died or been killed in the last three or four years. Vargha would be disappointed, maybe even angry, but Rebecca Molinere and Wolf Johannsen would be safe. And so would he.

Perelli was fairly certain that Vargha had not seen or heard his assassin, thus giving the operative much greater leeway in locating a deceased agent. Man or woman, English-speaker or not – all that was necessary was that the entity behind the kill be affiliated with one of Russia's enemy states. Unfortunately, Perelli couldn't just pick up the phone and start calling the C.I.A., M.I.6 or any other covert government agency. The kind of information he sought needed to come from someone like himself, an agent on the ground and with personal knowledge of the how, when, and why the agent whose identity he intended to use was killed.

Perelli would have one chance to fool Vargha. If he

failed, if Vargha saw through the ruse or simply didn't believe him, Perelli knew he would not live long enough to warn Rebecca of the danger she would then most surely be in. He needed more time, more time to make contact with the right people, more time before Vargha turned his attention to Rebecca Molinere, or even to Wolf Johannsen.

He would warn Rebecca now. Retrieving his cell phone, Franco Perelli made the call.

# CHAPTER THIRTY-ONE

Allison was nothing, if not thorough, when preparing for a case. While many lawyers disliked the discovery process that preceded actual trials, Allison found interrogatories and depositions to be some of most effective tools available to her. Allison had served a set of interrogatories, which were written questions for an opposing party to answer under oath, on Mona Phillips' lawyer before she left on the trip with Wolf. The responses were awaiting her when she returned, and Allison had referred to them several times when preparing the questions she intended to ask Mona at today's deposition.

Numbered questions in Allison's handwriting filled the yellow legal pad before her. The procedural rules in both State and Federal courts allowed very far-ranging questions during a deposition, even if the questions and answers might, ultimately, be ruled inadmissible as evidence at trial. Because of this laxity, Allison liked to have all of the questions she knew she wanted to ask actually in writing before she began a deposition. In that way, she was able to follow a line of questioning that might take her fairly far afield should the deponent say something interesting, but would always allow her to come back to the line of questioning that she deemed necessary for the defense of the case.

Mona Phillips' answers to the interrogatories were lacking in Allison's opinion and she intended to delve further into Mona's answers during the 2:30 deposition. Allison wasn't surprised at the thinness of Mona's responses. Litigants gave away as little as possible in discovery, providing only the narrowest of answers, both to interrogatories and in depositions. Allison, herself, had advised her own clients to answer only the questions asked, preferably with just a "yes" or "no" response. Getting more out of an opposing party was the lawyer's job.

Allison's legal opponent, Michael Baker, was a sole practitioner in Montgomery whom Allison had never met. In his mid-50's and known primarily as a plaintiff's lawyer, Baker was, according to the Montgomery lawyers Allison had spoken with, a decent guy. Nevertheless, decent guy or not, Allison figured her opponent would be expecting to threaten her client with a big jury award, given the impact of the current "#MeToo" movement.

A smile crept over Allison's face as she thought about the surprise that awaited Michael Baker after his client's deposition.

A glance at the grandfather's clock in the corner of her office informed Allison that she had five minutes before her early luncheon date with Wolf. Satisfied that she was as prepared as she could be for Mona's deposition, Allison gathered her files and headed for the door.

"I'm meeting Wolf at the diner," Allison called to Donna Pevey as she hurried past her secretary's desk. "I'll leave for Montgomery from there. See you in the morning."

Edna's Café was one of Allison's favorite Ft. Charles eateries. A purveyor of home-cooked Southern favorites, Edna's also offered lighter fare as a nod to its more health conscious patrons. With summer making its arrival, Allison knew the day's menu would include plenty of vegetables straight from local farms. Fried okra might not be that healthy, but if it was on the menu, Allison wouldn't be able to resist.

The whir of the café's ancient AC wall units hummed pleasantly, adding a recognizable accompaniment to the lively conversations that greeted Allison as she entered the small restaurant. Since the outside temps were only in the low 80's, the air coming from the three small air conditioners was fairly cold. Once the Ft. Charles summer was in full swing, those same three units would barely be able to waft any semblance of cool air over the diners. Allison hoped that maybe this year, Edna would decide to trade out the old units for modern Mitsubishis.

Wolf was seated in the far corner of the café, his back to the wall. Like her F.B.I. friend Jake Cleveland, Wolf always positioned himself in a restaurant where he could see all the entrances and exits. Wolf's instinct for self-preservation had remained with him after he left the covert life. Given the recent events in Rome, Allison had to admit that Wolf's precautions were a habit she hoped he would never break.

Toby Trowbridge, Calhoun County's popular sheriff, was seated at the table with Wolf. Allison hadn't seen Toby since her return and wondered if something was going on that she should know about. Making her way past two and four tops that would soon be filled with noontime customers, Allison greeted Wolf with a kiss and Toby with a smile.

"How're you doing, Toby?" Allison pulled out a chair and joined the men. "Anything interesting happen while Wolf and I were gone?"

"It's been duller than a butter knife," Toby laughed. "I reckon all the bad guys have been waiting for your return." The sheriff enjoyed teasing Allison. "Now that you and Wolf are back, I can expect the pace to ramp up some."

Allison glanced at Wolf. She wondered if he had told Toby about Gyuri Vargha. Toby was aware of Wolf's history. It wouldn't surprise the county's chief law enforcement officer to hear about Rome. Wolf's barely perceptible nod told Allison the subject had been broached.

"I hope all the bad guys stay where they are," Allison replied to the sheriff. "I take it Wolf told you about what happened in Rome?"

"He did." Toby paused to finish off his coffee and signal the waitress for a refill. "He also told me that the appropriate authorities were following up on the matter." Conversation stopped while Edna's daughter refilled Toby's coffee and took lunch orders from Wolf and Allison. After the young girl moved out of hearing range, Toby continued, "I don't have to tell either one of you that if there is any hint that this problem has followed you to Ft. Charles that I better be the first person you contact."

"I can't imagine that would happen" Wolf assured the sheriff. "If this guy really is Vargha, he'll be completely dead soon. And not by my hand."

Conversation returned to more benign topics. When Allison's veggie plate and Wolf's BLT were delivered, Toby bade the couple goodbye. "Good to have y'all back. Stay in touch."

Allison picked at her food, thoughts she had pushed aside now re-emerging with Toby's comments. "You don't think there's any possibility of Gyuri Vargha showing up here, do you?" Allison watched Wolf's face. His words might say one thing while his face might reveal something else.

Wolf reached for Allison's hand. "The odds of him following me to Ft. Charles are astronomical. He doesn't know about my covert life – to him I am just a friend of Rebecca's who was in town and was invited to her party."

"But you said he was asking too many pointed questions," Allison interrupted. "I remember what you said that night at Rebecca's party. You were worried."

"Overly cautious, not worried. Vargha wouldn't take the risk of coming here without positive proof that I was the agent who tried to take him out five years ago. Anyway, like I told Toby, Vargha is already a dead man. I'm sure a current operative has already been given the assignment to eliminate him." Wolf's face betrayed no sign that his words weren't true. "Quit worrying."

# CHAPTER THIRTY-TWO

Ned Bakke considered the information spread out before him. Franco Perelli, Rebecca Molinere, and Wolf Johannsen, three operatives whose judgement he trusted implicitly, had identified the man claiming to be Gyuri Vargha as the real deal. The decision Ned needed to make was whether to capture and interrogate Vargha or to dispatch someone to take him out permanently.

Drugs sophisticated enough to mimic death were things of the imagination, plots lines most often found in spy novels or made-for-TV movies. In his almost forty years with the Agency, Ned had never seen proof that such drugs actually existed. Ned wanted to know whether Vargha had fooled the medical examiner after his body was delivered to the morgue or if someone inside the Rome ME's office had been working for the other side and had simply forged Vargha's death certificate. If the staff at the Rome ME's office were innocent…well, the existence of a drug that could mimic death yet allow the user to survive was something the Agency would want to add to its arsenal. Unless the Agency already had such a weapon. Picking up the phone, Bakke punched the five digits to connect his call to the one person he knew would be straight with him.

"Johnson," A woman's voice answered.

"Meg, it's Ned Bakke. You got a minute?"

"When do I ever have a minute?" Meg Johnson, one of the Agency's in-house scientists, complained. "You know what a slave-driver McNair is."

Ned laughed. Fred McNair, the Agency's top scientific brain, was the least likely person to harass his employees about their work ethic, mainly because Fred never hired anyone who wasn't as intellectually driven as he was. "Well, if you can pull yourself away from whatever project Fred has you working on, I'd like to pick that scientific brain of yours for a few minutes."

"Give me a sec," Meg replied. "I need to capture this detail."

Placing his phone on speaker mode, Bakke reviewed the records that the Agency had acquired from the Rome ME's office after Vargha's supposed death. He doubted there was anything pertinent in those records since Vargha's body had disappeared before an autopsy had been attempted. It wouldn't hurt, though, to let Meg take another look at them.

"Alright, I'm ready. What's on your mind?"

"We've got an unusual situation," Bakke began. "Five years ago one of our operatives was given a target for elimination. The operative completed the mission, we thought, and the file on the target was closed."

"What do you mean, 'we thought'?" Meg interrupted.

"That's part of why I'm calling you," Bakke replied, "but let me finish. The hit took place in Rome, Italy. The target's body was delivered to the office of the Medical Examiner by the local authorities, but before an autopsy could be performed, the body vanished."

"So, you're calling me about a 'body-napping'? Really, Ned, I don't have time for this. Is this some sort of prank Fred put you up to?"

"No, Meg, it's not." Bakke forced himself to keep a civil tongue. Meg Johnson was both a brilliant scientist and a royal pain in the ass. "What has happened is serious. Potentially, deadly serious. Do you want to hear what I have to say, or should I enlist someone else's help?"

The interagency line buzzed quietly as Meg Johnson digested Ned Bakke's words and tone. "I'm listening."

"The target was a man named Gyuri Vargha. The kill was Wolf Johannsen's last assignment. We didn't immediately know that the body had been removed from the ME's office. What we did know was that a death certificate had been issued, and we assumed, wrongly, we now know, that Gyuri Vargha had died."

"What sort of incompetents run that office?"

Meg had no tolerance for ineptitude. "Either the man was dead, or he wasn't."

"That's why I'm calling you, Meg. Gyuri Vargha reappeared several weeks ago in Rome. He's returned to his cover identity as an art critic, and he's been very secretive about where he's been the past five years. When he reached out to one of our double agents, we got the call. Since then, Vargha has been positively identified by two other operatives, including Wolf Johannsen." Bakke waited for Meg's next question.

"Obviously, no autopsy was done, or we wouldn't be having this conversation. Were there any tissue samples taken before the body was removed?" Meg's curiosity was aroused.

"No. The man appeared dead – no noticeable respiration, greyish tint to the skin, the beginnings of rigor. According to the notes we obtained, Vargha's body was checked into the system, and he was placed in cold storage until an autopsy could be scheduled. My question for you, Meg, is this: is there a drug out there that could produce this effect? We know Vargha survived. We just don't know how."

"There are only two that I know of which can produce the appearance of death, but unless administered by a professional, actual death will most likely be the end result. Succinylcholine is a neuromuscular paralytic. It causes all of the body's muscle to be paralyzed, including those used for breathing. It's commonly used in anesthesia for surgical procedures, which is why a breathing tube is inserted by the anesthesiologist. It's highly unlikely that Succinylcholine was used in this case."

"And the other?" Bakke prompted.

"Potassim chloride. The right amount causes immediate cardiac arrest. In lesser amounts, it might mimic death, but frankly I doubt it. I think an injection of any amount of that stuff would truly kill the recipient."

"And that's it?"

"Maybe a modified form of Tetradotoxin. That's the poison in Pufferfish," Meg explained, "but I don't think there is an antidote to that nasty neurotoxin, so again, doubtful that this is what you are looking for either."

"Is the Agency working on anything that would mimic the symptoms I've just described, without killing the patient?"

"I can't share that information with you, Ned. Something like that would be classified, even if it existed."

Ned considered Meg's reply. If there was a message hidden in her words, he would have to figure out by himself.

# CHAPTER THIRTY-THREE

A cold front had swept through central Italy the night before, bringing unusually cool temps for a Rome summer. Sitting on her roof-top patio enjoying a morning cup of coffee, Rebecca Molinere thought life couldn't get any better. According to the weatherman, this delightful respite from the normal summer heat was going to last through the upcoming weekend.

The weekend. A contented smile spread over Rebecca's face. Two years earlier, the gallery owner had decided to splurge, buying a small cottage in Anzio. Just 51 kilometers from Rome, and an easy one-hour train ride on the Roma-Nettuno railway, Anzio's beach location provided Rebecca the perfect retreat from her hectic life in Rome. This afternoon Rebecca intended to close the gallery early and catch the 4 p.m. train. Even with stopping at the small market in Anzio to pick up groceries, Rebecca would be comfortably ensconced in her small cottage in time to watch the sun set over the Mediterranean.

Tourists, especially American and British tourists, remembered Anzio for its historical significance in World War II. A large and costly battle occurred in Anzio after an Allied landing, and in February of 1944, portions of the U.S. Fifth Army suffered significant casualties after being trapped in nearby caves by the German army. Rebecca had visited both the Commonwealth Anzio War Cemetery and the Beach Head War Cemetery on her previous visits. War was a terrible waste of life, but humanity had yet to learn that lesson.

Rebecca's Anzio realtor had shared a bit of trivia with her as the pair looked at properties for Rebecca to buy. An Englishman by the name of Lt. Eric Fletcher Waters had lost his life during a six-week battle in the area during the war. Years later, his son Roger Waters became the bassist and main lyricist for the rock band, Pink Floyd, and recorded a song in his father's honor. Rebecca had found the story somewhat serendipitous. Pink Floyd was one of the gallery owner's favorite older bands.

The Anzio of today had become a popular vacation spot. Replete with beautiful beaches, luxury hotels, and restaurants serving fresh-caught fish, Anzio provided a low-key escape for many, especially busy Romans who found the commute convenient for a weekend getaway.

Rebecca was glad she had purchased when she had. Real estate prices were only getting higher as the coastal town became more and more popular.

The cottage Rebecca had chosen was, in her mind, perfect. Located a few kilometers from city center and perched partway up a mountain, the two-bedroom cottage was just large enough for Rebecca to invite an overnight guest, but just small enough to be cozy when she came alone. For this trip, she had invited Charlene Jacobs to join her. Charlene was an enjoyable houseguest, actually one of Rebecca's favorites, but her invitation for this weekend hid an ulterior motive. Rebecca wanted to pick Charlene's brain about Gyuri Vargha.

Thinking about Charlene and Gyuri reminded Rebecca that she owed Franco Perelli a call. The message left on her cell phone late last night was concerning. Leaving the patio and beautiful morning behind, Rebecca walked inside to retrieve her phone. Hopefully, she would be able to reach Perelli before she headed to the gallery.

After several unanswered rings, it seemed that Rebecca and Perelli would continue to trade calls. The gallery owner had just begun to leave a message, when Perelli interrupted with a brisk "Pronto."

"Franco, it's Rebecca Molinere. I'm returning your call from last night. What is going on?"

Succinctly the double agent told Rebecca about his last meeting with Gyuri Vargha. "He's got his eye on you, Rebecca. You need to be very careful until he's taken care of."

"You're overly worried," Rebecca adjusted the volume on her phone to better hear Perelli's whispered warning. "All I am to Gyuri Vargha is Rene Depeche's granddaughter and a friend of his current bedmate."

"No, Rebecca. You're wrong. That's what I am trying to tell you. Having Wolf Johannsen at your party the other night spooked Vargha and got him to thinking. He's decided to take a hard look at you, and maybe, eventually, Johannsen. You made a mistake inviting Johannsen."

Perelli's condescending tone irritated Rebecca. "Who better to prove to Langley that Gyuri Vargha is who he claims to be than Wolf Johannsen? Gyuri was Wolf's target." Rebecca paused to light a cigarette. Inhaling the calming drug, she continued, "And Wolf is certain that Gyuri is the real deal. It was worth the risk to be certain."

"I thought you quit those things," Perelli interjected, hearing the soft exhalation at the other end of the line. Receiving no reply, he continued, "We could have confirmed his identity some other way but what is done, is done, and now Vargha has you in his sights. Just be careful."

"Don't worry about me, Franco. I can take care of myself."

Later, packing her overnight bag with shorts, t-shirts, a sundress, and a bathing suit, Rebecca replayed her conversation with Perelli. A part of her knew the agent was right – she should have been more circumspect in putting Wolf and Vargha face-to-face. Had she become careless? Were there red flags that she had ignored? Operatives who became careless, even those who merely gathered information, often paid a high price. Rebecca was still asking herself questions when she locked her apartment door and headed for the train station to meet Charlene.

# CHAPTER THIRTY-FOUR

Michael Baker's law office occupied a lovely, restored Victorian just a few blocks from downtown Montgomery. The driveway had been expanded into part of the house's side yard to accommodate a multiplicity of cars – lawyers, staff, and clients. Stepping out of her vehicle, Allison paused to admire the landscaping that someone had taken time to plan and execute. The setting for her opponent's office was an attractive combination of business and beauty.

A well-dressed receptionist greeted Allison, taking her name and telling her that "Mr. Baker" would be with her shortly. Allison wondered if Michael Baker played games with his opposing counsel. Making someone wait was a time-honored power ploy. Remembering what she had heard about her opponent, she didn't think hidden agendas were his style. Fifteen minutes later Allison had begun to think she had misjudged Michael Baker, when a harried looking man approached.

"Allison, I'm Mike Baker. Sorry to keep you waiting, but I've been trying to get in touch with my client. She was supposed to be here an hour ago."

A frown replaced Allison's smile. "We've had this deposition scheduled for weeks. Are you telling me your client's going to be a no-show?"

"No, no," Mike Baker rushed to assure Allison. "I just got ahold of her a minute ago. She's on her way. She ought to be here before too long." The attorney ran a shaking hand through his already disheveled hair. "I can't imagine why she got the times mixed up. But anyway, why don't I get you settled in the conference room? The court reporter is already in there."

An expert at picking up physical clues, Allison wondered what was causing Mike Baker's hand to noticeably shake. Was he ill? Was he nervous about the upcoming deposition? Maybe he was a drug addict and needed a fix? Allison discarded the latter thought as highly unlikely. "Mike, are you okay?" Allison watched Mike's reaction to see if a "tell" might give the lie to his answer.

"Hypoglycemic," Mike replied. "Missed lunch and my blood sugar's dropped. I'll grab a power bar before we get started." The lawyer gave Allison an apprising look. "Thanks for asking."

The conference room in Mike Baker's law office was

located directly off the large foyer which served as the law firm's reception area. Accessed by double pocket-doors which slid into the wall on either side of the room's entrance, the richly paneled walls suggested the conference room's first incarnation had been as a library or parlor of some sort.

Ginger Brooks, Allison's go-to court reporter, was already set up at the end of a large table. Efficient and professional, Ginger owned a chain of court reporting businesses from Montgomery to the Georgia state line. Whenever possible, Allison retained Ginger or one of her expert employees for depositions.

The slamming of a door caught Allison's attention. Glancing towards the sound, Allison saw a slim, raven-haired woman hurry across the foyer. Allison's seat at the conference table gave her a direct view of the newcomer who, despite the summer heat, was dressed in tight, black leather pants and a low-cut leather vest. Repressing the grin that was trying hard to escape her lips, Allison watched Mona admire herself in a large mirror that hung in the reception area. "This is going to be fun," Allison thought.

A few minutes later Mike Baker ushered his client into the conference room and made introductions. Mona Phillips' first words to Allison told the lawyer all she needed to know about the plaintiff. "You're a woman!" Mona Phillips gasped, eyeing Allison with surprise.

"Yes, indeed," Allison smiled in reply. "And you wasted your time on that outfit," she added silently.

Instinctively, the tactic Allison would use in the deposition came to her. Asking Ginger to "swear the witness," Allison prepared to lead Mona Phillips down the proverbial garden path.

Allison's first questions were standard and intended to lull Mona into a false sense of security. Allison kept her tone of voice gentle and non-confrontational. If the deposition went as she suspected, Mona Phillips would damage her case and her credibility without much help from Allison.

Thirty minutes into the deposition, Allison inquired innocently, "Do you work anywhere other than the Blue Moon Casino?" Allison knew full well where Mona held a second job, but she wanted Mona's answer under oath.

"Yes. I work at the Magic Lounge," Mona's reply was casual and matter-of-fact.

Allison feigned confusion, "Isn't that a strip club?"

Mona Phillips flicked an errant strand of hair from her face. "Yes, but all I do there is serve drinks."

Allison paused. Her next question would lay the trap. "Oh, you don't do any dancing, or whatever they do there?"

Mona Phillips shook her head, "No, I wouldn't want to do any of that stuff."

"No stripping, no lap dances, nothing like that?" Allison pressed.

"Look, lady, I already told you. I just serve drinks." Mona glared at Michael Baker, "Is she deaf?"

Reacting quickly to Mona's outburst, Allison affected

a chagrined look. "Ms. Phillips, I don't mean to offend you. I just wanted to make sure I understood exactly what you did at the Magic Lounge."

Mollified, Mona Phillips muttered a grudging, "Okay".

Deftly, Allison proceeded down her list of questions. By the time the deposition concluded an hour later, Allison was satisfied that she had covered all her bases and had put Mona Phillips and her lawyer in a corner from which they would find it difficult to escape. Driving home to Ft. Charles, Allison chuckled. What she would give to be a fly on the wall when Michael Baker watched the video she was going to send to him.

# CHAPTER THIRTY-FIVE

The otter that Wolf Johannsen was sculpting stood, belly protruding, hands clutching a small fish, on the workshop table. Wood shavings covered the floor, a testament to the detailed carving that was taking place. Wolf stepped back several feet to examine his work. The otter would be a surprise gift for Allison's birthday, and he wanted the otter to be perfect.

Picking up a spoon gouge, Wolf had just started to work on one of the otter's smaller details when the sounds of a piano scale interrupted him. Wolf recognized the ring tone. Laying aside the carving tool, Wolf reached for his cell phone.

"Yes?" Wolf wondered why Ned Bakke was calling. "Is there a problem?"

"Maybe," came Bakke's curt reply. "According to our

best scientists, there's no drug out there that we know of that could have successfully mimicked Vargha's death. That means he either had inside help, or the Russians have developed a new drug. Whichever it was, we need to know."

Wolf thought he knew what was coming next, and he wasn't biting. "I'm retired, Ned. I'm not going back out."

"I'm not asking you to," Bakke quickly interjected. "We've assigned an active agent to the Vargha matter. Capture rather than kill, if at all possible. We want to interrogate Gyuri Vargha."

Wolf considered another reason for Bakke's call. "Has the Agency picked up intel that affects me?"

"Yes, and that's why I'm calling. We have a deep-cover double agent in Rome. You were never made aware of his status, although he was read-in on your assignment five years ago."

"You what?" Wolf's ire began to rise. "I was sent on a kill mission, and you didn't see fit to tell me that we had a double agent in play?"

"Need to know. You didn't then," Bakke explained, "you do now. We've just received an encrypted message from him. Gyuri Vargha believes you may be the agent who tried to take him out."

A chill ran down Wolf's spine. He had feared this would happen, not because he was worried about Vargha killing him, but because of the collateral damage that might occur now that he was living in Ft. Charles.

"How certain are you of this information?"

"Our source is solid. And you aren't the only one in danger." Bakke paused. Wolf would not want to hear what Bakke was going to say next. "Vargha told our agent that he suspects Rebecca Molinere was somehow involved in the assassination attempt. She has been warned."

Wolf cursed silently. The news was going from bad to worse. Wolf knew Rebecca Molinere, and he knew she wouldn't take the warning as seriously as she should. Informational operatives never truly understood the danger of the business in which they were only peripherally involved. Passing information generally didn't place one's life in danger. "You need to do more than warn Rebecca. She needs protection until Vargha is removed."

"We can't spare one agent to babysit another. Rebecca knew what she was signing up for. She'll take precautions." Bakke hoped he was right.

"What about the double agent, the person whose name you still haven't shared with me?" Wolf inquired. "What's his role in all of this?"

"His name is Franco Perelli. We recruited him fifteen years ago. He allowed Vargha to recruit him a few years before you were assigned the hit. Vargha thinks Perelli is his agent on the ground in Rome. Perelli is the one who told us the Russian had survived."

"And his role in the current situation?" Wolf pressed.

"To keep his ear to the ground and report on Vargha's

plans. As soon as the operative we've assigned to bring in Vargha arrives in Rome- which should be later today – Perelli will contact him and coordinate the snatch."

"Let me know when Vargha has been neutralized," Wolf demanded, "or if our operative somehow loses him."

#

Wolf Johannsen may have been retired from the covert life for a while now, but he had never lost situational awareness, nor had he become complacent. The Old Fort Inn which Wolf had purchased upon his move to Ft. Charles offered both privacy and security, the latter enhanced by the tall wrought-iron fencing and hidden electronic surveillance equipment that Wolf had installed around the property's perimeter. A visitor to Wolf's home would merely see beautiful and tasteful fencing surrounding a lovely antebellum residence. The keypad adjacent to the large double gate was in place for the innocent. Wolf's high-tech surveillance equipment picked up visitors, legitimate or otherwise, well before their arrival at the gate.

Good security required more than one level of protection. A trained operative might bypass Wolf's fencing and initial warning system, although he thought that an unlikely possibility. But planning for unlikely possibilities kept a man alive, so Wolf had armored his home accordingly. Again, the casual visitor would see nothing alarming, but in each room and hallway

Wolf had hidden guns, extra ammunition, knives, and assorted weaponry which he could access if needed. A part of the ex-operative had felt foolish outfitting his home in such a manner. Now he was glad he had taken the extra precautions.

One more detail remained. Picking up the hall phone, Wolf placed his call to the Calhoun County Sheriff. If Gyuri Vargha came calling, Wolf wanted Allison and her children protected.

# CHAPTER THIRTY-SIX

Gyuri Vargha surveyed the items spread on the kitchen table of his flat. These were the tools of his trade, tools intended to hurt, to kill, tools that were as familiar to Vargha as any part of his body. Over the years, Vargha had used numerous guns, but the Walthar P99 remained his favorite. The 3-DOT polymer sights allowed for rapid aiming and target acquisition, while the low profile made it easily removable from inside a jacket or pocket. Picking up the semiautomatic handgun, Vargha tested the slide before placing it in a small overnight bag where it rested next to a tuckable holster and five clips of ammunition. In an abundance of caution, the Russian added a 9mm silencer. Depending on the proximity of Rebecca Molinere's cottage to its neighbors, Vargha might need it.

Unwrapping a soft chamois cloth, Vargha considered his collection of knives. Some he used to inflict pain in order to gather information. Some, like the slender blade to his left, he used to slit an opponent's throat. For the trip to Anzio, Vargha might need all of them. Carefully wrapping the weapons in the cloth, he added the blades to the leather bag.

The bag was almost full when Vargha added a coil of rope, several strips of muslin fabric, and a small bottle of chloroform. His victims would need to be incapacitated quickly. Satisfied that he had not forgotten anything necessary for the successful completion of the task before him, Gyuri Vargha zipped the black bag and headed out. He had plenty of time for a leisurely drive to Anzio. His work wouldn't begin until many hours hence.

The drive from Rome to Anzio was unremarkable. Staying well below the posted 150 km speed limit, Vargha kept a low profile. The last thing he needed was to be pulled over by some hotshot officer looking to make his quota on speeders. Killing a member of the "polizie" in broad daylight would be difficult. Difficult, but not impossible. Still, Vargha didn't need the hassle. He had more important work to do.

Dusk was falling as Vargha entered the outskirts of his destination. According to what he had gleaned from Charlene Jacobs at dinner the night before, she and Rebecca had planned an early evening for their first night at the cottage. If the women stayed true to their planned agenda, Vargha would be in no danger of running into them in town.  Nevertheless, Vargha wasn't taking any chances.  Selecting a café far from town center, the spy ordered food and a glass of wine.  He'd spend a few leisurely hours over a good meal before beginning the killing that awaited him.

Normally, Vargha would not have made himself noticeable in a public place like a restaurant.  While most people paid no attention to other diners, there was always the possibility that someone would remember the man sitting alone and be able to give the police an accurate description.  Vargha had planned for this possibility and wasn't worried.  If, by any remote chance, the police interviewed the wait staff at this café about any strangers, Vargha's current disguise would prevent his identification.  Besides, an old man walking with a cane was a danger to no one.

Vargha lingered over his meal of pasta and prawns.  The food was surprisingly good.  Maybe, he thought, he'd come back some day and sample more of Anzio and what her small cafes might offer.  Signaling to the waiter for another espresso, Vargha began a mental dry run of his plans for Rebecca Molinere.  For a brief minute, he felt bad about Charlene Jacobs.  The American expat had been a good lay and a sometimes-entertaining distraction, but he couldn't let her go.  If only she hadn't made the trip with Rebecca.  Shaking his head, Vargha allowed himself a small frisson of regret.

After the café closed, the spy ambled slowly past closed shops and trattorias.  The drive up the mountain to Rebecca's cottage was no more than a couple of kilometers. The moon was still on the ascendant and wouldn't be high in the night sky for another hour. Walking allowed Vargha to expend the last remnants of nervous energy as he watched the moon traverse its path. By the time he reached his car, Gyuri Vargha was focused on the task ahead.

# CHAPTER THIRTY-SEVEN

Wolf Johannsen pulled his Mercedes coupe into the last available parking space in the paved lot that served the Calhoun County Sheriff's office. After calling Sheriff Trowbridge, Wolf had spent some time on the phone with Ned Bakke. The folder Wolf clutched in his hand as he entered the county building had multiple photos of Gyuri Vargha and a brief dossier on the man. The photos were old – Wolf silently cursed his lapse in judgment. He should have taken a current picture at Rebecca's party. Thankfully, Vargha hadn't changed enough not to be recognizable from the file pictures Ned had emailed.

Beth Robinson, Sheriff Trowbridge's secretary, was waiting for Wolf in the lobby. "Sheriff is mighty anxious to talk with you," she advised Wolf. "You causing trouble again?"

"No ma'am" Wolf automatically replied. For the life of him, Wolf couldn't figure out why Toby's 70- something gatekeeper caused him to act like an errant school boy. "Just letting the Sheriff know about something that happened on my trip." Keeping information from Beth Robinson was a futile exercise, according to Toby and Frank Martin, but Wolf wasn't going to make it any easier for the woman by giving her specifics. Plus, with any luck, trouble in the form of Gyuri Vargha would be taken care of across the pond, leaving Ft. Charles well out of the line of fire.

"You mean your trip with Ms. Parker?" Beth grinned. "I didn't see a ring on her finger when y'all got back. When are you gonna ask that woman to marry you?"

In the year that he had lived in Ft. Charles, Wolf had become mostly accustomed to the Southerners' habit of asking personal questions and expecting an answer. To be fair, Wolf had to admit that not everyone asked the kind of questions Beth Robinson lobbed on a regular basis, but once a native felt that some sort of familiarity had been achieved, well – one never knew what topic of conversation might be introduced.

"Now, Ms. Robinson, you know that's between me and Allison," Wolf parried, depriving Beth of the gossipy tidbit she was hoping for. "How about taking me back to the Sheriff? As you said, he's anxious to talk with me."

Undeterred, Beth continued to pepper Wolf with questions about Allison and their trip before depositing him outside Toby Trowbridge's office. Leaving Wolf with "and I better be the first to know," Beth Robinson closed the Sheriff's door and left the men to their meeting.

One of the chairs in the Sheriff's office was already occupied. "I asked Frank to join us," Toby explained, "and I've got a call in to Jake Cleveland."

"The Agency hasn't notified the F.B.I. about this, so far as I know," Wolf interjected, hearing Toby mention the name of Wolf's F.B.I. friend. "I considered calling Jake, but decided against it. I'm not an active operative anymore. If I step on the wrong toes, I run the risk of being cut out of the information loop."

"Who gives a shit about that little detail?" Frank pointed at Wolf with a lit cigar. "I sure as hell don't, not if Allison might be in danger."

Wolf held his temper while Frank ranted. The P.I. was as protective as a mother grizzly when it came to Allison Parker, and his worries about her safety often presented as anger to the uninformed. When Frank gave a loud "harumpf," Wolf continued, "Since the call came from law enforcement Jake can run this up the line. I doubt Wilson Mackey will say no to Jake's involvement, at least to some degree."

As if to emphasis Wolf's point, the phone on Toby's desk buzzed with an incoming call. "It's Jake," the Sheriff told Frank and Wolf, punching the speaker button and answering the call.

"What's going on, Toby?" Jake Cleveland's deep voice boomed over the phone line. "Your message said it was urgent."

"I've got you on speaker," the Sheriff informed the F.B.I. agent. "Frank and Wolf are here. Actually, Wolf is the reason I called you, so I'm going to let him tell you what may be landing in our laps."

Quickly and succinctly, Wolf brought the agent up to speed, starting with his assignment to eliminate Gyuri Vargha, to Vargha's unexplained survival, to the Russian's re-emergence in Rome, and ending with the information provided by Franco Perelli. "Langley has sent a current operative to capture or kill Vargha. The Agency is particularly interested in how Vargha mimicked his death and would prefer to interrogate rather than kill him. With any luck, my concerns will be moot in another 24 to 48 hours, but Vargha escaped once before. If Perelli is right, and Vargha leaves Rome before the Agency's man can get to him, I think there's a pretty good likelihood that Vargha will come for me. I'm not worried about myself, but Vargha met Allison at Rebecca Molinere's party. He might target Allison or her family as leverage against me. That's why I called Toby, and that's why he called you."

"Well, crap and shit on a shingle!" Jake Cleveland cursed. "I thought you got out of the spook business, Johannsen. What in the hell were you doing exposing Allison to a maniac like Gyuri Vargha?"

"I didn't realize there would be face-to-face contact" Wolf retorted. "Rebecca told me Vargha would be at the party, but I expected to be able to surveille and ID him from a distance. It didn't turn out that way."

"The damage is done," Jake replied.

"If the man turns up here," Frank pointed out. "All we've got right now is speculation."

"What we've got is solid intel from a current operative that a killer wants to enact revenge against Wolf Johannsen." Toby paced the small office while he talked. "The C.I.A. has taken the threat seriously and my guess is the F.B.I. will, too. Ft. Charles is my home, and I've taken an oath to protect the citizens of Calhoun County. I don't intend to let some A-hole Russkie come in here and take out my people. If he tries, we'll be ready."

# CHAPTER THIRTY-EIGHT

The last golden rays of sun slipped below the horizon. "If we're lucky, those distant clouds will give us a show of pink and orange color before it gets completely dark. Something to do with reflected light and angles right after the sun sets," Rebecca explained to her houseguest.

"It's all beyond beautiful," Charlene Jacobs responded. "Thanks, again, for inviting me down for the weekend. Coming here never gets old."

Conversation lulled for a while as the women sipped wine, enjoying the view across the Anzio harbor. When the distant color-show had been replaced by a night sky and the earliest of the evening's stars, Rebecca broached the subject that had been on her mind all the way from Rome.

"Are you still seeing Gyuri?"

A slight smile lit the older woman's face, "Yes, and I still can't believe he's interested in me. I thought at first it was because I'm rich, but he won't let me pay for anything, and he seems to have plenty of money and other resources."

"I guess he's done pretty well over the years as an art critic and author," Rebecca replied, "but I'm not really familiar with anything he's put out in the past five or six years. He must have a good investment advisor."

Charlene didn't reply. Casting a sideways glance at her friend, Rebecca watched Charlene's expression change.

"Charlene?" Rebecca reached for her friend's hand. "Did I say something wrong?""

"It's nothing."

Charlene squeezed Rebecca's hand, as if to emphasize words which, spoken aloud, had seemed a bit hollow. The emotions rolling over her friend's face told Rebecca much more that the uttered denial. Charlene Jacobs had more to say. The question was whether or not she would. Rebecca waited patiently, refusing to release her friend's hand, hoping by her silence to encourage Charlene to share what was clearly disturbing the woman.

Charlene downed the remainder of her wine before speaking. "I think Gyuri is more than an art critic."

Stunned, Rebecca struggled to keep surprise from showing on her own face. Had Gyuri Vargha revealed himself to Charlene? Carefully, she asked, "Why do you think that, Charlene?"

Charlene Jacobs refilled her wine glass and gathered her thoughts. Admitting the truth, even to her friend Rebecca, was humiliating. "I think he's an art thief."

"What?" Rebecca was both relieved and confused. "What in the world makes you think Gyuri Vargha is an art thief?"

"I overheard a phone call he was on the other morning. Gyuri asked the person he was talking to how much he would pay for the package."

"Well, that could mean anything," Rebecca countered. "He must have said something else for you to decide he's an art thief."

"When he realized I had overheard his conversation he threatened me," Charlene's voice quivered. "He told me to mind my own business. Given his connections to the art world, I figured he was involved in something illegal."

"Charlene Jacobs!" Rebecca exclaimed. "Why are you even still seeing this man?"

Charlene began to cry. "I don't want to be alone."

Rebecca wrapped her arms around her friend. "Charlene, you're not alone. You have so many people in Rome who love you."

"It's not the same" sadness coated Charlene's voice. "I'm tired of waking up alone every morning, and going to bed the same way every night."

Rebecca debated. Should she tell Charlene the truth about Gyuri Vargha? Would Charlene believe her? Rebecca needed more information. "Charlene, tell me everything you overheard the other day."

"It wasn't that much." Charlene reached for the bottle of Pinot Noir and topped off her wineglass. "It was about nine in the morning. I stayed over at Gyuri's flat after a late dinner. I was walking through the main room on my way to the kitchen for a cup of coffee when I saw Gyuri was on the phone."

"Had you heard the call ring?" Rebecca interrupted.

"No, and that's really what caught my attention, because Gyuri hadn't said anything about needing to make a call so early." Charlene poured another portion of wine into her now-empty glass. "So I walked past the doorway and then stopped to listen. I thought maybe he had met someone at your party the week before and was giving her a call."

"Do you remember anything Gyuri said, other than about delivering a package?"

Rebecca watched as Charlene processed Rebecca's question. After a few minutes her friend replied, "He said the package would be large. That's all I remember." Charlene began to cry again. "Why did I have to eavesdrop? This is all just one big mess."

Charlene's inebriated condition made Rebecca's decision for her, at least for the evening. Telling Charlene who Gyuri Vargha really was would serve no purpose that Rebecca could imagine, other than to make her friend feel even worse about herself and her choice in men.

Charlene's sobs had faded, overtaken by soft snoring.

Grabbing a light blanket from the cottage, Rebecca gently covered her friend's sleeping body. The night would be chilly but not cold, and leaving Charlene in the recliner would be much easier than trying to move the woman to a more comfortable bed.

Rebecca gathered the empty wine bottle and glasses, depositing them on the kitchen counter before heading to her own bedroom. Morning would come soon enough. Whether she would share what she knew about Gyuri with Charlene was yet to be determined. Maybe the answer would come while she slept.

# CHAPTER THIRTY-NINE

Vargha had parked his car in a wooded area about one kilometer from Rebecca's cottage. He would have preferred a closer location in the event he needed a quick getaway, but the copse of trees had offered the best concealment for his dark-colored vehicle. Other than killing, stealth was one of Vargha's greatest assets. And tonight, his ability to move undetected had played to his advantage, confirming his decision to eliminate both women after interrogating Rebecca. Charlene Jacobs was too suspicious, and Rebecca Molinere – well, if he killed one of the women, he'd have to kill both of them.

Vargha waited patiently, concealed by the dark and the surrounding vegetation that grew close to the cottage. The snores coming from Charlene Jacobs assured Vargha that his first target would be easy to take.

The phrase "dead to the world" flitted through Vargha's mind, causing the man to stifle a laugh. Charlene Jacobs would, indeed, shortly be good and dead to the world.

The sounds coming from the cottage slowly diminished, soon followed by the extinguishing of light from the room Vargha figured likely to be Rebecca Molinere's bedroom. Checking his watch, Vargha decided to wait another thirty minutes before making his way first to Charlene Jacobs, and then to the cottage. Although Vargha intended to kill Charlene quietly, so much the better if Rebecca had time to enter a REM sleep cycle.

At a quarter past midnight, Vargha emerged from his hiding place. Withdrawing a stiletto, Vargha made his way to the sleeping figure of his intended victim. The rising moon illuminated Charlene's face with a silver glow, giving the older woman a softer visage than the harsh sunlight which cruelly accentuated the age lines around her eyes and mouth. Studying the sleeping woman, a part of Vargha, which he had hidden away decades earlier, rose to his consciousness. Regret? Sorrow? Vargha wasn't sure what the feeling was, but it no longer mattered. Taking up a position directly behind the American ex-pat's head, Gyuri Vargha made a deep and precise cut, left to right, across Charlene Jacobs' throat.

The blood-splatter propelled forward, across Charlene's blanket-covered body, spraying iron-scented liquid several feet over the stone patio. Leaning carefully around the corpse, Vargha wiped his blade on a cushion that had somehow escaped being stained. Turning towards the cottage, Vargha sheathed the blade and reached for the small duffle bag he had laid aside before killing Charlene. Incapacitating Rebecca before she could react or fight back was paramount. Vargha uncapped the vial of chloroform, soaked a small handkerchief with a portion of the powerful anesthetic and turned towards the cottage.

The front door opened easily, left unlocked, he supposed, in the event Rebecca's houseguest had roused during the night and sought a bed softer than the patio chaise lounge. Donning night-vision goggles, Vargha surveyed his surroundings. The main room where he was standing included a large fireplace at the back and an open kitchen to the far left. A doorway to his right revealed a short hallway. Heading in that direction, Vargha sought his target. The chloroform would dissipate soon.

The first bedroom was empty. Moving quickly, Vargha reached the next doorway. Rebecca Molinere lay on her back, her left arm encircling her head, the slow rise and fall of her chest confirming a deep sleep. In a matter of seconds he reached his victim. Pressing the soaked fabric over Rebecca's mouth and nose, he used his body weight to forcefully hold the woman against the bed as Rebecca's body instinctively struggled to breathe.

Rebecca's eyes flew open, shock followed by recognition registering in her green eyes before they rolled upward, signaling unconsciousness. Vargha waited. If Rebecca Molinere were the operative he suspected, making certain the drug had done its work was paramount. A few minutes more for certainty wouldn't matter.

Once satisfied that Rebecca Molinere was actually unconscious and not faking, Vargha slung the woman's inert body over his shoulder and moved to the main room. He had noticed a stout wooden chair there, and it was to this piece of furniture that Vargha now tied the cottage's owner, using rope to tightly hold her upper body upright against the back of the chair, and tying her legs and arms to its wooden ones.

Rebecca's head hung limp across her chest. However, small moans coming from the woman told Vargha that Rebecca would soon regain consciousness. Reaching into the black valise, the spy withdrew his preferred instruments of torture. In truth, Gyuri Vargha disliked inflicting pain on his victims. A clean kill, like the one with Charlene, was much more professional in Vargha's opinion, and certainly less messy and much quicker, but when his work necessitated extracting information, he was willing to do whatever was necessary. If Rebecca Molinere was innocent, he would know soon enough. Either way, her life would be over before the sun rose again.

# CHAPTER FORTY

Rebecca opened her eyes slowly, keeping her head down and feigning unconsciousness. Her head felt cloudy, obviously a response to whatever potion Vargha had used to knock her out. Rebecca had no illusions about what lay ahead of her. Gyuri Vargha was here to gain information, to find out what Rebecca knew, to discover who had tried to kill him over five years earlier. The only question that Rebecca could not answer was how long she could hold out.

Footsteps approached the bound woman. Inadvertently, Rebecca jerked, fear overcoming her intention to stay still. Steeling herself, Rebecca raised her head and glared at Gyuri Vargha.

"I don't recall inviting you for the weekend," Rebecca's calm voice concealed her anxiety. "It's rather rude, don't you think, to just show up, and particularly, at this hour?"

Gyuri Vargha smiled. Rebecca's words told him all he needed to know. She was, indeed, an operative. A civilian would have responded much, much differently. "I must apologize for the lack of advance warning, but I'm afraid circumstances made that impossible."

"Where is Charlene?" Suddenly Rebecca realized she and Vargha were alone. "What have you done with her?"

Vargha stepped close to Rebecca. Grasping Rebecca's chin, Vargha lifted the woman's face towards his own. "Charlene won't be interrupting us." Vargha roughly shoved Rebecca's head. "Ever."

"You bastard!" Rebecca spat. "You total, fucking bastard!"

Vargha laughed, "I've been called worse, and most of the names fit. Now," Vargha reached for a slim pointed instrument, "let's quit playing word games and get down to a little business. Who is Wolf Johannsen?"

"He's an old friend. I told you that when I introduced you to him at the party." Rebecca stared calmly at her captor, "He's an international businessman."

Vargha moved closer to Rebecca, "Yes, you did tell me he is an old friend, but I asked you who he is, not what his business interests are." Without warning Vargha hit Rebecca's face with his fist. "We can do this the easy way, or the hard way. It's up to you." He paused. "Now, tell me, who is Wolf Johannsen."

Blood spurted from Rebecca's nose. Broken, probably,

she thought. "What are you doing, Gyuri? I don't know who you think I am, so let me remind you – I'm René Depeche's granddaughter. The granddaughter of the man who you told me had been your friend." Rebecca fought the urge to sniff. All she needed was to choke on the blood that was coming in a steady stream from her nose. "You have made a terrible mistake."

A terrifying grin spread over Vargha's face. "René Depeche? You think René was my friend?" Vargha placed the silver blade against Rebecca's cheek. "René Depeche was a double agent who paid for his deceit with his life."

Disbelief coated Rebecca's reply. "What are you talking about? My grandfather was an artist. He despised politics. There is no way he would have been involved in such a deception. His years of eating and drinking finally caught up with him. The doctor said my grandfather died of a massive coronary."

"He did," Vargha nodded in agreement. "With a little assistance from me. And now I see that his granddaughter took up Rene's side job, so to speak, how many years ago? Well, no matter. Unfortunately, she will end up the same way as her grandfather."

"Misdirection," Rebecca told herself. Misdirection enough to buy time for the authorities to find her body, and for word to reach someone who could warn Wolf Johannsen. Could she make Vargha believe her lies? Would she be able to lie? She couldn't give up immediately – Vargha would quickly see her ruse. Pain would be her companion for as long as she could bear.

She wouldn't be able to save herself, that much was now clear, but maybe she could save someone else.

Rebecca jerked her head away from Vargha's knife. "I own an art gallery in Rome. That's all I do. I'm not some, what did you say, operative? I know Wolf Johannsen because he bought artwork from me for his London office several years ago. That's it."

Rebecca's response surprised Vargha. This was the first he had heard about a connection to London. Maybe MI6 was behind the attempt on his life. If he couldn't get what he needed from Rebecca Molinere, he could certainly get information from an employee in Johannsen's London office. "Rebecca, you still haven't told me who Wolf Johannsen is." Vargha pressed the point of steel against the corner of Rebecca's right eye. "I'm getting tired of waiting."

The agonized screams which poured forth from the sall cottage echoed over the hillside. The solitude that had attracted Rebecca to her weekend retreat now prevented anyone from hearing her cries. Had anyone been close enough to hear, they would not have believed the sounds to be human, so terrible was the sound and so long in duration. By the time Gyuri Vargha closed the cottage door behind him and walked quickly to his hidden vehicle, Rebecca Molinere's blinded and mutilated body hung lifeless, surrounded by an expanding pool of blood. She had lasted almost an hour.

# CHAPTER FORTY-ONE

It had been a good week, Allison reflected as she slid a slim casefile into her briefcase. She had waited a few days after Mona Phillips' deposition to send Mona's lawyer a copy of the surveillance tape Frank Martin had made at the Magic Lounge. Pictures were worth a zillion words in Allison's estimation, and it had not taken long for Michael Baker to call, telling Allison that his client would accept the paltry settlement offer that Allison had tendered along with the video which showed Mona Phillips to be a liar. The tape hadn't disproved Mona's claim against Allison's client, but it had dramatically decreased the likelihood that a jury would have awarded her much in the way of damages. Allison made a mental note to send Frank a bottle of his favorite Scotch as a bonus for a job well done.

At the beginning of the week, a new matter had come into the law offices of Parker & Jackson, a larger piece of commercial litigation on which her partner David Jackson would take the lead, but which would ultimately require Allison's participation as well. Allison enjoyed trial work, even when outside her normal employment practice, and she looked forward to delving into the new case. The client, a large business in Montgomery, had retained the firm for a smaller matter the previous year. With the much more complicated matter that had now been presented by the client, Allison figured the first case had been a way for the business to gauge her firm's expertise. If she and David could provide a positive outcome in this case, Allison knew Parker & Jackson would have a permanent client.

Flicking the wall switch to extinguish her office lights, Allison waved a goodbye to her secretary, "I'm heading out, Donna. Don't stay past five."

"Don't worry," Donna laughed in reply. "Scott and I are heading to the coast for the weekend. I've got strict orders to be home by 5:30."

David Jackson was still at his desk when Allison passed his office on the way to the firm's back door and shortcut to the firm's parking lot. "Don't you have something better to do late on a Friday afternoon?" Allison paused at the doorway to David's office.

David Jackson was a few years younger than Allison. It was his wife Sarah who had urged Allison to take the trip with Wolf. Tall, lanky and known for wearing cowboy boots, even in the courtroom, David Jackson's laid-back personality was the perfect accompaniment to Allison's more A-type behavior. Both lawyers had been partners in Johnson & Merritt, a regional law firm with its main office in Ft. Charles. After the suicide of Ben Johnson, Johnson & Merritt's managing partner and Sarah Jackson's father, the large firm had dissolved and Allison and David opened their two-person firm, Parker & Jackson.

"Sarah's got the whole weekend planned," David grinned. "The kids are staying with her mother until Sunday afternoon. I'm finishing up a few matters here so I'll have an entire weekend free of take-home work. What about you and Wolf? Anything in particular going on with y'all?"

"Not much," Allison allowed, "just a quiet weekend. I think both of us are still recovering from jet lag, maybe me more than Wolf." Setting down her briefcase, Allison eased into David's office and sank into one of the overstuffed chairs Sarah had picked out for her husband's office. "I'm hoping Wolf will have an update on that Vargha character."

David Jackson knew all about Gyuri Vargha, but more from what Frank Martin had told him rather than from what Allison had shared with him. Choosing his words carefully, David asked, "Isn't that being handled by one of our intelligence agencies?"

"Well, that's the last I heard, but it's been over a week now since we got home." Allison tapped her fingers nervously on the chair's padded arms. "I'll feel much better when I know someone has captured that man."

"I'm sure our guys are on top of this," David assured his partner. "And, you know the old saying 'no news is good news.' If I were you, I'd head to the house and enjoy your weekend."

"You're right," Allison admitted, leaving the comfort of the upholstered cocoon and retrieving her briefcase from the doorway. "And you need to take your own advice. Get out of here and start your romantic weekend." Allison mimicked a kiss. "I wonder what Sarah is wearing right now?"

David Jackson waited until Allison's departing laughter was silenced by the closing of the firm's back door. Then, picking up the phone, David placed a call to the sheriff's office. With a little luck Toby would still be at work. He was.

"What's up, David?" Toby Trowbridge was surprised to hear from the lawyer so late on a Friday afternoon. "Everything alright at Parker & Jackson?"

"Everything's fine at the firm. I'm calling about Allison. And about some disturbing information Frank Martin passed on to me last night."

Toby Trowbridge stifled a curse word that attempted escape. One of these days he was going to put a muzzle on Frank. "What information might that be?"

"Come off it, Toby," David retorted. "You know exactly what information I'm talking about. I want to know everything Wolf Johannsen told you. If Allison is in potential danger — and Frank is worried that she is — then this office and its employees may be, as well." The more David Jackson thought about being left out of the loop by Wolf and the Sheriff, the madder he got.

"Look," Toby interrupted, "you know how Frank is about Allison. Wolf doesn't think there's any real danger. He was just covering all his bases by giving me and Frank a heads-up."

"If Wolf Johannsen didn't think there was any real danger, he wouldn't have come to you in the first place," David pointed out what he thought was obvious. "Wolf Johannsen dealt in a very dangerous business for many years. I think it's highly likely, given what Frank told me, that some of that dangerous business may follow him to Ft. Charles."

David Jackson's spoken words were the same ones that Toby Trowbridge had thought, more than once, since his meeting with Wolf Johannsen, but right now Toby needed to reassure Allison's partner that he had nothing to worry about. "If I get any more information, from any source, about this Vargha situation I'll call you. But for now, I'm telling you, there is nothing to be concerned about."

"Does Allison know Wolf talked to you and Frank?"

"No, Wolf didn't want to worry her," Toby replied, "so don't you go telling her either."

The Sheriff's reply told David Jackson all he needed to know. Wolf Johannsen was worried. If Wolf Johannsen was worried, David knew things were much more serious than the sheriff wanted him to believe. Thanking Toby for taking his call, David Jackson terminated the connection. He didn't want to ruin the weekend Sarah had planned, but first thing Monday morning, he and Wolf Johannsen were going to have a serious conversation.

# CHAPTER FORTY-TWO

The London offices of Johannsen Consulting occupied a building on Crutched Friers, a weirdly-named street in the London business district, not too far removed from the Tower of London. Vargha had traveled from Rome to London under an alias, using one of the several passports he owned. For this trip Vargha had become Gunthur Weber, a German businessman passing through London on his way to a holiday in the Cotswolds. A change of hair color, accompanied by a realistic short beard, had completed the transformation. Only someone very familiar with Gyuri Vargha would discern the real man underneath the disguise.

Time was of the essence. Today was Monday, and when Rebecca Molinere didn't show up to open the gallery or answer her cell phone, someone would be dispatched to the Anzio cottage to check on her. The gruesome murders would certainly make the Rome TV stations. It would not take long for the news to reach the covert intelligence agencies. Vargha didn't kid himself about what was coming next. Interpol, MI6, the C.I.A. – those agencies and more would see his handprints, figuratively of course, all over the Anzio murders.

Just how much time did he have? That was the question. If he were able to get information out of one of Johannsen's London employees, if he could get out of the U.K. and into the states undetected, Vargha thought he might have as much as a forty-eight hour lead. He was fairly certain the authorities would look for him first in Rome. How long it would take them to look elsewhere – well, he didn't think the intelligence agencies would be as slow as the Italian police.

Vargha had arrived in London the day before. Scouting the city with which he had once been familiar, Vargha selected a small rental in one of the immigrant neighborhoods that had sprung up. The refusal of the recent immigrants to assimilate into their new environment fit Vargha's needs perfectly. Local police steered away from those neighborhoods, reluctant to engage a population that remained openly hostile to its hosts while accepting every handout offered by a government that was quickly becoming stretched financially.

The landlord, or maybe he was only the on-site manager, hadn't been too keen on renting to Vargha, but the amount of money Vargha offered had been too much for the man to resist. In Vargha's estimation, procuring the man's silence was paramount and well worth the expenditure. When the police arrived – if the police arrived – the man would be unlikely to share any worthwhile information with Vargha's pursuers.

Vargha glanced at his watch. Quarter 'til four. London's northern latitude delayed sunset in the summer months until almost ten o'clock. The spy contemplated his dilemma. The extended daylight would make it nearly impossible to successfully grab a departing employee to interrogate. Perhaps a more genteel method would provide the information Vargha sought. Decided on a plan of action, Vargha crossed the street to Wolf Johannsen's London office.

The firm's main door opened onto a small but stylishly decorated reception area. A young, redheaded woman sat behind a mahogany desk. A leather sofa and several upholstered club chairs completed a welcoming sitting area. Soft lighting gave the area more of a residential feel. Vargha was surprised. He had expected something much more contemporary.

"May I help you?" The receptionist smiled at Vargha.

"I was hoping Mr. Johannsen might be in town," Vargha countered with a smile of his own. "I had the pleasure of meeting Mr. Johannsen in Rome recently, and when my business here unexpectedly concluded early, I thought, perhaps, I could take Mr. Johannsen to dinner and continue our conversation from last week." Give enough of the truth to be believable. The receptionist would remember a blond German man if anyone asked.

"Oh, I'm sorry. Mr. Johannsen has returned to his home in America," the red head explained. "He won't be back in this office until next month."

Vargha affected a show of regret. "That's right. I remember now. He lives in one of those Southern places doesn't he? I can't recall the name."

The young receptionist had been trained to be accommodating to the firm's clients. From what the well-dressed gentleman in front of her was saying, not only was the man a potential client, he sounded like he might be her employer's friend. "It's Ft. Charles, Alabama. We were all surprised when Mr. Johannsen decided to move there, but I guess you can work anywhere these days, so long as you have access to the internet."

"Indeed you can," Vargha agreed. "Well, perhaps next time I'm in London our paths will cross." Vargha started to leave, then hesitating asked, "You wouldn't happen to have his actual address would you?"

Tapping quickly on her desktop computer, the receptionist retrieved the desired information. "It's called the Old Fort Inn. Apparently, that's all that is required for postal delivery. Just the Old Fort Inn, Ft. Charles, Alabama."

A corner coffee shop offered internet and a small repast while Vargha googled the exact location of Ft. Charles, Alabama, and its nearest international airport, Atlanta. Opening a second browser, Vargha scoured the available flights from London to Atlanta. Delta Airlines had a 9 o'clock flight with one seat remaining in first class. It would be cutting it close, but if he left now, there would be just enough time to grab his belongings from the rental and make it to Heathrow. Vargha booked the flight, powered down his Ipad, and hailed a cab. He was taking a slight risk booking under the Weber alias, but he didn't have time to change his appearance. After he got to Atlanta, Gunthur Weber would disappear. The seven-hour flight over the Atlantic would give Vargha time to decide which of his remaining aliases would make its way to Ft. Charles, Alabama.

# CHAPTER FORTY-THREE

Antonio Bendidi didn't start worrying until the church bell in the nearby square struck 2:00, and Rebecca Molinere still hadn't appeared at the gallery. Antonio knew his boss had gone to her Anzio cottage for the weekend and had asked him to open for her Monday morning, allowing her to take the early train back to the city. Nothing odd about that. Antonio was Rebecca's assistant manager and often opened the gallery when Rebecca was out of town or running late. What was odd, however, was the fact that his boss had neither shown for work nor called, and she wasn't answering her cell phone.

When the church bell rang again, denoting the passing of yet another hour without an appearance or call, Antonio Bendidi called the Anzio police station.

Initially an argument ensued, the in-take officer in the small police station refusing to take Antonio's call seriously, thinking Bendidi might be checking up on a cheating wife. The Anzio police had better things to do than to get involved in a domestic situation. It was only when Antonio invoked the name of one of the gallery's patrons, a man well-known across Italy, that the in-take officer paid attention.

"We will dispatch an officer to Signora Molinere's cottage," the officer advised Antonio. "You can expect a call from us, or more likely, from Signora Molinere, in a few hours."

When the call came, the news delivered by a man, who identified himself as an Anzio homicide detective, took Antonio to his knees. Who would do such a thing? Antonio gagged at the bile which rose in his throat as he listened to the detective describe the condition of Rebecca's body, and that of her friend Signora Jacobs.

The detective's instructions were terse. Antonio was ordered to close and lock the gallery. Admittance would be allowed only to the Rome police who had been contacted and should arrive soon. Antonio was to touch nothing in Rebecca Molinere's office, and under no conditions, was he to enter her nearby flat.

Stunned and trying to assimilate the terrible news he had just received, Antonio Bendidi remembered a conversation Rebecca had initiated with him a week earlier. "If anything ever happens to me, it's very important that you contact two people. Their names and numbers are on the back of a small black book in the middle drawer of my desk." When Antonio had protested that nothing was going to happen to his boss, Rebecca had laughed reassuringly. "It's just a precaution, Antonio. I don't expect anything to happen either."

But now he wondered. Had the Signora been in some sort of trouble? The police might arrive at any minute. Hurrying to the gallery's private office, Antonio searched feverishly for the book. There, at the very back of the drawer, Antonio's fingers felt a smooth leather cover. This must be it.

A loud pounding on the gallery's front door sounded. Secreting the small book in his pocket, Antonio rushed to open the door and allow the police to take over. One officer took Antonio aside and began to question him. "When had he last seen Signora Molinere? When had he last spoken to her? Was he aware of anyone who would want to hurt her? Were there any disgruntled clients? Did he know Signora Jacobs?" On and on the questions went, including a question of where Antonio had spent the weekend and who had seen him in Rome during that time. The last question both startled and unnerved Antonio – he was being looked at as a possible suspect. Finally, after what seemed an eternity, the police escorted Antonio from the gallery, locked the door and placed yellow police tape across the entrance. Given the conversations Antonio had overheard, he knew the same search-and-closure had been conducted at the homes of both of the murdered women.

It was midnight before Antonio Bendidi reached the safety of his own apartment and pulled the small black book from his pocket. Flipping quickly to the last page, Antonio recognized Rebecca's neat handwriting. Two names and two numbers were inscribed – Franco Perelli and Bastien Dubois. Looking at the names of men he had never heard of, Antonio remembered Rebecca's instructions." If you ever need to call the names in the book, use the title of the painting which hangs behind my desk to introduce yourself."

With shaking hands, Antonio Bendidi dialed the number for Bastien Dubois. A nondescript recording instructed Antonio to "leave a message." Rebecca hadn't told him what to do if no one answered. Berating himself for being so indecisive, Antonio terminated the call and dialed the number for Franco Perelli. If he got another answering machine, this time he would leave a message.

"Pronto," A man answered on the second ring.

"Is this Franco Perelli?"

"Si."

"Uh, Rebecca Molinere told me to call you and one other person if anything happened to her. I couldn't reach the other man. Signora said to tell you "Phoenix Rising." Antonio's voice quivered as tried to explain why he was calling.

"Identity yourself!" Perelli demanded.

"I'm Antonio Bendidi, Signora Molinere's assistant manager at the gallery. Signora has been murdered. And her friend, too."

A sharp intake of breath followed by a curse preceded Perelli's next questions, "Where, when, and how. Tell me everything you know."

Antonio began, "When Signora didn't show up for work today, and I couldn't reach her by phone, I called the Anzio police. I knew Signora and her friend Signora Jacobs had gone to the cottage for the weekend. The police found the bodies. Signora's Jacob' throat had been cut. Signora Molinere had been tortured." Antonio paused. The visual of his employer's destroyed body was almost too much to bear. "She had been blinded. And cut. Who would do such a thing?"

"Who knows you are calling me?"

"No one. As soon as the Anzio police called me. I followed Signora's instructions and found the book with your name and number. I hid it before the Rome police arrived at the gallery."

"Did the police say when they thought the murders had occurred?" Perelli knew this information was of utmost importance.

"They asked me where I was Friday and Saturday, so I assume that's when they think the Signoras were killed. The police wanted my alibi." Antonio was glad he could provide witnesses to his whereabouts over the weekend.

"Who was the other person you were to call?"

"Bastien Dubois. Do you know him?"

"I will contact Dubois. Now, destroy that book and forget everything Rebecca told you about calling anyone." Perelli considered his last sentence. "Your life may depend on it."

# CHAPTER FORTY-FOUR

Without hesitation, Franco Perelli dialed the number which he had been required to memorize years earlier. Regardless of the time of day or night, his call would be answered on a secured and scrambled line. Continuously updated by the Agency's tech geniuses, the emergency line provided the highest security possible for the agents who found themselves needing to call for help or to raise a warning.

Perelli didn't think he was in danger, at least not imminently. If Gyuri Vargha had suspected Perelli was an agent, Franco believed Vargha already would have have moved against him. But there was always the chance that, under torture, Rebecca Molinere had let slip his name. Leaving Rome would be a wise move, one Perelli intended to take as soon as he could.

Perelli's call was answered on the second ring. Identifying himself with the appropriate code, Perelli reiterated every detail that he had been told about Rebecca Molinere's murder. The conversation was being taped, he knew, and would be replayed numerous times as the information made its way up the chain of command. Terminating his call by advising of his plans to go into temporary hiding, Franco Perelli turned his attention to warning Bastien Dubois. It was now closing in on four in the morning. If Rebecca had been killed as early as Friday evening, Gyuri Vargha could have as much as a 72 hour advantage.

"Allo?" Bastien Dubois' sleepy voice answered.

"Bastien, it's Franco." There was no need to give his last name. Dubois would recognize Perelli's voice, and anyone tapping Dubois' phone line – unlikely, but not impossible – would have one more hurdle to jump in identifying him.

Bastien Dubois was instantly awake. His counterpart in Rome would not be calling at this early hour unless something dire had happened. "This line is not secure," he reminded his caller.

"It can't be helped," Perelli replied. "Rebecca is dead, murdered most likely at the hand of the man we both know. Her friend Signora Jacobs as well."

"Mon Dieu." Anger, coupled with a dozen other emotions, spilled over Bastien Dubois. "I warned her to be careful. What happened?"

Again, Perelli recited the information he had received.

"Everything I know is second-hand, third-hand actually, because the person who called me was relaying what he had been told by the Anzio and Rome police."

"Poor Rebecca." Bastien saw no reason not to use the deceased woman's name. No more harm could come to her. "And her friend, too. Wrong place at the wrong time?"

"I've been thinking about that. I don't think the friend was collateral damage. I think her murder was intentional, as well. If she is who I am remembering, Vargha was seeing her. That's how Rebecca realized he was back in play. I think Vargha was getting rid of someone who knew too much about him, whether or not she actually did. He wouldn't want to take any chances."

"He hasn't come after you or me," Dubois stated the obvious. "Given what you've described to me, the damage done to Rebecca's body, I have to believe she not only gave up you and me, she probably gave up Wolf Johannsen, as well. If Vargha decided to leave us alone… well, we both know what that means."

"He's after Johannsen," Perelli agreed. "I called Langley before I called you. They'll contact Wolf, probably are doing it as we speak. I'm going under until this situation is contained. If Vargha gets to Wolf and succeeds without losing his own life, he'll be after one of us next."

#

Washington, D.C., was six hours behind Rome. Perelli's call on Langley's emergency line was logged in at 9:00 p.m. local time. Per procedure, the agent receiving Perelli's information immediately contacted his superior, who, in turn, emailed a secure alert to three people - the head of European Operations, the Assistant to the Director of the C.I.A., and Ned Bakke. By 10:15 p.m., all three men and several of their team members had returned to headquarters and had been directed to the large conference room outside the Director's office. Now, murmuring quietly, they awaited the man who ran the nation's covert intelligence agency.

Director Burwell Vance had served at the helm of the Central Intelligence Agency through three different Presidents and two political parties. Of medium height and physically nondescript, not a man or woman in the room doubted the keen intelligence that lived in a brain that forgot nothing. When Vance walked through the conference room doorway with the head of the F.B.I., every participant in that evening's meeting understood the significance of that partnership. The two agencies did cooperate now, mainly as a result of legislation passed after 9/11, but it was highly unusual to see Wayne Lesinger actually in a meeting with C.I.A. personnel. Of course, Lesinger wasn't alone. Trailing him were two other people, both women, and presumably high ranking F.B.I. officials as well.

Vance dispensed with introductions, "Thank you for arriving so promptly. We have a high priority situation unfolding." The Director's presence and use of the term "high priority situation" brought the room to attention. In the clipped and concise manner that was his trademark, Burwell Vance laid out the Agency's known history on Gyuri Vargha, ending with the recent events in Rome. "The covert operative who was sent to eliminate Vargha was, unfortunately, too late to prevent the murder of Agent Molinere and her friend. Our most current intel indicates that Vargha has likely left Rome, and perhaps Italy. We believe – and this is why Director Lesinger is here – we believe Vargha is making his way to the States to track down and exact retribution on one of the Agency's retired operatives. That places this problem under the F.B.I.'s jurisdiction." Vance motioned to Wayne Lesinger, "Wayne, tell us what you know."

Wayne Lesinger, Vance's counterpart, was, in appearance, Mutt to Vance's Jeff. Tall, lanky, and bespeckled, Wayne Lesinger towered over Director Vance. Physical appearances, however, were just about the only traits the two men didn't share. Possessed of a steel-trap mind, Wayne Lesinger was a man to both respect and fear. The agents of the F.B.I. loved him.

"Our Birmingham Field Office received a call from local law enforcement in Ft. Charles, Alabama a few days ago." Lesginer knew this would be news to Vance. Before Vance could interrupt, Lesinger continued, "The call wasn't through regular channels, just to a field agent who the Sheriff down there knew from an earlier case in the area. That agent," Lesinger referred to a note handed to him by one of his associates, "is Jake Cleveland. Cleveland passed the information to the head of that office where it went no further. When Burwell called me earlier this evening and told me he thought one of his retired agents now living in Alabama might be in danger, I placed a call to the Birmingham office and discovered the agents there were already aware of the possibility. I've instructed that office to coordinate with your Agency until we've got this threat contained."

It peeved Lesinger to admit to the C.I.A. that one of the F.B.I.'s field offices had sat on intelligence of this magnitude, but the security of the nation was more important right now than Lesinger's feelings. Wilson Mackey ran a tight ship in the Birmingham office, but if his lapse in judgment resulted in civilian deaths at the hands of Gyuri Vargha, the head of the Birmingham Field Office would be looking for another job.

# CHAPTER FORTY-FIVE

Early morning light filtered through the plantation shutters covering the windows in Allison's bedroom. Carefully, so as not to awaken her, Wolf Johannsen gazed at the face of the woman with whom he had fallen desperately in love. They were both still young. With luck, he and Allison would have many more years together. Once he was assured that Gyuri Vargha was dead, and that Allison was out of danger, Wolf intended to ask Allison to marry him.

Unable to resist, Wolf brushed his fingers over Allison's cheek. In response, a sleepy voice asked, "How long have you been awake?'

"Long enough to enjoy the view." Wolf placed a kiss on Allison's forehead. "I enjoy watching you sleep."

"Sleeping is nice," Allison agreed, "but maybe we

should take advantage of an empty house. Charlotte and Mack will be home later this morning, and I don't want them to find us in bed."

Wolf grinned. As modern a woman as Allison was, she had been adamant about concealing the couple's sexual relationship from her children. Enjoying an overnight with Allison in her home was a first and had only happened because Charlotte and Mack had been at an overnight "lock-in" hosted by their church youth group.

Allison's suggestion needed no verbal reply. Quickly, Wolf removed the loose, grey t-shirt that covered Allison's breasts, hardened nipples telegraphing Allison's readiness. With a groan, Wolf's hand and mouth sought one breast while his other hand pushed inside Allison's bikini panties.

Wolf's insistence on sleeping nude offered no obstruction for Allison's groping hands. She loved his hardness, his size, the way his penis filled her completely. Pulling Wolf closer, Allison struggled to get rid of the offending panties. "Get rid of them!" Allison ordered.

With a violent rip, Wolf obeyed, tossing the ruined lace garment to one side. No further words were needed. Leveraging his lean body over Allison's smaller one, Wolf thrust himself inside his lover. Slowly at first, and then increasing in rapidity, their bodies moved against one another, joining in desire, need and deep love, until in a violent release, they lay exhausted, bodies entwined, their breath struggling to return to a more normal pace.

"My god!" Allison gasped "This will never grow old."

"Unless it kills me first," Wolf joked.

Allison turned to look at Wolf. Trying for a serious demeanor, she asked, "Are you complaining?"

"Do I look like a man who is complaining?"

"I'm not sure. Perhaps we should try something more sedate." Allison traced a question mark on Wolf's chest.

"Like this?"

An hour later, Wolf's question had been answered. Showered and dressed, Allison and Wolf had barely seated themselves at the kitchen table for morning coffee when the sound of a car coming up the long driveway met their ears.

"That was cutting it close." Allison's raised eyebrows accompanied a grin.

Wolf's reply was interrupted by a loud, "Mr. Wolf!" followed by Mack Parker-Kaufman's imitation of a howling wolf. Gleefully, the young boy jumped into Wolf Johannsen's lap. Although both of Allison's children had quickly accepted Wolf Johannsen into their lives, Allison's son Mack had formed an almost immediate bond with the Swede. Mack missed his father, and Wolf Johannsen had helped to ease that loss.

"Hey, Mr. Wolf" Charlotte Parker-Kaufman's voice carried over her brother's animated conversation. With her teen years just around the corner, Mack's older sister exhibited the see-saw of emotions that went along with the emergence of hormones. Allison knew her daughter well enough to discern the pre-teen's affection for Wolf

Johannsen, but she also recognized Charlotte's growing need to seem uninterested in the goings-on of the adults in her world. Not for the first time Allison wished her mother Helene were still alive to guide her through her children's teen years.

Allison fixed a light breakfast for herself and Wolf while Mack regaled Wolf with stories from the previous night's lock-in. Without asking, Allison prepared a stack of pancakes for her children. Whatever they had eaten for breakfast was now several hours in the past, and pancakes were one of her children's favorite meals, regardless of the time of day.

The last of the breakfast dishes had been loaded into the dishwasher when Wolf's cell phone buzzed. Working remotely, Allison knew Wolf's "office" was more often than not his cell phone, so initially, Allison paid no attention to the call, even when Wolf left the room to continue the conversation. Some of the projects Wolf's company worked on were sensitive, and oftentimes, Wolf needed to take some of his calls in private.

It was only when Wolf returned to the kitchen and softly called Allison's name that she knew something was wrong.

# CHAPTER FORTY-SIX

"Jake Cleveland and Sheriff Trowbridge are on their way out here." Wolf stopped and nodded towards Allison's children who were happily destroying the blueberry pancakes their mother had fixed. What Toby Trowbridge had told Wolf on the phone was not something for young ears to hear.

"Charlotte, Mack, I want to show Mr. Wolf something in the garden." Allison brushed her hand over Charlotte's blond curls as she headed towards the back door. "When y'all finish your pancakes, please rinse your plates and put them in the dishwasher."

"Mummm," Mack replied.

"What was that?" Allison paused at the back door and gave her son a look.

Swallowing a mouthful of sweetness, Mack answered,

"Yes, ma'am."

"Thank you, Mack," Allison rewarded her son's manners with a smile. Instilling manners in her children was important to Allison. Allison also recognized the diversionary tactic she had inadvertently employed. She was afraid she already knew why Jake and Toby were on their way to the Farm. Hearing the news would make it real.

Wolf was standing a few feet away, gazing at the bucolic view that comprised the Farm's ten acres. Allison had seen the expression that covered Wolf's face only once before. Memories of the event that almost cost her life caused Allison an involuntary shudder.

"It's Vargha, isn't it?" Allison wondered why she was even asking. Of course, it was Vargha.

"I never intended for my past to bring danger to your doorstep." Wolf turned to face Allison, "I should never have agreed to go to Rebecca's party, or to take you with me."

Allison grabbed Wolf's hands, drawing him closer to her. "Wolf, I'm sure whatever is going on, if the F.B.I. is already on it, we'll be fine." Allison didn't believe her own words, but she needed to assure Wolf that she wasn't afraid.

"Rebecca is dead."

The three words stunned Allison. "She's what? How?"

"Most likely, Friday night, maybe Saturday morning. The Italian medical examiner hasn't issued a time of death, yet, that I'm aware of."

"Then, how can you or anyone know for certain Rebecca was murdered?"

Wolf looked directly into Allison's questioning eyes. He hated giving her specifics, but he had no choice. "The police found Rebecca's body tied to a chair inside her cottage. Her right eye had been gouged out and there were other signs of torture."

Allison's hands flew to her mouth. "Nooo," she moaned. "How horrible."

Wolf continued, "She wasn't the only victim. Her friend Charlene, the lady we met at Rebecca's party," Wolf watched Allison's nod of recognition, "she was at the cottage, too. Her throat had been cut."

"Oh, Jesus," Allison whispered. "How could this happen? I thought all Rebecca did for the Agency was pass information."

Wolf began to pace. "This is my fault. If I hadn't been at that party, Vargha would never have suspected Rebecca."

"You can't know that," Allison grabbed Wolf's arm. "You've told me more than once, no one in that business can be too careful. Rebecca asked you to come to the party to see if the man passing himself off as Gyuri Vargha was who he claimed to be. I'm sorry she's dead, but Rebecca put herself in danger as much as you did. Maybe more. When she introduced you to Vargha as her friend, she put herself right in the middle. You can't blame yourself for her death."

A part of Wolf knew Allison was right. Even operatives

who generally didn't get their hands dirty, so to speak, were advised of the dangers inherent in working for the Agency. Still, the part of Wolf which held himself to an impossible standard castigated himself for not predicting, and preventing, Vargha's subsequent actions.

Silence accompanied the pair for several minutes as they walked along the garden's pea-graveled path. The fears that had assaulted Allison in Rome when she had learned who Gyuri Vargha was and what Wolf's connection was to the Russian rose again. This time, though, the fear was not for herself, but for her children. Gyuri Vargha was an animal. A rabid animal. And rabid animals needed to be put down.

"We're going to kill him, aren't we?"

"You are not going to do anything." Wolf was certain of that fact. "Toby, Jake, and I will work out a plan for ensuring your safety and that of your children. Gyuri Vargha may have escaped death once on my watch, but it won't happen a second time."

Exasperation coated Allison's retort, "I'm getting really tired of telling you and every other penis-toting human that I am not some helpless female. Yes, I'll listen to what you and the others propose, but if that son-of-a-bitch comes anywhere near me or my children, he's a dead man." Allison's eyes burned intensely, "And you damn well better believe me."

Wolf did believe her. He'd seen Allison in action, seen her handle a gun as well as any law enforcement man or woman he knew. But he also knew the kind of man

Gyuri Vargha was. No act would be too depraved for Vargha if it allowed him to reach his goal. And Vargha's goal, Wolf was now completely certain, was him.

# CHAPTER FORTY-SEVEN

The sound of a car engine coming up the long driveway caught Wolf's attention. "Looks like Jake and the Sheriff are here." Motioning to Allison to follow, Wolf trotted towards the house.

Jake Cleveland emerged from the Sheriff's cruiser before Toby had a chance to cut the engine. Seeing Wolf and Allison approaching, the F.B.I. agent raised a hand in greeting. "Johannsen, I really am getting tired of running into you like this."

"You and me, both," Wolf replied, the look of chagrin on his face underscoring his agreement with the agent's attempt to infuse humor into the situation. Cleveland's half-ass joke was, Wolf knew, intended to convince Allison that things weren't as serious as they sounded.

Allison knew better. She and the F.B.I. agent had

first crossed paths several years earlier when Allison had unwittingly uncovered an old murder-for-hire plot which had placed the young lawyer in mortal danger. But for the fact that Jake Cleveland had stumbled onto the plot during an undercover operation, Allison would have been killed. Then, just a little over a year ago, as the result of another undercover operation, Allison found herself involved once again in a life-and-death situation with Jake Cleveland. Allison knew Jake Cleveland well. The F.B.I. agent was worried, and his attempts at levity didn't fool her.

"Jake, Toby," Allison acknowledged the two men with a grim smile. "Charlotte and Mack are in the house, and I don't want them to overhear any of what we are getting ready to discuss. Let's take this to the guest cottage."

The Farm's guest cottage was rarely used anymore. Allison's father, Matthew Parker, had spent his last days there, and after his death, Allison and her husband Jim had closed up the one bedroom tiny house. There were simply too many sad memories attached to the structure. But this past October, Allison and her children decided to reinstate their annual Hallowe'en party, and the cottage was aired out to double as a food and beverage station. Since that time, Allison had kept the cottage clean, if unused on a regular basis.

"This will work just fine." Jake Cleveland looked around the cottage's interior.

"Just fine for what?" Allison asked.

"Bennett Shealy and a couple of his team will be here

by mid-afternoon. Bennett will shadow you 24/7, and his team will set up a perimeter around your property. With the kids out for summer break, keeping them contained and safe will be easy," Jake explained.

Allison threw up her hands. "Now wait just a minute!" Allison glared at the three men standing in front of her. "I don't have any problem with protecting my children, but there's no way I'm going to allow that ex-Navy Seal to follow me around town."

"As the head law enforcement officer in Calhoun County, I'm not giving you a choice." Toby Trowbridge handed Allison a manila folder. "Take a look at those pictures. I think you'll change your mind."

The color photos, shot with a high-quality camera, were shocking. Allison knew Rebecca had been tortured and Charlene Jacobs' throat cut, but seeing the bodies brought the reality front and center. Allison could not imagine what Rebecca Molinere's last hours of life must have been like. An inadvertent shudder passed over her body as Allison handed the photos back to the Sheriff.

"I can't confine my children to the property constantly. Charlotte goes to the Overlook Riding Club every day. She's training with Jerry Kennedy for an upcoming competition." Allison worked the problem out loud, "If one of Bennett's men can go with her, I don't see why that won't work."

Toby and Jake considered Allison's suggestion. Both men would prefer keeping the children at the Farm, but Toby, in particular, understood Allison's desire to keep her children's lives as normal as possible.

"Let me talk to Jerry and Marion later today. I don't want to put any other civilians in potential danger. If they're okay with Charlotte being there with a bodyguard, and if Bennett agrees, then I'll sign off on this." Toby glanced at Jake for agreement.

"And," Jake added, "that will be the only time either of the children leave this property until this is over. Agreed?"

Allison nodded. She didn't think Vargha would go after her children, but she knew better than to risk their safety. Her own safety was another matter. "As for me," Allison looked sharply at the three men, "like I said, I can't have Bennett following me around Ft. Charles."

"This is not negotiable," Wolf's voice was harsh. "Even though you've seen those pictures, you still don't understand who we are dealing with. Gyuri Vargha is a dangerous man for whom killing has been a way of life for years."

"I know exactly what kind of man we're dealing with," Allison's ire was evident. "He's the Russian equivalent of Jefferson Boudreaux. And like I told you earlier, rabid animals like that need to be put down."

Allison's reference to the serial rapist gave Toby an entrée. "Jefferson Boudreaux almost killed you. You spent a week in the hospital recovering. Based on what Jake and Wolf have shared with me, this Vargha character is ten times worse. You will have protection while you live in my county, and I won't have it any other way."

# CHAPTER FORTY-EIGHT

Allison fumed. The intelligent part of her knew Toby was right, but the stubborn part of her hated, yes, really hated, being told she had to basically be babysat until the Russian was caught. Toby had walked outside to place a call to Jerry Kennedy, and Jake was walking the perimeter to make an initial exposure assessment before Bennett and his team arrived, leaving Wolf to take the brunt of Allison's ire.

Wolf held his tongue as Allison paced the cottage's main room. "Best to let her wrestle with her emotions for a few minutes," he thought. Wolf was certain that Allison wouldn't do anything that would endanger her children, but he was far from certain that she would apply the same precautions for herself.

"How certain are you that Vargha is coming here?"

Allison asked her question with her back to Wolf. She was still angry.

"He's not in Rome. That much has been confirmed by the operative Langley sent. Interpol reports no travel under Vargha's name but that doesn't surprise me. An experienced spy like him would have multiple passports and identities."

"So, not only do the authorities have no idea where he is, they don't even know who to look for." Allison's anger was beginning to fray around the edges as fear replaced the former.

"Interpol is using facial recognition. If Vargha left Italy in a hurry, and that is likely, given the bodies he left behind him, he probably only had time to change his hair color and name. With the kind of advanced technology Interpol uses, we've got a decent chance of spotting him going through customs somewhere."

"So, how certain are you that he's coming here?" Allison asked for the second time.

"If I were a betting man, this is a bet I'd take." Wolf placed his hands on Allison's shoulders, turning her so they were face to face. "He'll know Rebecca's and Charlene's bodies have been found by now, and he'll know the intelligence agencies will be looking for him. But, he will have planned for that eventuality, because he's smart."

"Ok, fine, the guy is on the lam somewhere in Europe, but you still don't know whether or not Vargha is after you," Allison interrupted.

"Allison," Wolf caressed Allison's face. He wished he could assure Allison that they were safe, but he could not. "Rebecca knew I was the operative who was assigned to kill Vargha five years ago. There is no way she could have withheld that information under the kind of torture Vargha inflicted on her. No one could. Gyuri Vargha has my name, and even more troubling, he likely knows where I live, given my stupidity in taking you to Rebecca's party."

"How long do we have to prepare?" There was no doubt now in Allison's mind that serious danger was headed their way.

"A few days, if we are lucky. Jake says the F.B.I. is already looking at surveillance footage from the Atlanta and Dallas airports. There are multiple agents on the ground in both airports covering departing passengers on flights from Europe. It's a long shot, though, because by now, Vargha will have improved on his disguise. I'm not relying on them spotting him."

Allison pondered Wolf's answer. Rebecca and Charlene had been murdered sometime over the past weekend. Today was Tuesday. How important was time to Vargha? A thought began to form. "Wolf, if you were Vargha, how would you plan this?"

"I've been thinking along those same lines," Wolf replied. "Vargha would have planned on leaving Italy as soon as he gathered the information he needed from Rebecca. The M.E. places time of death between two and five a.m. Saturday. My guess is that Vargha was out of Italy by Sunday, at the latest. He would be too smart to have flown to the States directly from Italy, so if I were him, I'd have flown to a city with a large international airport."

"Paris, Berlin, London?" Allison offered up some possibilities.

"And any of those would have direct flights to the States. But, if I were Vargha, I'd want at least one day of hiding, a day to regroup and make sure my plans were still solid." Wolf worked the details in his mind. "Yes, I'd definitely have a stop-over, maybe gather additional intel on my target."

A thought that had been niggling at the back of Allison's mind erupted in full force. "Wolf, do you remember the conversation at Rebecca's party? Gyuri Vargha knows about your London office. Would he be so bold as to actually go there?"

"He wouldn't go there under his own name. If there had been an incident of any kind, I'd have been contacted. But you raise a good point. I'll give Nigel a call and see if anyone came in asking for me."

"So, he may have gone to London. Or Paris. Or somewhere else. If he stayed over one night – and that's just supposition – he could be in the States as soon as "Allison calculated the days, "good lord, as soon as today!"

"Which is why you are going to agree to Bennett's protection detail, not just for Charlotte and Mack, but for you as well," Wolf was firm. "My attention will be focused on finishing the job I undertook five years ago. Worrying about your safety is a distraction I can't afford."

# CHAPTER FORTY-NINE

"What is the purpose of your visit?" The customs agent at Atlanta's Hartsfield-Jackson airport barely glanced at the middle-aged man standing before her. Molly Clark had been on duty since 10:00 the night before. Pissed about having to work overtime to cover the shift for another agent who had called in sick at the last minute, Molly had ignored the "flag" that had come across her terminal earlier in her second shift.

"Just a small vacation," Gunthur Weber replied pleasantly. "I've been saving up to make this trip."

"Uh huh." The customs agent, whose only thought was getting home at a reasonable hour, asked the next required question, "Where will you be staying?"

"I've hired a car so I can travel leisurely. I've read about those mountains called "the Smokies." That's my destination this trip." Weber/Vargha allowed a benign smile to crease his face. The geographic misdirection might prove helpful if the authorities started looking for him in the States before he completed his task. The odds of them tracking him to Atlanta were slim, Vargha thought, but taking the extra precaution wouldn't hurt.

"Follow the line to your right. Baggage claim for international flights is over there." With a bored expression, the customs agent stamped Gunthur Weber's passport and started to hand it back to him, for the first time comparing the face of the man standing in front of her to the face staring from the passport she was holding. Travelers often looked somewhat different from their passport pictures, especially now that passports were valid for ten years, but Molly Clark's instincts told her something was off about the picture and the man. She hesitated. Protocol required her to call a supervisor, but Molly Clark was tired and she wanted to go home. Telling the traveler to "have a nice day," the customs agent returned the passport and motioned for the next person in line to step up to the desk.

Adept at reading people, Vargha knew he had barely escaped a closer look. Hurrying to the baggage claim in the new Maynard H. Jackson International Terminal, Vargha grabbed his suitcase and carryall from the conveyor belt and headed towards the nearest bathroom. The cramped quarters of a public restroom stall weren't ideal for a change of identity, but Vargha didn't want to leave the airport matching the description of Gunthur

Weber.

Vargha selected the stall furthest from the restroom entrance. Locking the door, the spy opened the first of three bottled waters he had purchased after clearing customs, leaned his head over the toilet, and poured. Next, Vargha massaged a dissolving agent into his hair, waited three minutes, and then emptied the contents of the second bottle over his head. The red residue from the earlier dye job circled the toilet bowl as Vargha flushed away that part of Weber's disguise, returning Vargha's hair to its natural color.

Rifling through his carryall, Vargha retrieved a pair of scissors and mirror. Attaching the mirror to the side of the stall, Vargha cut his hair as short as possible. Then, applying an adhesive to a fake pepper-and-salt moustache, Vargha pressed the realistic looking hair to the skin above his upper lip. A pair of thick, horn-rimmed glasses completed Vargha's new look. Gunthur Weber was no more, replaced by Stanley Middleton, professor of economics, Cambridge, England.

Exiting the bathroom, Vargha tossed Gunthur Weber's passport in the nearest waste receptacle. Not the best way to dispose of that identity, but Vargha couldn't chance keeping the passport with him. With any luck it would never be found, and if it was, Vargha would be well on his way to Ft. Charles, Alabama.

Renting an upscale vehicle proved easier than Vargha had expected. Vargha's slight British accent, affected to fit with his new British persona, had charmed the young woman working the Hertz rental desk. Heading onto I-75 north towards the I-20 interchange, Vargha settled comfortably onto the plush leather seats of the Lexus sedan the agent had rented him for the price of a much smaller vehicle.

The navigation system displayed the arrival time in Ft. Charles as 4.5 hours hence. The driving map of Georgia and Alabama that the man had purchased from a convenience store before he got on the interstate lay open on the passenger seat. Vargha had not brought any of his killing tools with him. Checked luggage was examined as closely as carry-on bags. The chance of detection was simply too great in this day and time of exploding underwear and laptops.

Vargha wasn't particularly worried about finding what he needed. America's gun laws were not always enforced in the shadier parts of urban centers, especially if cash was offered. Pawn shops in the rundown areas of Birmingham or Montgomery would do just fine. Vargha wanted a good night's rest before finding a hidey-hole near Ft. Charles. If he couldn't find anything in Birmingham later this evening, he'd look tomorrow in Montgomery.

Two hours later, when the headlights on Vargha's rental illuminated the sign indicating he had reached the city limits of Birmingham, Alabama, he was still undecided as to how he wanted to enact his revenge. Of course, killing Wolf Johannsen was his ultimate goal, but Gyuri Vargha had suffered grievously during the years of his recovery. Simply killing Johannsen was too quick. Vargha wanted his almost-assassin to suffer as much has he had. Obviously, he didn't have five years to torment Johannsen, but he would have enough time to inflict emotional and physical pain on his target before ending the ex-operative's life.

Reflecting on the information he did have, Vargha remembered the woman Johannsen brought to Rebecca Molinere's party. A lawyer, he thought he had overheard the woman tell Charlene Jacobs. Well, there couldn't be too many female lawyers in some back water Southern town. Finding her would just be a matter of a quick internet search. Perhaps this lawyer, whoever she was, would be one of his weapons against Johannsen.

# CHAPTER FIFTY

Jerry Kennedy watched her star pupil take the Appaloosa through its paces. "That's right, Charlotte. Keep your reins loose. Diamond Girl will respond just as well to your knees, and the judges will award you higher points for less obvious control." Saturday's competition was only a few days away, and both Jerry and Charlotte had great expectations for Diamond Girl's performance. "Better. Better," Jerry encouraged her young charge, as Charlotte followed her coach's instructions. "Okay, I think that does it for today," Jerry nodded approvingly. "Take Diamond Girl through her cool down, and then I'll meet you back at the barn."

"I'll stay with Charlotte until she's finished," the young man who had driven Charlotte to the Overlook Riding Club called softly to Jerry without looking in her direction.

Outfitted in jeans and a t-shirt, the communication device resting in Nixon Oehmig's left ear identified the man as the bodyguard Jerry had been told would accompany Charlotte for the next few days. Oehmig's casual appearance didn't fool Jerry Kennedy one bit. Given the way he repeatedly scanned the property's perimeter, this guy was far more than a bodyguard. Allison hadn't said much when she called earlier that day, but then, Allison never did when things got really serious. The manner in which Nixon Oehmig carried himself, the military buzz cut, a body with a fat percentage of maybe 6 or 7% , the continual situational awareness – Jerry Kennedy was willing to bet next week's paycheck that Charlotte's "bodyguard" had spent some time in one of the Special Forces deployed by Uncle Sam's military.

"Are you freakin' kidding me?" Marion Hutcheson's deep voice carried from the barn office to Jerry's ears as she approached the structure.

Entering the smallish office which also doubled as a tack room, Jerry watched her partner's face grow red. Whatever the person on the other end of the telephone line was telling Marion, it was making her really angry.

"I can't just shut down the club. I've got three students preparing for the competition in Montgomery this weekend." Marion began to strum her fingers on the desk top. Recognizing her partner's tell, Jerry knew her partner didn't like what she was hearing. "I don't give a shit what the F.B.I. says. I've got a gun and I damn well know how to use it." Marion slammed down the phone, disconnecting the bearer of bad news, and glared at Jerry.

"That seems a little drastic," Jerry observed, keeping her tone neutral. "And I bet it has something to do with the fact that Charlotte Parker-Kaufman arrived with a bodyguard today."

"She what?"

"Allison called me early this morning. Said there was a safety concern." Motioning towards the practice arena, Jerry pointed, "See that guy leaning against the railing? He brought Charlotte for her session today. He's wearing some sort of communication device in his ear. I think he's more than a regular bodyguard."

A deep sigh escaped Marion's lips, "You won't believe what Toby Trowbridge just told me. And yes, you're right. That guy out there is much more than a bodyguard."

Jerry poured two cups of coffee from an ancient, battered percolator. Handing one to Marion, Jerry settled into the only other chair in the office and asked, "How bad is it?"

"Well, it depends," Marion blew on her coffee. "That machine makes this way too hot."

"Don't change the subject. What did Toby tell you?"

At 6' 2", Marion Hutcheson presented an imposing figure. Short-cropped hair, arms muscled from years of manual labor running the riding club, and a no-nonsense manner, Marion Hutcheson was the perfect visual counterpoint to her life partner Jerry Kennedy, who in her early 40's, still looked like the debutant she once was. But as many people learned, sometimes to their chagrin, Jerry Kennedy was made of much stronger stuff than society balls and parties.

A tall gun safe stood in one corner of the office. Deftly, Marion rotated the cylinders on the metal lock. The gun safe was old and well made. Pulling open the iron door, Marion peered inside. "According to Toby," Marion pulled out a shotgun and inspected it, "there's a Russian spy probably headed this way to kill Wolf Johannsen."

In any other universe, the idea of a Russian spy in Ft. Charles would have been ludicrous to Jerry, but Ft. Charles had seen more than its share of unimaginable occurrences in the last four years, so why not a Russian spy? "Well, that would explain Rambo out there," Jerry commented. "I take it Toby wanted us to close down for a while?"

"Not happening," Marion nodded. "However, I'm not taking any chances, either." Pulling out another shotgun, two rifles, and three pistols, Marion moved a stack of papers from the desk and laid out the weapons. "After Charlotte leaves, you and I are having target practice. I don't think trouble will come here, but if it does…."

"Ms. Marion," Charlotte Parker-Kaufman's lilting voice sounded from the open doorway. "Diamond Girl's been rubbed down, and I put fresh straw and water in her stall. Is there anything else you need me to do before I go home?"

Jerry moved to block Charlotte's view of the desk. No need for Charlotte to see a display of so many weapons. Nixon Oehmig stood behind his charge. Seeing Jerry's action, and noting what lay on the desk, the young man gave a slight nod of approval.

"Sounds like you've taken care of everything," Marion replied. "I'll expect you tomorrow at 9:30. I've asked Chase McDonald to join us."

"Chase!" Charlotte expelled a tortured groan, accompanied by exaggerated eye-rolling.

Ignoring Charlotte's theatrics, Marion continued, "You and Chase both do better when you are competing against one another. This will be good for both of you."

After Charlotte and her bodyguard were gone, Jerry turned a questioning eye to Marion, "Are you sure you want to have practice tomorrow?"

"I refuse to live in fear of what might happen. According to Toby, the protection detail for Allison's kids is just a precaution. No one thinks this Russian nutjob is going after kids." Marion returned all of the firearms to the gun safe, except for a semi-automatic handgun and a shotgun. "We'll be wary, but I don't think there's really anything to worry about. Here," Marion handed the long gun to Jerry, "You're a better shot with this than I am. Let's get in some practice. Just in case."

# CHAPTER FIFTY-ONE

The Motel 6 outside Birmingham proved sufficient for Vargha's needs. A no-questions-asked clerk took the cash Vargha used to pay for his room, handed him the key, and told him check-out time would be 10:00 the next morning. The pimply-faced clerk returned his attention to the Kung Fu movie playing on the small TV behind the counter before Vargha exited the lobby.

The rented room boasted two double beds, paper-thin bath towels, pint-sized bars of soap, and not much else. A musty and unpleasant smell hung over the room. Flipping the AC switch to "on," Vargha doubted running the air would make much of a difference. The motel was old and off the beaten path, a place for illicit rendezvous more than honest travelers.

Signing into the motel's internet, Vargha searched

for pawn shops in the area. He had considered asking the reception clerk for a recommendation, but the less anyone remembered about him, the better. Finally, Vargha settled on two possibilities, both within a ten mile radius of his motel, and both open until midnight. Pocketing the room key, Vargha headed out.

The marquee for Sam's Pawn was half-lit with neon lights. Vargha wondered if the shop's owner was too lazy to get the signage fixed, or just cheap. Chuckling, Vargha added another possibility for the sign's disrepair. Maybe the owner just didn't give a shit.

Surprised by the number of vehicles in the parking lot, Vargha contemplated trying the other pawn shop with less potential witnesses. While Vargha didn't plan on resorting to mayhem, he did plan on making the shop owner an offer he couldn't refuse. Money wasn't the issue. The Russian was willing to part with a large chunk of cash to get what he needed. But the items he intended to purchase might raise some eyebrows, especially if said eyebrows belonged to some nosy hick. After a moment of internal debate, Vargha decided to survey the shop's interior. Depending on what his instincts told him, he could always leave.

To his surprise, other than the middle-aged clerk standing behind a glass front counter displaying a variety of knives and jewelry, Vargha counted only two other people. Where were the owners of the vehicles parked outside? That question was answered within minutes when a door in the back of the shop creaked open, revealing what appeared to be a poker game in full swing. The two men Vargha had observed upon entering the pawn shop scooted quickly inside the open doorway, likely to join the illicit game.

Vargha knew he had selected well. Whoever owned Sam's Pawn obviously didn't care about breaking the law. Approaching the grey-haired man guarding the knife display, Vargha made his opening gambit.

"Looks like a nice selection of blades," Vargha affected a nonchalant tone and waited for a reply.

"Yep," The clerk acknowledged Vargha's observation with a curt nod.

Taking his time, Vargha wandered the length of the glass case. "Mind if I take a look at that one?" Vargha pointed to a slim switchblade.

Taking the blade from the clerk, Vargha noted the weapon's heft. It opened easily and quickly, and was of a size that he could easily conceal on his person. "How much?" he asked.

The price quoted was reasonable, but Vargha didn't want to be too easy of a sell. "Well, I'd like to look at some of your semi-automatics before I decide." Vargha glanced at the locked case hanging on the wall behind the display counter. "What do you have?"

The pawn shop clerk eyed his customer. "You aren't from around here, are you?"

"I guess my accent gave me away," Vargha smiled innocently. "I'm taking a holiday in the States." Vargha leaned on the glass case, placing himself closer to the man he might need to disable quickly.

"Why would you need a gun for a holiday? You planning on making the news?"

Vargha wasn't sure whether a problem was developing or not. Better to keep things civil. The spy knew he could take out the clerk, but he wasn't sure how many men were playing poker and might hear a commotion out front. That was a complication he didn't need right now. "I read the news," Vargha huffed. "Your country can be dangerous. I just want some protection."

"You limeys are all the same." A loud guffaw erupted from the clerk's lips and relief passed over Vargha. "There's no trouble here 'less you bring it on yourself." Still laughing, the clerk retrieved a key and opened the gun cabinet. "Any of these should do."

Vargha debated between the Sig Sauer P226 and the Beretta 92. "You have a Walther P99?"

The clerk's genial smile was replaced by a suspicious look, "You seem to know a good bit about guns."

"Oh, I read up on them before leaving England," Vargha kept his tone light. "The Walther P99 was well-reviewed."

A few tense minutes passed. Vargha could almost see the wheels turning inside the clerk's head. Finally, the clerk replied, "Sold the last P99 a week ago. What I've got is what you see."

"How much for the knife, the Sig Sauer, and a box of ammunition?" Vargha pulled a wad of cash from his pocket.

The clerk never asked for identification, and Vargha never blinked at the price. Driving back to the Motel 6, Vargha began to plan.

# CHAPTER FIFTY-TWO

David Jackson arrived at the offices of Parker & Jackson just as Donna Pevey was unlocking the firm's employee entrance. A quick perusal of the parking lot assured David that he had made it to the office ahead of Allison and the rest of the staff, just as he had planned.

"Hey, Donna!" he called. "I need to talk to you before anyone else arrives."

"Give me a minute to get the coffee started." Donna held the door open until David joined her, then headed towards the firm's break room. "I've only had one cup of caffeine this morning, and I need another shot before the commotion begins."

When David and Allison opened their two-person firm, David had selected the office at the rear of the building for himself. Spacious and quiet, its location allowed David to come and go during the work day without disrupting the rest of the firm's small cadre. Sometimes David missed the anonymity of a large firm, but deep down, he recognized there were many more benefits to being his own boss. After his recent discussion with the Sheriff, David was grateful for his serendipitous selection of office space.

"What's up?" Donna Pevey handed David a cup of fresh brewed coffee and settled in the nearest chair to sip her own. "You're usually not here this early."

"I wanted to talk to you before everybody else got here." David shifted in his seat struggling to decide where to start, "We may have a problem, a safety problem."

"Yes?" Donna's raised eyebrows encouraged David to continue. "Spit it out."

"It's really Wolf Johannsen's problem, but I'm afraid Allison may be targeted, too, and that, potentially, places everyone in this office in danger."

"What in the world are you talking about?" Donna jumped out of her chair and leaned across David Jackson's desk. "Is someone after Mr. Johannsen? Why would Allison be targeted? Has something happened I don't know about? And why, in the good Lord's name, would anyone in this office be in danger?"

"Let me start over." David laid out the facts as he knew them, starting with Wolf's last assignment for the C.I.A. and concluding with the murder of Rebecca Molinere and Charlene Jacobs.

"Damn!" Donna shook her head. "Damn, damn, and

damn!" Donna knew her boss had had some close calls in the past several years, but this Vargha character seemed much more deadly than any of the other criminals that had crossed Allison's path. "Okay, so there's a pretty high probability that this creep is coming to Ft. Charles. What are the Feds doing about it?" Donna doubted whatever was being done would be enough.

"The F.B.I. has taken over now that they suspect Vargha is coming into the U.S. Jake Cleveland has been assigned lead since he is already familiar with Ft. Charles from last year's sting operation. Allison's house and property are pretty much on lockdown. Charlotte and Mack have bodyguards, and Bennett Shealey will be shadowing Allison." David gave Donna a knowing look, "She's refused to change her work schedule."

"Of course she has," Donna interjected. "Does that come as some big surprise to you?"

Ignoring Donna's comment, David continued, "Even with that level of security, a determined assassin – and that's what this Vargha guy is – a determined assassin can get through. If that happens here, we need to be ready."

A thought crossed Donna's mind. "Why are we having this conversation without Allison? I get not telling Susan and Alice," Donna agreed, referring to Susan Craig, the firm's paralegal, and Alice Eason, David's secretary, "but why are you not including Allison in this discussion?"

"If I know Allison, she will be working overtime to convince herself that she isn't in any real danger. Toby told me last night, Allison is furious about having

Bennett Shealey assigned to shadow her, thinks it is totally unnecessary." David finished the last of his coffee. "In this instance, asking forgiveness later instead of permission now is, in my estimation, the better route."

"But you'll talk to the guy guarding Allison, right?" Donna didn't want any mistakes causing more problems.

"Already in the works. I briefed Toby last night about my plan and he's giving this Shealey guy a head's up."

"Well, speaking of plans, what's yours?" Donna glanced at her watch. "Alice will be here any minute. If you want to keep this between us you better start talking."

"No one in this office is that proficient with firearms," David began.

"Speak for yourself," Donna snorted. "Why do you think I have a concealed-carry permit?"

"You may be the exception, but shooting is the last option." David reached for the cardboard box he had brought with him that morning. Placing it on his desk, David opened the container and retrieved several objects.

"That looks like a gun to me," Donna observed.

"Taser," David replied. "Police grade. Toby gave me four last night. You'll have one in your desk, I'll have one in my office, and we are going to hide the other two, in case we need them and can't get to the ones we have."

"What's in that case?" Donna examined the enclosed cylinder that David had laid next to the tasers.

"A last resort." David carefully removed the top portion of the container. A syringe lay on a bed of thick cotton, its needle encased by a protective covering. "A paralytic that will incapacitate within seconds."

"Where in the world did you get something like that?" Donna gazed suspiciously at the dangerous object.

"Let's just say a vet I know owes me a favor. I'd rather leave it at that." David closed the container and placed it in his desk drawer. "And let's hope I can return it, unused, when all this is over."

Donna stood to leave David's office. "And how do you think you'd have the chance to even use that? I doubt the Vargha guy is going to stand there while you prepare the syringe."

"It's like using an Epi pen," David explained. "All I have to do is jab him with the needle. It injects immediately."

Shaking her head, Donna left David's office. She didn't like David's plan one little bit, but for the life of her, she couldn't think of a better one.

# CHAPTER FIFTY-THREE

Wednesday afternoon found Gyuri Vargha on the outskirts of Ft. Charles, Alabama. The killer had taken a leisurely morning at his flea-bag motel near Birmingham before filling up on the nasty, sugary foods Americans called breakfast at a Huddle House near Montgomery. No wonder Americans were so obese, he thought. Even the somewhat healthy foods were cooked in grease.

Now Vargha had a decision to make. According to the census information he had perused on the Internet, Ft. Charles was a fairly small town. Taking accommodations there could be problematic. Better, he decided, to backtrack to a small, roadside motel he had passed thirty minutes earlier.

The motor lodge Vargha selected had seen better

days. Eight rooms lined the L-shaped, one-story motel, each opening directly to a cracked concrete parking lot. What Vargha presumed was the establishment's office occupied the far right side of the long building. Like the clerk in the dump he had stayed in the previous night, the pimpled-faced teenager manning the front desk paid Vargha scant attention. In under three minutes Vargha had paid for a three-night stay and closeted himself in a shabby motel room.

Vargha knew the address of Wolf Johannsen's place. He would locate the property tonight when he would be less likely to be spotted. Later today, he planned to drive into Ft. Charles to get a better feel for the town and find the law offices of the Parker woman. Having a hostage might prove the perfect leverage. Vargha smiled thinking about the attractive lawyer and what he could do to her.

The Walmart bag lay on top of the ragged bedspread covering the sagging double bed. Picking through the contents which had spilled across the chenille coverlet, Vargha selected a box of hair dye. The temporary rinse he had used in the Atlanta airport was fading. Before heading into Ft. Charles, Vargha planned to re-dye his short hair and to replace the moustache he had plastered on his face two days earlier. The horn rimmed glasses he had purchased would add a nice touch to his disguise.

Vargha retrieved the gun and ammunition he had purchased at Sam's Pawn. He liked the Sig Sauer's weight. Hefting it from one hand to another, Vargha sighted the weapon. Naturally ambidextrous, he had been trained by his spy masters to shoot with either hand.

Vargha had purchased two different-sized magazines for the weapon. The longer magazine, of course, held more rounds, but it would be harder to conceal. He would start with the standard magazine of nine rounds but have the larger magazine ready. Vargha had paid a premium for the hollow-point bullets that he loaded into the two magazines. The clerk at the pawn shop had been very reluctant to sell him such destructive bullets, but several Benjamin Franklins had proved persuasive. Laying aside the Sig Sauer, Vargha turned his attention to the wicked looking blade that had completed his purchase.

Guns were a necessary evil in Vargha's opinion. Necessary for distance and self-protection, but guns didn't give Vargha the rush that killing with a knife always did. The blade was personal in a way that a gun never could be. The pleasure Vargha derived from close-up work was almost sexual in nature. Vargha fondled himself as he thought about using the blade on Johannsen's woman.

The shadows playing out on the thin carpet from the room's sole window had lengthened considerably, indicating the arrival of late afternoon. Satisfied with the new hair color and matching moustache, Vargha tucked the Sig into the back of his jeans. It was still summer, so a heavy jacket would draw suspicion. The thin cotton windbreaker that had been on sale at Walmart would be fine, although on this scouting trip, Vargha intended to stay inside his vehicle. Taking the gun with him was merely insurance that the spy didn't plan on needing for this brief excursion.

The drive into Ft. Charles was uneventful. Staying five miles under the speed limit, Vargha cruised into the small Alabama town and headed toward town center. According to Mapquest, that was where he would find the law offices of Parker & Jackson. Vargha figured he would recognize the office from the Google Earth picture he had pulled up before he left the motel.

Ft. Charles was a busier town than Vargha expected. Traffic was brisk, likely due to the fact that he had arrived a tad after 5:00. Irritated initially, Vargha quickly realized that the heavier traffic was good cover. As he turned the corner onto Main Street, Vargha recognized the older building that housed the law office. From what Google Earth had shown, Vargha thought the law firm occupied the entire building. Driving past, Vargha noted a second tenant in the one-story building, a private investigating firm from the sign in the front window.

Vargha decided he needed a closer look. Pulling into a parking spot a block away, Vargha placed the Sig Sauer under the driver's seat and pulled on the Atlanta Braves ball cap he had purchased in the Atlanta airport. The jeans and workshirt from Walmart completed his disguise. As long as he didn't speak to anyone, Vargha thought he would easily pass for a local.

Walking on the same side of the street as the law office was too risky. He had only met the Parker woman once, and he did not believe she would recognize him through his disguise, but Vargha wasn't a man who took unnecessary chances. Fortunately, a hardware store was located directly across the street from the law office. The sidewalk displays of tools, plants and other miscellaneous products allowed Vargha to feign interest in the store's wares while surveilling Parker & Jackson. With time to really look, Vargha realized the law offices had two entrances, the main one that fronted on the sidewalk and a side entrance near the back of the building, accessed by the adjacent parking lot. As he was mentally cataloguing this information for possible future use, the side door opened, disgorging two women, neither of whom were Allison Parker. The women climbed into older model cars and left. Staff, Vargha estimated, given their dress and the age of their vehicles.

Satisfied with the information he had gleaned, Vargha turned to head back to his car when the firm's side door opened again. Allison Parker and a man Vargha did not recognize stepped out, engaged in what appeared to be a heated argument. The pair stopped in the middle of the parking lot, with the Parker woman shaking her finger at the man in some sort of reprimand. Vargha had not paid the unknown man much attention, so focused was he on his possible hostage, when something about the way the man moved caught Vargha's eye.

Military, or ex-military. The Parker woman was being protected. And that could only mean that the authorities had arrived in Ft. Charles ahead of him. Would the same be true of Wolf Johannsen? The element of surprise that Vargha had based his plans on had been removed. Or had it? Driving to his motel, Vargha began to reassess.

# CHAPTER FIFTY-FOUR

Allison was pissed. Arguing with Bennett Shealey was like arguing with a brick wall. The ex-Navy Seal wanted her to ask for a continuation in a wrongful termination case that was set for trial next week.

"The courthouse is wide open. Anyone can come in. The courtroom isn't much better. You know as well as I do that, in small towns, people watch trials for entertainment, and the judges let them. I'm good, but trying to protect you in that sort of environment exposes you to an unnecessary risk."

"I'm not continuing this case. It's taken us a year to get to trial. My client wants this over." Allison headed toward her car, high heels tapping angrily on the pavement. "If you can't protect me, find someone who can."

The Seal moved around Allison, stopping her. "No one can protect you in a crowd. No one." The pair stared at each other, neither willing to concede to the other. "This is an order from the F.B.I. If you don't ask for the continuance, the Agency will do it for you."

Stunned by this information, Allison retorted, "Well, I'm surprised Jake hasn't closed down the entire town."

"There are two objectives here. First, to keep you and your family safe. Second, to eliminate the danger," Shealey lectured. "It makes my job harder when you refuse to follow orders."

"I don't take orders from Jake Cleveland." Allison stepped past the man blocking her path. "I agreed to have my home occupied by snipers and god knows who else, because I intend for my children to be protected from this maniac. They are my first priority!" Allison unlocked her car and slid into the driver's seat, motioning for her bodyguard to get in on the passenger side. "My second priority happens to be my clients. We're going to trial next week. I strongly suggest Jake reconsider telling Judge Costner what to do, too. That conversation won't be well-received."

Silence filled the car during the entirety of the twenty minute drive from downtown Ft. Charles to Allison's home. Allison knew Jake was worried she might be a target and his request that she ask for a continuance of next week's trial was based on a legitimate logistics decision. Gyuri Vargha wouldn't hesitate to kill. Was she putting her fellow citizens at risk by refusing the agent's request?

"I can't ask Judge Costner for a continuance by lying," Allison began as she turned the car into the long driveway which led to her house. "I would have to tell him about Vargha and counsel opposite, as well. Maybe Jake really should have someone higher up in the Agency make a call to the judge, explain this has to do with national security or something."

"You can tell him yourself," Shealey saw the dark SUV parked near the cottage. "He's here."

Jake Cleveland wasn't alone. Wolf Johannsen and two other men stood nearby. Allison recognized Pete Pantsari, one of the F.B.I.'s tech geniuses, but the other man was a stranger.

"What's going on?" Allison asked Wolf, greeting him with a kiss. "Has Vargha been caught?"

Wolf put his arm around Allison, hugging her closely. "No, unfortunately. And the news Jake has brought isn't good."

"Which is?" Allison stared grimly at the F.B.I. agent.

"Mackey got a call this morning." Wilson Mackey was the head of the F.B.I.'s regional office in Birmingham and Cleveland's direct boss. Allison had met him several times, usually under dire circumstances. "Vargha was wearing a disguise, but we're pretty certain he entered the country yesterday through the Atlanta airport."

"How certain are you," Allison pressed. "if he was wearing a disguise?"

"The Customs Agent who processed him didn't pick

up on him initially, even though an alert had gone out. Apparently, she was at the end of a double shift, was tired, and hadn't read the alert when it came across her screen." Jake paused to reflect. The Customs Agent would probably lose her job over her error. "Anyway," he continued, "when she finally saw the alert the first thing that came to her mind was this German fellow who had cleared customs on a Delta flight from London. She passed the information on to her supervisor, who in turn alerted us. Post 9/11, all incoming International travelers are caught on camera. Facial recognition placed the man at a better than 90% match for Gyuri Vargha."

"He was traveling under a German passport as Gunthur Weber," Wolf interjected. "He will have ditched that identity, probably before he left the airport. Pete will be going through airport surveillance videos for rental cars, buses, taxis, etc., using an upgraded facial recognition program the Agency has. We'll find him, and then we'll have a better idea of what he looks like now."

At Wolf's urging, Allison agreed to let Pete set up in the guest cottage. The small space was already occupied by members of Bennett Shealey's protection detail. One more person wouldn't matter.

This latest and disturbing information made up Allison's mind about next week's trial. Pulling Jake Cleveland aside, Allison shared her concerns. "If you want to keep this as quiet as possible, I suggest you have Wilson Mackey or maybe even someone from D.C.

reach out to Judge Costner. If the continuance comes from the judge, I won't have to lie, and my client won't need to know why the case is being postponed until after all of this is over."

"I'll ask Mackey to think about who should make the call for the most optimal result." Jake knew judges were not used to being told what to do. "If we're lucky and can track Vargha...." Jake didn't need to finish his sentence. If the stars aligned in their favor, Vargha would be dead, and life would return to normal well before Allison's scheduled trial.

"Jake," Allison reached for the agent's arm, "if Vargha arrived in Atlanta yesterday, he's either already in Ft. Charles or very close."

"I know."

# CHAPTER FIFTY-FIVE

It had been difficult to tail the Parker woman and her guard. Traffic thinned out once they left the environs of Ft. Charles proper, so Vargha had stayed well behind the white SUV with the Overlook Riding Club bumper sticker. Ten minutes outside of town, Vargha decided the risk was too great and turned off onto a side road. All his planning would be for naught if he were spotted following the pair.

Pulling up the rental car's navigation system, Vargha entered the address for the Old Fort Inn. He knew from looking at Mapquest the evening before that his real target's home was on the other side of Ft. Charles, out a two-lane state highway. It was too early to head in that direction. Vargha wanted the cover of darkness before he surveilled Johannsen's property. The sun wouldn't set for another three hours.

Vargha figured enough time had passed, however, for him to continue down the road the Parker woman had taken. With luck he would be able to determine where she lived. If not, he'd google the Overlook Riding Club and see if that was a connection he might take advantage of. Making a three point turn, Vargha pulled back onto the main road and continued east.

The countryside was mostly farmland, interspersed with a house here and there. Interesting that the Parker woman lived in a remote area, he thought, and to his benefit, if he decided to go after her. In the distance Vargha noticed a stone farmhouse set well back from the highway. A long drive meandered past a small pond before terminating near the house. Satisfaction at the sight of the white SUV that he had followed from Ft. Charles was immediately replaced by a sharp intake of breath when Vargha spied the other two vehicles parked nearby. Black SUVs with tinted windows belonged to only one entity – law enforcement. Vargha was too far away to note the plates, but he was willing to bet they were Federal government issue, most likely the F.B.I. or even Homeland Security. Cursing, Vargha forced himself to maintain a moderate speed as he passed by the property. For now, Allison Parker was out of his reach.

Out of sight of the farmhouse, Vargha pulled over and considered his options. Amazingly, his phone had a signal, so he clicked on a web browser and entered the words "Overlook Riding Club." Another click and the riding club's homepage filled the small screen. Vargha skimmed the offerings listed. Students could board their horses, as well as take group and individual lessons. The main menu displayed a link to upcoming events. Clicking on the blue line, Vargha continued his search for information. Several competitions were listed in chronological order. Clicking on the event scheduled for the upcoming Saturday, Vargha was rewarded with a list of the riding club's students who were competing.

Charlotte Parker-Kaufman. What were the odds that this girl was the Parker woman's kid? 100%? "Had to be," Vargha told himself. Opening a second browser, Vargha entered the name of the upcoming competition. A satisfied smile covered the killer's face. If no other opportunity presented itself between now and Saturday, Vargha would attend the event and conceal himself in the large crowd. Allison Parker would certainly be there to watch her daughter, and with luck, Wolf Johannsen would accompany her.

Powering down his phone to conserve battery-life, Vargha checked the time. A quick supper somewhere outside Ft. Charles, and then a leisurely drive towards the Old Fort Inn. He ought to arrive just as the sun was setting.

#

Several older model trucks and a couple of newer cars were parked outside Roy's, the restaurant on the far side of Ft. Charles where Vargha planned to grab a quick dinner. Removed from the main part of town, and in the direction of Johannsen's place, Vargha figured he would be mostly unnoticed in the semi-rundown appearing eatery.

Pulling the bill of his ball cap further over his forehead, Vargha pushed open the restaurant door. Six or seven tables were already occupied, even at this early hour. Casually, as not to draw too much attention, Vargha surveyed the mostly male crowd. Tired-looking men, overalls or wrinkled jeans, heavy work boots – Roy's was obviously supported by the Ft. Charles' working class. Two women occupied a lone two-top, the only females in the place other than a harried, middle-aged waitress and a younger, pony-tailed one.

"Just sit wherever's open," The pony-tailed waitress grinned cheerfully. "I'll be with ya in a sec'."

A spot in the back corner was open. Situating himself to face the restaurant's front door, Vargha opened the slim menu that was already on the table. What the hell was red-eye gravy? Fried okra? Collards? Vargha searched for a familiar food. These Southerners were heathens. The first thing Vargha planned to do once he had taken care of business in this hick town was treat himself to real food.

"Know whatcha want?" Pony-tail inquired.

Hiding his disgust at the menu choices and the

unappetizing view of the waitress's mouth full of chewing gum, Vargha ordered chopped sirloin, no gravy, with green beans and a side salad. "And a cup of coffee," he added as the waitress turned to leave.

The kitchen at Roy's was, if nothing else, efficient. Vargha's order appeared in under ten minutes, and to the Russian's surprise, actually was fairly delicious. He was on his third coffee refill when the tinkling of the bell on the restaurant's main door announced the entrance of more customers.

# CHAPTER FIFTY-SIX

Jake Cleveland liked Roy's. The food was good, the price was right, and it was the closest food-joint to Wolf Johannsen's place to get take-out. The F.B.I. agent had dispatched Rick Miller, one of Bennett Shealey's men assigned to the Old Fort Inn, to pick up a supper order for the group.

Gyuri Vargha had never laid eyes on Rick Miller, but the way in which Miller moved, the way he checked out the room, his physical presence – all of this and more told Vargha that this man was a potential disaster. Above all else, Vargha must not draw attention to himself.

"Kin I getcha some dessert?" Pony-tail smacked her gum.

Seizing on the opportunity, Vargha feigned discomfort. "My food hasn't agreed with me. Is that the loo?"

"The what?" Pony-tail frowned. "I don't think we have that on the menu."

Vargha bent over, grabbing his stomach, "I think I might be sick."

Still flummoxed by the unknown menu item, Pony-tail immediately recognized the beginnings of a diarrhea attack. "The bathroom's just over there."

Vargha's problem had his back turned, talking to a woman at the counter. Quickly, Vargha rose from his table and headed towards the door which sported a picture of a cowboy. Locking the door behind him, Vargha searched for a way out. He didn't think he had been made, but he wasn't taking any chances.

A rickety window above the urinal looked promising. Balancing on the porcelain rim, Vargha pushed open the window and released the screen covering. Hoisting himself through the opening was difficult, but on the third attempt, he achieved success. Dropping to the ground, Vargha made his way to his rental car and fled.

#

A high school drop-out, Pony-tail liked her job at Roy's. It wasn't too hard, the pay was decent, and the tips from her regular customers helped pad her monthly income. Eventually, maybe she would take a class at the community college and get her GED, but for now, the simple job of waiting tables sufficiently taxed her brain.

Pony-tail glanced at the man's empty table. He must be really sick to still be in the bathroom. Maybe she ought to get someone to check on the guy. He looked pretty old, maybe even fifty. The cute young guy who had come for the take-out order was still at the register. She'd ask him to check on the sick older man.

"Scuse me, sir" Pony-tail tapped Rick Miller on the shoulder. "Kin I git you to do me a favor?" Close-up, the young stranger was even cuter. Pony-tail twisted her hair nervously.

Rick Miller smiled at the young woman standing beside him, "Sure, I will if I can. What do you need?"

"I think one of my customers might be sick. He's been in the men's room for a while now."

Miller thought the waitress might be exaggerating. "How long is a while?"

Pony-tail pondered Miller's question. She didn't want to seem stupid. "I don't know. Maybe five minutes?"

Rick Miller grinned at the young waitress. He thought the customer-in-the-bathroom story might be an excuse to flirt with him, and now he was pretty sure that was the case. Miller liked women and women liked him. A come-on such as this one was nothing new. No need, though, to be cruel. The waitress was sort of cute, and no telling how long his current assignment might last. "Five minutes isn't that long. I'm sure he's fine." Miller turned to pick up the Styrofoam containers of food. He needed to get these back before the food got cold.

Pony-tail grabbed Miller's arm. "Please, just check on him. He said he didn't feel good after he ate his food."

Miller reconsidered. Another minute or two wouldn't matter. The agent walked over to the men's bathroom door and knocked. "Hey, man, you okay in there?" Miller placed his ear against the door. Either the door was too solid for sound to travel through it, or the guy really was sick. Miller called out again and pounded on the locked door.

"You have a key for this?" Miller turned to question Pony-tail. Seeing her affirmative nod, he ordered, "Go get it, quick!"

A red-faced man wearing a chef's apron returned with Pony-tail and handed Miller a key. "I'm Roy," he introduced himself. "Penny says one of her customers is sick."

The bathroom door unlocked with a loud click. Pushing open the door, Rick Miller called out, "You okay in here?" and walked through the opening. There was no one inside.

"What the hey?" The restaurant's owner exclaimed. Turning to the pony-tailed waitress, Roy scowled. "Is this some sort of joke, Penny?"

"No, Mr. Roy, I swear. He told me he felt sick, and I showed him where the men's room was." Pony-tail

Penny paced. "He seemed fine when he was eating. He even asked for refills on his coffee." A look of despair came over the young waitress as she processed the fact that her customer had disappeared. "Does this mean I'm stuck with his bill?"

"Had you seen him in here before?" A disturbing niggle was beginning to tingle at the back of Rick Miller's mind.

Penny shook her head, "No. He talked funny so I just thought he was passing through."

"Talked funny in what way?" Miller pressed.

"You know, like one of them fer'ners. Sort of prissy-like, but nice enough," Penny wiped away a tear. "I never took him for someone who'd run out on his bill."

Rick Miller pulled a twenty from his wallet and handed it to the crying waitress. "This ought to cover his bill. Tell me, was he sitting here when I came in?"

Penny tried to remember. She wanted to help this nice man who had saved her from losing money on the evening's shift. "Well, I had just put Billy's plate down," Penny motioned towards a nearby table, "when I heard the bell ring. I reckon that was you, comin' in." Penny scrunched her face, concentrating. "Yep, he was still here, facing towards the front of the restaurant. It was right after that he told me he didn't feel good."

Rick Miller pulled his cell phone from a back

pocket. Punching in a series of numbers, the agent turned the phone towards the waitress. "Does this look anything like the man who was here?"

Penny studied the picture on Rick Miller's phone. "He was wearing a baseball cap, so I don't know about the hair. But he does favor the man in this picture some. Close enough to be his brother, maybe."

The niggle in Rick Miller's brain exploded. Leaving the carry-out boxes on the counter, the agent ran for the parking lot.

# CHAPTER FIFTY-SEVEN

Rick Miller set a land-speed record as he tore down the two-lane road from Roy's and raced up the driveway towards the iron gate guarding entry to the Old Fort Inn. Caught on Pantsari's hidden cameras as he turned off the main road, Miller's approach had been noted, and the gate opened in advance. Gravel flew as the agent wrenched the wheel to the left, causing the back of the government vehicle to slide ninety degrees before coming to a stop, barely shy of the Inn's front steps.

"He's here!" Rick Miller shouted, taking the front steps two at a time. Bursting through the front Inn's front door, Miller repeated his pronouncement to the trio of men who emerged running from Johannsen's office at the rear of the long, open foyer.

"Report!" Jake Cleveland's sharp order brought the young agent to attention. "Every detail, Miller. Start at the beginning."

Succinctly, as he had been trained, Rick Miller recited the events that had unfolded while he waited for the carry-out order at Roy's. "I really thought that waitress was hitting on me," Miller admitted sheepishly, "and I didn't take her seriously at first."

"Thinking with his dick, again," Pete Pantsari muttered just loud enough to be heard.

"Later, Pantsari," Jake dismissed Pete's observation with a wave. Returning his attention to Rick Miller, Jake reconsidered and asked, "How much time passed while you were deciding whether or not this girl was trying to get in your pants?"

Rick Miller cringed at the deserved reprimand. "Not long, sir. Maybe thirty seconds." When Cleveland simply nodded Rick continued, "Anyway, I knocked on the bathroom door and didn't get an answer, asked the girl for a key, and then went in. The window over the john was open, and the guy was gone. When I realized the guy had slipped, I thought about Vargha. Didn't really think it could have been him, but …."

"Your training kicked in, finally," Wolf Johannsen observed. "Did she ID him?"

"I showed her the picture from the Atlanta airport. She said he was wearing a ball cap, so she wasn't sure about hair, but she thought it was the same guy. Or a close relative."

"And you think this was Vargha because?" Pantsari inquired.

"Because according to the waitress, the guy was facing the front door, and after I walked in to pick up our order, he bolted." Rick Miller put his hands in his jeans pocket and waited. Would he be pulled from this detail for letting Vargha escape?

"Good work, Miller," Jake acknowledged. "We know our target is in the area, and now he knows we are, too. That ought to worry the son-of-a-bitch."

#

Gyuri Vargha wasn't so much worried as he was irritated. Now he'd have to re-evaluate both his plans and his targets. First, though, he needed to find a new place to hide. The Feds would start checking every motel and hotel within a wide radius now that he had likely been spotted.

Packing up didn't take long. Before he left the shabby room, however, an idea came to mind. Logging onto the motel's internet, Vargha clicked on Home Away and looked. Private, one bedroom cottage, convenient to Ft. Charles and Auburn. Perfect, Vargha thought, and available. The Russian didn't like having to use a credit card, but the ones he had with him were well protected, and by the time their use was linked to him, his work here would be done.

Dusk was settling its purplish haze over fields of

soybean and cotton as Vargha made the drive to his new hideout. The moon wouldn't rise for another couple of hours, and the in-between time would offer the dark cover that Vargha sought.

Darkness had fallen by the time the car's Nav system announced, "You have arrived at your destination, on the left." As anticipated, the cottage's owner was waiting for him with a key and instructions.

"Thank you for renting to me on such short notice." Vargha smiled benignly at the white-haired woman standing under the small structure's front porch light. "I was beginning to think I'd have to sleep in my car. I hope your husband isn't too upset with me coming in so late."

The owner's answer sealed her fate, "Oh, it's just me. Never been married." The older woman laughed, "Men are too much trouble."

"May I see the inside?" Vargha continued to smile. "I'd really like to get settled. It's been a long day."

"Why, of course," his hostess replied. "Where are my manners?"

The old woman focused her attention on the cottage door, fiddling with the key. "This key can be obstinate," she called over her shoulder to her renter. "You may have to jiggle it somewhat to make it work."

She was still intent on her task when Gyuri Vargha slid the sharp edge of his knife across her throat. Without a sound, the woman's frail body fell to the ground, the blood spraying from the severed carotid, barely visible against the darkness. Wiping his dirtied blade against the old lady's cotton housecoat, Vargha waited until the blood had stopped before gathering the woman in his arms and heading towards the farmhouse adjacent to the rental cottage.

As he had hoped, the old lady had left her house wide open. The screen door slammed loudly as Vargha moved rapidly across the enclosed porch and into the farmhouse proper. No need to go further, he thought. Dumping the old woman's body to the kitchen floor, Vargha paused to wash his hands in the old-fashioned farm sink. Blood on the cuff of his jacket caught his attention. Peeling off the Walmart special, Vargha tossed the discarded jacket on top of the woman's cooling body.

A few minutes later, armed with food and drink he had taken from the old woman's refrigerator, Vargha closed the kitchen door and made his way to the nearby cottage. With any luck, no one would miss the old biddy until next Sunday when she didn't show up for church, assuming she even attended services. By then, he would have formulated and executed a new plan and be well on his way back home.

# CHAPTER FIFTY-EIGHT

Toby Trowbridge sprinted across the blacktop parking lot and into the brick building housing the Calhoun County law enforcement complex. For the umpteenth time, the Sheriff had misplaced his umbrella and was running hard to avoid a complete soaking from the unexpected shower. Toby grinned, thinking about the lecture he was sure to get from his octogenarian secretary Beth Robinson when she saw his wet shirt.

The Sheriff's office occupied the back, west corner of the law enforcement complex with the county jail garnering most of the building's square footage. A secured entry segregated the regular folk from deputies, staff and other legit employees. Melinda Maddox, one of the county's first female deputies, manned the desk behind the large plate-glass panel that separated the entryway from the rest of the building. Nodding at the Sheriff, Melinda buzzed her boss through the heavy, metal door marked "No Admittance."

An unlit office greeted the Sheriff as he entered his quarters. Strange, Toby thought, that Beth wasn't already in. In all the years she had worked for the Sheriff, and before him his predecessor, Beth Robinson had been late to work less than two or three times. Flicking the light switch, Toby dialed the front desk.

"Melinda, has Beth called in this morning?"

"No, sir. Not since I've been here, and I came on at 6:00."

Thanking the deputy, Toby placed the phone in its cradle. Beth Robinson would never just not show up for work. Picking up the phone for a second time, Toby called Beth's house. No answer. Maybe she was running late and had already left. It would take her at least thirty minutes to drive into town. Her refusal to have a cell phone meant he couldn't try to reach her that way.

The Sheriff had tried several times to convince his secretary to move closer to town, to one of the newer retirement communities. Living so far from town on her family's old homeplace, he had told her, wasn't a good match for a woman alone in her late 70's, but Beth Robinson would have none of it. Well, now her stubbornness had probably gotten her in trouble, Toby thought. He'd be willing to bet Beth had fallen down her back step, or slipped in the bathtub. Maybe this would convince the intractable woman to make a move to town.

Convinced of his scenario, Toby figured he'd better send someone out to check on his missing secretary.

"Hello, Martin Investigations," Sheila McMurray's familiar voice answered Toby's call.

"Sheila, it's Sheriff Trowbridge. Is your boss in yet?"

"Just a second, Sheriff. I'll put you right through."

After exchanging greetings, Toby asked Frank if he would mind running out to the Robinson home place and checking on Beth. "I'm afraid the old girl has gotten herself into some kinda fix. I really can't spare a deputy right now for an hour round trip, but I'm worried about her."

"Not a problem," Frank replied without hesitation. "I've got a free morning. I'll head out now and give you a call as soon as I get there."

#

The down-home beat of George Straight poured from the dual speakers of Frank's Ford behemoth as he cruised down the state highway to Beth Robinson's house. Frank's favorite country singer had been gone now for several years, but Frank hadn't found any of the younger Nashville stars he liked any better. George was singing, "I ain't got a dime but what I got is mine," when Frank topped a small hill and spied Beth Robinson's house in the distance. Yep, that looked like Beth's car parked up next to the farmhouse. Toby must have been right.

Beth had gotten herself hurt or sick.

Slowing to make the turn into the gravel drive, Frank noticed another vehicle parked further back on the property, near the small cottage Beth rented out on Home Away. Frank couldn't get a good look at the plates, but from the distance they didn't look like Alabama issue. Probably a guest, Frank figured, dismissing the vehicle and its owner from his mind. If Beth wasn't in the house he'd check with her renter.

The Ford's engine rumbled loudly when the P.I. cut the ignition. Frank didn't like that sound. He'd need to take it to Charlie's pretty soon for a tune up. With his mind on how much money a tune-up might set him back, the sound coming from the back porch didn't immediately catch Frank's attention. Whack, whack, whack. The staccato sound registered at about the same time the P.I. saw the source of the noise. The red screen porch door was slamming against its frame. Odd, Frank thought, that Beth would leave the screen door unlatched overnight. The sound, alone, would have interrupted a night's sleep.

Frank pushed open the screen door and stepped inside the long, narrow porch that ran the length of the house. Nothing seemed out of place. Frank tried the door to the house. It was locked. Pounding forcefully, Frank called out, "Beth? Beth, it's Frank Martin. Are you in there?"

Frank's concern began to grow. If Beth was inside,

she must be hurt. He'd apologize later for what he was about to do. Stepping back, Frank readied himself for contact and then slammed his considerable bulk against the locked door. His efforts were rewarded with a sharp crack. Beth's farmhouse was over 100 years old, and the door looked to be original. Frank's second assault brought success. The door swung open on one hinge, allowing Frank access to Beth's kitchen.

"Mother of God!" The sight of Beth Robinson's body shocked the veteran P.I. Kneeling beside the still form, Frank felt for a pulse, knowing as he did so that the deep wound to Beth's throat had stolen her life. "Oh, Beth," Frank whispered, "who did this to you?"

Stepping around his deceased friend, Frank picked up the receiver on Beth's ancient telephone and dialed the Sheriff's direct line. "Toby, you need to get out here. Bring Andy Dabo with you," Frank referenced the Calhoun County Medical Examiner. "Beth's been murdered."

"Murdered? Beth? How?" Rapidly, one word questions spilled from the Sheriff.

"Her throa,t" Frank started to give Toby details when the sound of footsteps caught his attention. "Hang on a minute!" Frank placed the receiver on the kitchen counter.

The first bullet hit Frank Martin in the upper middle of his back, its violence causing Frank's body to arch unnaturally. Automatically, Frank reached for the weapon he always wore in a shoulder harness beneath his coat jacket, adrenaline powering his actions. But he was too slow. Falling to the ground, Frank's last thought was "Fuck me. Not again."

# CHAPTER FIFTY-NINE

"He's one lucky son-of-a-bitch," Andy Dabo's voice seemed far, far away. "Any closer, and the back of his head would be on the front of that counter over there." Frank struggled to make sense of the words he was hearing. "I've packed the back wound with pieces from one of Beth's kitchen towels. EMS ought to be here any minute."

A soft groan escaped Frank's lips. Struggling, the P.I. forced his eyes to open. The Calhoun County Medical Examiner knelt by his side. "I'm still alive?" Frank asked, his words barely audible, "Or am I on your cadaver table?"

"You're alive," Dabo allowed, "and lucky as hell. I reckon with the blood pouring from that grazing shot to the head your attacker thought he'd killed you, and hauled ass outa here."

Frank rolled to one side and instantly regretted it as pain exploded across his head. Still, he needed to look. And ask. "Beth?"

"She's gone," Toby Trowbridge answered Frank's question. The Sheriff squatted beside his friend. "From the state of rigor, Andy figures she'd been dead at least twelve hours when you got here." Toby grasped the P.I.'s hand. "Damn good thing you kept the phone line open. I heard the gunshots. Do you remember anything, anything at all?"

Two years earlier, Frank had suffered traumatic amnesia after being shot and had never been able to recall the events surrounding that attack. This time, however, Frank's memory remained intact. "There was a car parked by the cottage Beth rents out. Is it still here?"

Frank's non sequitur took the Sheriff by surprise. "Uh, no, just your truck and Beth's car."

"There was a car back there when I arrived. Took it for a guest renting out the cottage. Didn't pay it any mind." Frank grimaced as a sharp pain stabbed at his head. "Whoever that car belongs to either heard what happened, or was the person who shot me and probably killed Beth."

"I take it you didn't get a look at your assailant?"

"Not good enough for much of a description, tho' I'm pretty sure the shooter was male, maybe 5'8" or so." Frank tried to sit up as a horrific thought occurred to him. "Jesus, Toby, do you think it could have been that guy the Feds think is after Wolf Johannsen?"

"If it was, why would he be staying out here?" Toby turned the possibilities over in his mind. "On the other hand, what better place to hide? He'd have to know the motels around here would be checked, but who would think about these VRBO places?" The sound of an approaching siren telegraphed the imminent arrival of an ambulance and EMS crew. "Do you remember the make and color of the car?"

"Light-colored, looked like a newer model. Florida plates, I think – I remember thinking it was probably a rental." Frank struggled to pull up more details. "That's all, Toby. I can't remember anything else."

Leaving Frank to the ministrations of Andy Dabo and the EMS crew rushing through the kitchen door, Toby stepped outside for a better signal. Beth Robinson's murder would stun Ft. Charles' law enforcement community, and many of the officers would want to avenge her death. Better to hold that information close until he had a chance to talk with Jake Cleveland about his and Frank's suspicions. The BOLO that the Sheriff issued for the car and assailant only warned that the assailant was armed and dangerous. There would be time to mourn Beth Robinson later.

#

Gyuri Vargha pulled into the parking lot of the Glenndean Shopping Center in Auburn, Alabama. He needed to switch vehicles as soon as possible. In his rush to get away from the dead woman and the fat guy who had stumbled upon his victim, Vargha had left most of his belongings in the rental cottage. It was his bad luck that the fat guy had called the sheriff, but it was his good luck that he had overheard the conversation in time to make his escape. Ft. Charles was too dangerous for him right now, and he was certain that law enforcement was already on the lookout for his car.

The small bag beside him on the passenger seat contained all Vargha needed. Gun, ammunition, blade – anything else he could easily acquire. The shopping center was an older style strip center. Several retail establishments, a bowling alley and a Brazilian Jui Jitsu studio occupied most of the mall, with only one empty space advertising a "for rent" sign.

Preferably, Vargha would have stolen a new ride under the cover of darkness, but circumstances were dictating otherwise. It was now close to noon. With any luck, traffic would increase as people ran errands during their lunch hour or picked one of the mall's small eateries for a quick repast.

Parking his car in the middle of the lot, Vargha waited. Hot-wiring a new vehicle would take time and draw unwanted attention. Carjacking, although also risky, offered him a faster getaway. He could easily disable the driver and dispose of the body later if necessary.

Vargha's patience was soon rewarded. Loud music blared from the open windows of the dark green Kia hatchback that pulled into the empty slot next to Vargha's car. A young man, maybe still in his teens, gyrated behind the wheel, keeping time with the beat. He was alone.

Quickly, Vargha leapt from his car and yanked open the Kia's passenger side door. Pointing the Sig, he ordered, "Drive!" Instead, however, the tattoo-covered teen replied, "It's yours, man" and, before Vargha could react, had jumped from the car and run.

Vargha cursed. The kid could describe him to the police. Speeding from the mall, Vargha muttered angrily. The element of surprise, the component so necessary to his plans, was completely destroyed. The American authorities weren't stupid. If they hadn't already figured out he was in the country, the fiascos of the past twenty-four hours ought to illuminate even the dullest law enforcement mind.

But he would not be denied his revenge, even it was the last act of his life. All he needed was to stay one step ahead of his pursuers until Wolf Johannsen was dead.

# CHAPTER SIXTY

By Thursday evening, the BOLO had yielded results. Not only was Vargha's rental located abandoned in the strip mall in Auburn, the Lee County Sheriff had immediately put two and two together after hearing about the carjacking in the same mall parking lot. In response, Toby and one of his deputies made the short drive to Auburn and interviewed the teen whose car had been taken at gunpoint.

The description the teen gave both sheriffs matched the one Frank had given. There was no doubt in Toby's mind now that Beth Robinson's killer and Frank Martin's assailant was the same man who had carjacked the Auburn teen's Kia. A second BOLO was issued, this one identifying the target as wanted for murder and attempted murder. But for the teen's quick thinking,

Toby knew another body would be at the coroner's.

Then, the trail went cold. Friday passed without even a hint of a sighting. Every motel and hole-in-the-wall in Calhoun and Lee Counties was searched. Local TV stations ran an artist's drawing of the suspect being wanted by state and federal law enforcement. The public was warned not to approach the suspect if seen, but to immediately call 911. No tips came in. The phone lines remained silent.

Calhoun and Lee Counties were quite rural. Even so, neither Toby Trowbridge nor Jake Cleveland thought Gyuri Vargha would be able to slide under the radar of country folk who were naturally suspicious of folk who didn't look or sound like them. When thirty-six hours passed without any calls coming into the sheriff's office in either county, a meeting was called at the Old Fort Inn to consider the possibility that Vargha had fled.

"I'm telling you, there's no place for him to hide for any length of time," Toby argued. "My deputies have been all over this county, more than once since Thursday. The man has vanished. And that's good news for my way of thinking."

Jake Cleveland nodded, "I tend to agree. We can deduce from his recent actions that he was afraid he'd be made when Rick walked into Roy's, otherwise he wouldn't have bailed through that bathroom window. He probably thought he was safe at Beth's, figuring he'd kill her and buy himself some time."

"And it was his bad luck that I sent Frank to check on

Beth," Toby interjected. "He's on the run. Got to be. He knew to dump his rental but carjacking that kid was a dumb move."

Leaning against the open doorway to his office, Wolf Johannsen listened to the state and federal lawmen try to convince themselves that the danger posed by Gyuri Vargha was over. Finally, he could listen no longer, "He's still here." Wolf's voice halted all other conversation.

Pete Pantsari pulled his attention from a large computer screen he had set up the week before. "I've spent the last several hours going over traffic cameras in Auburn, Ft. Charles and everywhere in between. I've accessed private surveillance as well. Vargha is nowhere in the vicinity. I'd bet money on it."

Wolf walked into the office, opened a small fridge and pulled out a Coke Zero. No one spoke, watching the Swede pop open the can and take a long swig. "Gyuri Vargha is not your normal criminal. His life has been spent evading capture, concealing his identity, blending in with the unsuspecting civilian. He is disciplined and goal-oriented." Wolf finished the soda and tossed the empty can into a nearby trash basket. "Gyuri Vargha came here to kill me, and he won't leave until he accomplishes his mission, or I get to him first."

"Are you suggesting we just sit around and wait?" Jake Cleveland didn't like that idea at all.

"Yes," Wolf agreed. "That's exactly what I'm suggesting, only I think we ought to send him an invitation. Speed things up, so to speak."

"By doing what?" Toby asked.

"Make it easy for him to get to me. Vargha will have surveilled this property, probably more than once, and most likely, as soon as he got to Ft. Charles. The man is smart. Even if he didn't ID the surveillance cameras on the perimeter, he would plan as if they were there."

Pete Pantsari slammed his fist on the table. "There is no way in hell he saw my cameras."

Wolf cast a rueful glance at the F.B.I.'s tech guru. "No offense, Pantsari. Just stating a fact."

"Ain't seen no facts yet," Pantsari mumbled, returning his attention to the glowing screen in front of him.

The outdoor lights had responded to their automatic timers, spreading a soft glow around the Inn's exterior and down the long drive before the group reached a consensus. Toby Trowbridge didn't like Wolf's plan, but he hadn't been able to think of a better one. Jake Cleveland didn't particularly like it either, but he understood the Swede's reasoning. Too many people had died already. If Wolf Johannsen thought he could take Gyuri Vargha, Jake was willing to give him a shot.

"We'll move out tomorrow. Make a point of stopping at the diner in Ft. Charles so the gossip can get started." Jake pulled out a rumpled pack of Winstons. "Taking it outside," he added, seeing Wolf begin to object. "By noon the word will be all over town that the Feds have left."

"What about you, Sheriff?" Wolf asked.

Toby smiled grimly, "I'll see what I can do to spread

the word. I don't like deceiving my constituents, especially when a killer is on the loose. But if this is our best option, I'll do my best."

# CHAPTER SIXTY-ONE

"Mom, we're gonna be late!" An exasperated Charlotte Parker-Kaufman yelled down the hall. "Hurry up!"

Toweling her wet hair, Allison emerged from the master bedroom. "Honey, we have plenty of time. You don't compete until this afternoon."

"I know that," Charlotte retorted. "Jerry wants me to run Diamond Girl through her paces once more before the competition. We need to get there now!" Allison's daughter argued, placing teen-age emphasis on the word "now".

Allison paused at the bedroom door. "Charlotte, don't use that tone with me. I am well aware of what needs to be done today." Giving her daughter "the look," she continued. "Tell Mack we're leaving in thirty minutes. And I'll expect you to have all your gear in the car by then, as well."

Hair dried, Allison selected a pair of jeans, a red t-shirt, and debated over her choice of footwear. It would be hot today, no doubt, but spending most of her time at the riding club and, later at the horseshow, dictated a pair of comfortable cowboy boots. Flicking her long hair into a tight chignon, Allison pronounced herself ready to deal with the emotionally charged, almost-teenager that her daughter had become.

The small cooler that Allison intended to take with her sat empty on the kitchen counter. As she was loading it with water and ice, movement out by the guest cottage caught her attention. Moving closer to the large windows that ran the length of the breakfast area, Allison was surprised by what she saw. Bennett Shealey and two of his men appeared to be moving out of the cottage. If the security team was packing up, Gyuri Vargha must have been caught. The cooler could wait. Allison needed to find out what had happened.

"Bennett." Stepping out the back porch, Allison called to the man who had shadowed her for over a week. "What's going on? Did they catch him?"

The ex-Seal paused, giving Allison a confused look. "Hasn't Johannsen called you?" Bennett wasn't sure what he could share with Allison Parker about the new plans.

"No, I haven't talked to him since yesterday morning." Bennett's men continued to remove boxes from the cottage, nodding to Allison as they walked past her to several SUV's parked in the upper driveway. "Bennett, what's going on?" Allison asked again.

"You need to call Mr. Johannsen. He'll explain." Bennett picked up the stack of boxes he had laid down when Allison had stopped him. "My men have been assigned elsewhere, but I'll be going with you today to the show."

In the time it took her to cover the twenty feet back to the main house Allison had become more than irritated. First, an army of ex-Seals and other assorted security types had descended upon her home, supposedly to protect her and her children from the maniac who wanted to kill Wolf. Okay, she was fine with that, but she expected to be kept in the intelligence loop as a quid pro quo. No one had said a thing to her about most of the security detail moving out, and come to think of it, Bennett had never answered her question about Gyuri Vargha. Allison's ire rose with every button she pressed on her cell. By the time Wolf Johannsen's accented voice answered, Allison was ready for battle.

"You've got ten seconds to tell me what in the hell is going on," Allison hissed in response to Wolf's hello. "And I mean everything, starting with why Bennett's men are leaving when, a week ago, protecting me and my family was paramount to you and Jake Cleveland."

"I'm on my way to your house right now." Wolf did not want to have this conversation on the phone. "A lot has changed in the past thirty-six hours."

Allison paced her kitchen, listening to Wolf's excuses. "Thirty-six hours? And I'm just now being brought into the loop?"

"You weren't in danger," Wolf interjected. "And I don't think you are now either. Things have escalated, and we've made a decision to change tactics."

Allison knew her lover well enough now to know he was withholding some piece of information, probably an important piece, but she didn't have time to argue any further. "I can't wait on you. Charlotte has one last practice at the riding club before this afternoon's competition, and we're already running late because of having to talk to Bennett. You can tell me what's so important out there."

Charlotte and Mack were already in the car, having honked the horn twice trying to get their mother's attention. Under normal circumstances Allison would have discussed her children's rude horning-blowing behavior, but right now she shared her children's feelings. Without waiting for Bennett Shealey, Allison sped down her driveway and onto the state highway heading to Overlook Riding Club.

Only one car was parked in the unpaved lot when Allison pulled her car into a shaded area near the riding club's main buildings. By this time of day, and especially preceding the afternoon's scheduled events, Allison expected to see the practice ring being used by several riders. The absence of activity registered briefly at the back of Allison's brain, a soft whisper telling her that things weren't quite right, but the warning faded quickly, replaced by her children's excited voices.

"Mama, can I stay outside while y'all talk to Miz Jerry? The black nanny might have had her babies by now."

The riding club kept a small number of goats that intrigued Allison's son. Nodding her permission, Allison added, "Just don't go so far you can't hear me when I call for you."

Gathering Charlotte's practice helmet which lay forgotten in the back seat, Allison closed the car door and headed towards the barn's entrance to follow her daughter inside.

# CHAPTER SIXTY-TWO

Bennett Shealey gunned the black SUV, urging the government-issued vehicle well past the posted speed limit. Allison Parker had just about tried the last of his limited patience. She knew damn good-and-well, the ex-Seal muttered to himself, that she wasn't supposed to go anywhere without him until told otherwise by Jake Cleveland.

Bennett didn't really think Allison was in danger. Based on the intel state and local authorities had gathered since Thursday mid-day, it seemed fairly obvious to everyone except Wolf Johannsen that the Russian had left the area. Bennett didn't know the specifics about the new plan, just that the focus had shifted. But for the fact that Johannsen was romantically involved with Allison Parker, Bennett figured he'd have been pulled off guard duty just like the rest of his crew. The ex-Seal didn't mind, though, so long as Uncle Sammy paid his fee. Guarding Allison Parker had been frustrating at times, but he hadn't had an assignment this easy as far back as he could remember.

Thinking about Allison Parker reminded Bennett of why he was breaking the speed limit on the two-lane Alabama highway. Would it have hurt his strong-willed charge to wait an extra ten minutes so he could accompany her to this riding club?

Nixon Oehmig had described the place to him after taking Allison's daughter to practice. Out in the middle of freakin' nowhere. Two gay women run the place. Looks like they've done pretty well for themselves. Bennett didn't give two hoots about anyone else's sexual orientation, but the remoteness of the riding club could have presented a problem logistically. Thankfully, that wasn't going to be an issue going forward.

#

The silence should have warned her, but Allison was thinking about other things as she crossed from the bright sunlight of the grassy yard into the darkness of the dimly lit barn.

"So nice to see you again." The press of cold steel against the back of her neck accompanied an even colder voice, a voice she had last heard in Rebecca Molinere's flat. "Now that you have arrived, the party can begin.

Gyuri Vargha grabbed Allison's arm roughly, pushing her into the riding club's office. The sight that greeted Allison was even more alarming than the gun against her neck. Marion Hutcheson's body lay unmoving, whether dead or simply unconscious, Allison was unable to discern. Charlotte and two other young riders were huddled together in the corner of the room, the youngest of the trio crying. Jerry Kennedy was nowhere to be seen. Was she dead? Incapacitated? Did Vargha know enough to realize an adult who should be here was missing?

"Mr. Vargha, what is going on?" Allison feigned confusion. "Why do you have a gun? Did someone hurt Marion?"

"Sit down." Removing the gun from the back of Allison's neck, Vargha motioned towards a nearby straight-backed chair. "If you move, I'll kill one of those kids." Vargha grabbed a length of rope hanging on the wall, tucked his weapon inside his waistband and began to tie Allison tightly to the wooden chair. For a brief moment Allison considered making a play for the gun, but her opportunity was short-lived, and she knew, too risky.

"Why are you doing this?" Allison continued her charade. "I don't understand." If she could buy time, maybe Jerry would be able to get help - if Jerry was still alive and not dead in the yard somewhere. Allison didn't care about herself, but she needed desperately to think of some way to get Charlotte and the others to safety. "If you're mad about something, at least let these children go."

Vargha began to laugh "Mad about something? Oh, I'm mad about something alright." Vargha gave the rope a last vicious twist. "And you don't fool me for one minute, Ms. Parker."

Allison carefully considered her response. Gyuri Vargha had a plan, of that she was certain, and now she was the bait. She knew the truth about how Beth Robinson had died. The man standing in front of her wouldn't hesitate to kill her or the children if it furthered his goal of getting to Wolf.

"You're right. I know all about you and what you're capable of doing." Allison glared at Vargha. "Killing adults is bad enough," Allison nodded towards Marion's body, "but only a coward hurts children."

Allison felt the bone crack from the intensity of the blow Vargha landed against her face. She couldn't lose consciousness. Struggling against the sharp pain and fighting to control her breathing, Allison raised her head and forced herself to look her attacker in the eye.

"And women," Allison spat, grateful that she could still talk.

"You leave her alone." Charlotte Parker-Kaufman hurled herself at the man who had hurt her mother, pounding her fists on Vargha's back. "I hate you!" she yelled.

Gyuri Vargha flung the girl from his back with the ease of a man flicking lint from his suit. Before Charlotte could scramble to her feet for another attack, Vargha gave the child a vicious kick. "Do that again and I'll kill your mother."

Fury overtaking her, Allison struggled against the ropes that bound her, adrenaline-fueled strength causing the chair to bounce violently. As she had hoped, her attempt to break free drew Vargha's attention away from Charlotte.

"Charlotte," Allison's voice was calm. "I'll be fine. Mr. Wolf will be here soon, and this will all be over."

Vargha began to laugh again. "Yes, I am certain Mr. Wolf will be here soon. And you are correct, Ms. Parker. Then this will all be over."

# CHAPTER SIXTY-THREE

About a quarter of a mile down the road, Bennett could make out a small figure jumping up and down and waving its arms. Bennett slowed, coming to a stop as he recognized Mack Parker-Kaufman.

"Hey, buddy, are you supposed to be out here?"

"A bad man has Mama," Mack began to cry. "When I told Miss Jerry that Mr. Wolf was on his way, she sent me out here to tell him. But I'm telling you, too."

"Slow down, Mack. And start over." Bennett opened the passenger side door. "Get in and tell me what's going on."

Mack sniffled. He needed to be strong, like Mr. Wolf and his daddy in Heaven would want him to be. Slowly, interrupted by hiccups brought on by his crying, Mack recited everything Jerry Kennedy had told him. "And when we got there, Mama and Charlotte went inside the barn. I went up to see the baby goats, and that's when Miss Jerry found me and sent me out here to the road."

Bennett Shealey grabbed his cell phone praying for coverage in the rural countryside. "Thank you, Jesus" he whispered when two bars appeared. His first call went to Wolf Johannsen. Mack thought Wolf was supposed to meet them at the riding club. With any luck, the Swede was close by.

"Yah." Wolf answered on the second ring.

"It's Bennett. I'm up the road from the Overlook Riding Club. Allison's son is with me. Vargha has everyone else except one of the owners hostage. How far away are you?"

"Less than five minutes out. Have you contacted anyone else?" Wolf's tone was all business but Bennett could detect an undercurrent of fear. The ex-Seal knew not much scared the Swede. If Wolf was even a little bit frightened by this turn of events, it couldn't bode well for a positive outcome.

"Called you first. As soon as you clear the line, I'll contact Jake and he can get everyone out here."

"Listen, I'm Vargha's end game. If Vargha feels cornered by a show of force, he'll kill the hostages just for the hell of it." Wolf pushed aside the thoughts of what Vargha might do to Allison before killing her. But Wolf knew there was no way the Sheriff or the F.B.I. were going to let Wolf handle the situation by himself. "Tell Cleveland to coordinate with Sheriff Trowbridge and keep their guys away from the barn."

"You can't just walk in there, Johannsen," Bennett replied. "That fucker, sorry Mack," Bennett apologized to the young lad for the slip of profanity, "that jerk will shoot you first and still kill everyone else."

"I wasn't the best wet agent at the C.I.A. for no reason," Wolf reminded the younger man. "And to use one of your Southern expressions, I didn't fall off the turnip truck yesterday. I have no intention of 'just walking in'."

Before Bennett could ask what Wolf planned to do, the Swede's roadster crested the hill and came to a stop behind the black SUV. Quickly, Wolf exited his car and climbed into Bennett's.

"Hey, Mack," Wolf tosseled the lad's curly hair. "You okay?"

Mack began to cry again, "Mr. Wolf, a bad man has Mama."

"I know, Mack, and I'm going to make sure nothing happens to your mother, or to anyone else." This was Wolf's intent. Failure was not an option. Addressing the ex-Seal, Wolf continued, "Cleveland should be at the Inn. He and the sheriff were supposed to meet this morning. If Trowbridge is still there it'll save time. Put your phone on speaker. I want Mack to tell Jake everything he knows." Wolf leaned close, "Can you do that for me, Mack?"

Swallowing tears, Mack nodded.

"Is there a problem?" Jake Cleveland asked, recognizing the number calling him.

"Our target has been acquired, but he's taken hostages," Wolf answered, and you're on speaker with me, Shealey and Mack Parker-Kaufman. Where is Trowbridge?"

"Right here, along with the rest of the team." The sound of Cleveland's voice changed, indicating that he, too, had placed his cell phone on speaker mode.

"We've got a brave young man in the car with us," Wolf began. "Thankfully Mack and Jerry Kennedy didn't go into the barn, so they were able to evade capture. At this point, we don't know if Vargha is aware of their existence, or that we may be onto him. Mack is going to tell you everything Jerry Kennedy told him." Wolf paused. He didn't want to frighten Mack with what he needed to make clear to the team. "You'll need to set up a perimeter as soon as you can get here. If I'm successful you won't need to do anything." Wolf left unspoken what would be necessary, if he failed. "Mack, do you know where Miss Jerry is hiding?"

"Oh, I forgot that part!" Mack exclaimed. "She said to tell you she'd be in the goat house." Mack grimaced. "It smells really bad in there. I don't like it."

"Cleveland, I'm going to make contact with Jerry Kennedy, see what else she can tell us. Mack, think hard and tell Mr. Cleveland everything you saw or heard after you got to the riding club."

Bennett made no move to dissuade the Swede. They needed more intelligence, and Jerry Kennedy was their best source at the moment. Wolf might have been out of the business for several years, but he had been well trained. And, personally, Wolf Johannsen had a lot on the line. Bennett just hoped the Swede wouldn't do something stupid trying to save the woman he loved.

## CHAPTER SIXTY-FOUR

"Charlotte, are you alright?" Allison's daughter lay in a fetal position, arms wrapped tightly around her chest. Vargha's booted attack on the young girl had been short-lived, but vicious.

"It's worse than when Diamond Girl threw me last year," Charlotte moaned softly. "I think something's broken."

Allison kept her face expressionless. Diamond Girl had never unseated her mistress. What message was Charlotte trying to send her? Allison didn't think Charlotte would launch another attack at Vargha, given his threat. Was she offering her mother some other opportunity? Why, yes, she was, Allison realized as a thought came to her.

"You've badly hurt my daughter," Allison addressed

her captor. "She needs medical assistance."

Vargha scowled at the accusatory words. "It was her fault," he spat. "Next time it will be worse for her. And for you."

"You're a smart man. Use this to your advantage," Allison kept her tone light and non-threatening. "Call in an ambulance, tell them you've got other hostages. Wolf Johannsen will be here in no time, and you'll have the person you really want."

Gyuri Vargha paced. The assassin didn't have many ethics. In his line of work, ethics could get one killed, but he did have one. In all his years of covert work, he had never harmed a child. Until today.

He didn't need the children. The Parker woman was right about that. The large-boned woman who had attacked him earlier hadn't moved since he shot her. Dead probably, but no need for anyone other than himself to know that particular bit of information. Even if he let the children go, he would still have two female hostages…with Allison Parker as the bait for Wolf Johannsen.

A rotary phone sat on the edge of the office desk. Picking up the receiver, Vargha dialed "911" and waited. The emergency operator had barely asked her question before Vargha began his rapid-fire order. "My name is Gyuri Vargha. Dispatch an ambulance to the Overlook Riding Club. I'm letting some of the hostages go and one is injured. Tell the F.B.I. to send Wolf Johannsen to me. If he's not here in an hour, I'll kill his woman."

#

Wolf Johannsen's eidetic memory had saved his life numerous times. Not many people were blessed with the ability to recall images from memory with high precision after just brief periods of exposure, but the Swede had been genetically gifted in this regard. As he made his way through the trees on the perimeter of the riding club's property, Wolf knew exactly where the goats were kept from his earlier visits to the club to watch Charlotte practice. With luck, Jerry Kennedy would be waiting for him there.

At Jake Cleveland's instructions, each of the government SUVs used by the team had been outfitted with the latest mobile communication equipment. The high-tech earbuds Wolf grabbed from Bennett's SUV would enable him to receive real-time information.

Stepping from the protection of the tree line would be risky, but Wolf had no choice. He would have to cross an open area to reach the goat house. Fortunately, the barn's main entrance faced a full 180 degrees away from where Wolf needed to go. With any luck, his advance would go undetected. Wolf withdrew his weapon and ran.

The full-speed sprint left the Swede breathing hard as he ducked into the small shed that provided shelter for the small family of goats kept by the riding club as companions for the horses. There Jerry Kennedy sat huddled, arms encircling bent knees, her back against the far wall.

"Thank God it's you," Jerry whispered. "I was afraid you wouldn't come."

Wolf offered the slim woman a hand up. "Bennett Shealey is the one who found Mack on the side of the highway. It's a good thing, too, because Bennett's driving one of the decked-out SUVs."

"Is Mack okay? I didn't know whether to keep him here with me or send him for help," Jerry stood and brushed straw from her jeans. "That boy has been through more than any child his age deserves. If something happens to his mother and sister…."

Wolf tapped his left ear, held up one finger and motioned for Jerry to be quiet. His eyes narrowed as he listened to the new information Jake Cleveland was sharing. "Roger that," the Swede acknowledged as the transmission ended.

"What is it?" Jerry felt her anxiety rising. "What's happening?"

"The man in the barn is a wanted international criminal."

"I know who he is," Jerry interrupted. "Charlotte's bodyguard told us about the guy. I assume that's who's in the barn?"

Wolf nodded, "Vargha called 911. Said he had an injured hostage and wanted an ambulance."

All color drained from Jerry's face. "When I heard the gun shots in the office, I hoped Marion was the one doing the shooting. After what Charlotte's bodyguard told us we started practicing, thought we could protect ourselves if the bastard came our way." Jerry shook her head, "What fools we were. Oh Lord, please don't let anything have happened to Marion."

"Don't go there," Wolf admonished. "If Vargha is calling for an ambulance, whoever was hurt is still alive. I need to know how many people he is holding. We know Allison and Charlotte are inside. Do you know if there are any others?"

"Yes, the Smith twins had already arrived. Their dad dropped them off and is meeting all of us at the competition later." Jerry thought hard. Had she missed anybody? "I'm pretty sure that's it."

So, Wolf thought, three kids, Allison, and Jerry's partner Marion Hutcheson. Gyuri Vargha would have his hands full, especially if the two women had not already been incapacitated. He would know more after he learned the identity of the injured hostage. Then he could plan his attack.

# CHAPTER SIXTY-FIVE

Marion Hutcheson had been conscious and aware for several minutes, long enough to realize her life depended on not moving a single inch nor making any sound. Marion's left shoulder hurt like the son-of-a-bitch who had shot her. When she got out of here – and Marion refused to think otherwise – she was going to kill Gyuri Vargha, assuming someone else didn't get to him first.

Hitting her head on the side of the heavy wooden desk when she was shot was what had knocked her unconscious. Marion wasn't certain how long she had been out, but based on what she could hear, the fiend had hurt Allison's daughter. Marion added a second reason for killing Gyuri Vargha to her mental hit list.

The office desk hid most of Marion's body from view.

Unless Vargha actually walked around to the back of the massive piece of furniture, he would not know she was awake. Right now, Marion's head faced the barn's outside wall. If she turned her head in the other direction, she would be able to see under the desk. Should she take the risk? She had no way of knowing whether Vargha had seen her body fall into its current position. If he had, and he checked on her again... moving her head could be a fatal mistake.

The gun that she had concealed in the office after first learning that Vargha was on the loose lay in the bottom left-hand drawer of the large desk. Without a distraction, Marion knew she would not be able to reach the weapon in time to use it. Frustrated, Marion remained still trying to come up with options that might offer a better end result.

A small scratching sound caught Marion's attention. For all her bravado and strength, Marion Hutcheson was deathly afraid of mice, a fact which provided her partner Jerry with abundant opportunities to tease. No matter how clean they kept the horse barn, it was an older structure with all the issues attendant to a forty year-old wooden building located in the countryside. Hay and grain, two of the little buggers' menu delights, drew mice like a magnet. The scratching sound came again. If one of those tiny, four-legged creatures appeared next to her, Marion wasn't sure she would be able to stifle a scream.

Alert for any sign of the small marauders, Marion

watched in mounting horror as a small section of the back wall made an almost imperceptible movement. It was the loose board that Jerry had pointed out earlier in the week and which Marion had forgotten to repair. For a second, Marion thought she would be the victim of a mouse invasion before quickly realizing someone, not something, was pushing against the board.

The shrill ring of the office phone startled Marion. Closing her eyes, she feigned unconsciousness. Vargha would be only a foot away from her if he answered the phone.

"I'm sending two of them out now," Vargha spoke rapidly to the person on the other end of the line. "Any tricks, and the women are dead." Vargha slammed the receiver onto its cradle.

Marion listened as Vargha's footsteps moved away from the desk. He thought she was dead. Should she go for the gun? The scratching sound came again, drawing Marion's thoughts away from the contents of the desk drawer. Marion's eyes grew large as she watched Jerry Kennedy's fingers slip through a widening opening. "Ready Now." Jerry's fingers made the silent sign, the one she used to help her students focus right before they entered the competition ring. Marion understood immediately. Something was about to happen, but how did Jerry know Marion was lying just inches from the wall? After she killed Gyuri Vargha, Marion intended to find out.

"You two, get out," Marion heard Vargha address the

Smith twins. "If you tell them that other woman is dead, I'll kill your little friend here." Terrorizing children was not acceptable. Marion added yet another reason to her kill Vargha list.

"Charlotte, baby," Allison's quiet voice floated across the room. "The ambulance men will be here to get you next. Hang on baby. You'll be fine."

The desk phone rang a second time. "What?" Vargha demanded answering the call. "No. I've changed my mind. I'm keeping the other one."

"We had a deal!" Outrage coated Allison's words. "Let my daughter go."

The sound of Vargha's palm striking Allison's face, followed by an angry "Shut up, bitch" caused Marion an involuntary shudder. "He'll come now, for both of you."

Whatever was being planned outside the small office needed to happen, and happen now. Marion didn't think Gyuri Vargha would be able to control himself much longer.

# CHAPTER SIXTY-SIX

Wolf Johannsen moved slowly and carefully, his senses on high alert. The plan he had worked out with Jerry Kennedy was dangerous, but he knew a frontal assault would almost assuredly result in the loss of innocent lives. Vargha's life was already over, as far as Wolf Johannsen was concerned. It was the lives of those he loved which he intended to save.

The main barn at the Overlook Riding Club was enormous. Twenty stalls, ten on each side, lined the open expanse that ran the length of the barn. Normally, this time of the morning, the barn's inhabitants would be grazing in the adjacent pastures, but due to the afternoon's competition down the road, three of the horses had remained in their enclosures.

Horses were skittish with strangers, and none

of the three horses still in the barn were familiar with Wolf's smell. If any of them became alarmed by his presence, the element of surprise would be lost. To counter this possibility, Jerry Kennedy had removed the workshirt she was wearing, and using the garment's long sleeves, tied it around Wolf's waist. "They won't know you, but they'll recognize my smell. Hopefully, this will keep them from raising an alarm."

In the thirty minutes it had taken for the ambulance Vargha ordered to arrive, Wolf was certain that Bennett Shealey had moved his team into position. Pete Pantsari had also worked quickly, hacking into the surveillance system that Jerry Kennedy had installed in the barn and office just a few weeks earlier. Wolf hoped with Pete's eyes on the inside, so to speak, he could accomplish his mission without needing Bennett or his snipers.

Gyuri Vargha would be expecting him, of that Wolf had no doubt. The Russian would be prepared. And he knew from the latest intel that Vargha had refused to release Allison's daughter with the other young hostages. Only the element of surprise would give Wolf the edge he needed.

Creeping towards the barn office, Wolf wondered if Marion Hutcheson would live through the coming assault. Jerry told him Marion would do everything she could to save Charlotte Parker-Kaufman, including giving up her own life. Sending a prayer to a Deity whose existence he often questioned, Wolf asked for any help that might be sent his way.

"You know you won't get out of here alive." Wolf was close enough to hear Allison's voice. "Wolf is going to kill you, whether or not you kill me. Taking my child's life serves no purpose. Let her go."

"You think your lover is so smart," Vargha laughed. "He didn't kill me five years ago, and he won't kill me now. His love for you has made him weak. And a weak adversary is a dead adversary."

"You're a pitiful excuse for a human being!" Allison spat the words. "Only a coward hides behind a woman and a child!"

The earbud in Wolf's ear crackled. "You need to move!" Jake Cleveland's voice commanded. "It's about to get ugly in there. I'm giving Jerry the go-ahead. Get ready."

Almost instantaneously, the sound of splintering wood and an enraged "What the hell?" signaled the distraction Wolf desperately hoped would be enough. Smoke and noxious fumes from the canisters of Hot Shot Insect Fogger that Jerry Kennedy had rolled through the hole in the back wall filled the office space. Charging through the open doorway, Wolf drew down on Gyuri Vargha, only to note with despair that his nemesis held Allison prisoner, using her as the human shield Wolf had feared.

"Shoot him!" Allison's voice held no trace of fear. "Shoot the diseased motherfucker, Wolf!"

Insane laughter poured from Gyuri Vargha's lips. "She's got spunk. I'll give her that, Johannsen. Too bad neither of you will live much longer. You'll never take me down before I can take your woman with me."

The smoke and chemicals released by the bug bombs stung Marion Hutcheson's eyes. Ignoring the pain, Marion rolled towards the desk that shielded her from view, reached for the bottom left drawer and jerked it open. Calmly – an emotion she would later ascribe to her intense anger at the man who had terrorized her students– Marion Hutcheson withdrew the semi-automatic she had hidden there, checked the magazine, and stood.

The gun appeared in Wolf's peripheral vision mere seconds before Gyuri Vargha's head exploded, blood and brain-matter spewing partially over Allison's hair as the angle and force of the destructive bullet sent most of the nastiness towards the ceiling.

Marion Hutcheson struggled to stay on her feet, her hand seemingly glued to the instrument of Gyuri Vargha's death. "Thank you for the opportunity to put down that rabid piece of crap." The big-boned woman began to weep as the enormity of the situation dawned. "I wasn't sure my aim would be true, but I had to try."

"Mama, Mama!" Charlotte crawled across the floor. Allison knew only shock prevented her daughter from seeing the blood and gore which now dripped grotesquely from her mother's blond hair. Holding her child tightly, Allison allowed the two of them to be enveloped in Wolf's strong arms. They were safe.

# CHAPTER SIXTY-SEVEN

After puking his guts, the younger of the two EMS workers covered Vargha's body with a sheet. The deceased couldn't be moved until law enforcement finished with the scene and Andy Dabo had completed his pro-forma examination. There was no doubt Gyuri Vargha was dead, but the medical examiner had to follow the bureaucratic rules which required him to pronounce the cause of death.

The ambulance Gyuri Vargha had ordered made a fitting hearse for what was left of the man's mortal remains, but it would be a couple of hours before it could take its cargo to the morgue. In the meantime, the two First Responders hung out near one of the corrals, vaping and drinking sodas. The Sheriff would call them back inside when they could load Vargha into a black body bag and finish their job.

Toby Trowbridge and Jake Cleveland arrived at the barn within minutes of the shooting, having positioned themselves just outside the perimeter of the riding club's property after receiving Bennett Shealey's initial call. Now the representatives of State and Federal law enforcement expected Wolf to brief them on what had transpired.

"Pete's got everything that happened inside on video, but I want you to walk us through the details." Jake Cleveland lit a cigarette and waited for Wolf to start.

His years with the Agency had accustomed Wolf to debriefing sessions. The ex-C.I.A. agent described how the morning had unfolded. "Frankly, if Jerry Kennedy had been in the office when Vargha grabbed everyone, we might be looking at a different outcome. It was sheer, blind luck that she was at the far end of the barn, heard the commotion, and was able to make her escape."

"To my way of thinking," Sheriff Trowbridge added, "Allison's boy is the real reason no one other than Vargha died today. The presence of mind that kid had is impressive."

Marion Hutcheson and Jerry Kennedy sat on a nearby bench underneath one of the horse stalls, heads together, talking quietly. Motioning in their direction, Wolf continued, "I owe that woman over there Allison's life. There's no doubt in my mind that Vargha expected to die and intended to take Allison with him."

"Would you have taken the shot?" Jake asked the

question that had been on the mind of both lawmen.

Minutes passed silently as Wolf considered his answer. "I don't know," Wolf admitted. "Vargha told Allison my love for her had made me weak. Maybe he was right."

Jake Cleveland grunted his disagreement, "You'd have taken the shot. Marion Hutcheson just beat you to it."

#

"How in the world did you know where I was?" Marion asker her partner. "Or that I was even alive?"

Jerry Kennedy fidgeted nervously. Marion hated spending money, and the two women had argued extensively over the need for a surveillance system. The current system had been installed without Marion's knowledge or agreement.

"Well, I could see you." Jerry steeled herself for Marion's response.

"What do you mean you could see me? Have you developed x-ray vision?"

Jerry gathered her courage, "We've got a new surveillance system. One of the Feds hacked into it."

#

"We've got what? How much did that cost?" Marion Hutcheson's voice carried outside the barn, tickling Allison's ears and bringing a laugh to her lips. Marion's reaction to the life-saving installation was a sure sign that things would return to normal sooner rather than later.

Normal. The word was a conundrum. Three years ago, normal looked a lot different for Allison and her children than it did now. Three years ago Charlotte and Mack still had their father, a sexual predator had not yet kidnapped their mother, home grown terrorists from the University at Auburn had not tried to kill everyone at Ft. Charles' elementary school, and Beth Robinson had not been murdered. A tear slipped from Allison's eye, thinking about Toby's long time secretary. Beth Robinson had been a Ft. Charles institution. Her absence would leave a hole in the town's psyche for a very long time.

The sound of footsteps on gravel broke Allison's reverie. Wolf Johannsen stopped in front of Allison, as if asking permission to come closer. Wolf's clothes, like Allison's, displayed the sickening remnants of Gyuri Vargha's shattered skull.

"How is Charlotte?" Concern splayed across Wolf's face. "I heard she refused to go to the hospital."

"She's okay physically." Allison smiled ruefully. "The next few days will tell about the rest." Her children were tough, but they were still children. "We'll see how the nights go."

"And Mack?"

"He thinks this has been a great adventure. I guess that's good. He didn't have to see what happened in there." Allison nodded towards the barn. "Bennett Shealey took them to the house as soon as Jake let him leave."

Wolf reached for his lover, taking her smaller hands in his larger ones. "This is probably not the best place or time to ask this, but I swore to myself if we survived this, if Gyuri Vargha died, really died this time, that nothing would stand in my way of having this conversation with you." Dropping to one knee, he asked, "Allison, will you marry me?"

# CHAPTER SIXTY-EIGHT

## *Christmas Eve*

The Farm at Serenity Hill had never looked lovelier. Lush cedar garlands hung gracefully across the home's wide front porch. A pair of enormous cedar wreaths hung on the leaded glass double doors, welcoming the wedding guests inside for a celebratory reception.

In the middle of the entry foyer, a sixteen-foot Christmas tree glittered with white lights and gold ornaments. Beneath it, a red tree-skirt could be seen occasionally peeping out from between gaily wrapped gifts which would be opened the next day. In the den, at the back of the home, four stockings hung from the ancient wooden beam which served as the mantle for a stacked-stone fireplace. Three older ones, plus one newly purchased.

The dining room, located to the right of the foyer, already held a large number of the couple's friends. Jake Cleveland and Bennett Shealey had driven down from Birmingham together, arriving earlier in the afternoon and helping with last minute setup as directed by Allison's friend and party planner, Dawn Deakins. Grabbing a beer from the bar which had been set up in one corner of the expansive room, Jake gave a wave to Toby Trowbridge and ambled over his way to catch up.

Only the couple's closest friends had been invited to the small wedding ceremony at the Episcopal Church-David and Sarah Jackson, Donna and Scott Pevey, Frank Martin and Marty Hampton – along with, of course, Allison's children Charlotte and Mack. Practically the entire town of Ft. Charles had been invited to the reception.

The sounds of car horns coming up the long driveway announced the arrival of the wedding party. Guests gathered on the front porch poised to throw red, green and gold confetti in happy greeting to the couple.

Wolf Johannsen exited the shiny black limousine that had been hired for the special occasion. Resplendent in formal attire, the tall blond Swede grinned as he helped his beautiful new wife step from the vehicle. And beautiful she was. Dressed in a simply cut, off-white gown which clung to her shapely figure, long blond hair pulled into her signature chignon, Allison Johannsen's smile told the guests all they needed to know.

"I'm so very happy," Allison whispered to her husband, as they climbed the front stairs to greet their friends and neighbors. "Thank you for bringing joy back into my life."

Leaning down to kiss Allison's cheek, Wolf whispered back, "And you to mine."

Made in the USA
Columbia, SC
20 February 2021